PRIVATE FOUNTAINS

Volumes 1-5

JEREMY EDWARDS

1001 Nights Press

Table of Contents

Volume 3

Volume 4

Volume 5

Volume 1

Undercurrents

"ABOUT HOW MANY TIMES A DAY DO YOU PEE?" HORACE ASKED Evelyn.

"What?"

"On average. How many times?" He smiled charismatically.

"I don't know … four or five, maybe. A bunch."

"Excellent."

The wine bar was hopping. Other couples huddled at every point of the compass—engaging in less peculiar conversations, Evelyn wagered.

"Why do you ask? Do you keep tallies?"

"Oh, no," he chuckled. "I'm an enthusiast, not an accountant."

"An enthusiast?"

He leaned in closer. "Do you like it?"

"Hmm?"

"Do you like *peeing?*"

She smirked. "What do you mean? I—"

"I mean, do you enjoy yourself with it?" His hand touched her knee.

"What a question, Horace."

"And here's another: If you could wave a magic wand and never have to pee again, would you take advantage of that? Or would you miss how luxurious it feels to pull your panties down and piss? Would you opt out of the magic-wand thing, Evelyn?" He broke eye contact long enough to help himself to a piece of focaccia, giving her a moment of space.

This had definitely turned into an interesting date.

"You like how it feels, don't you?" said Horace, promptly back on her ass.

"Doesn't everyone?"

"But you like it a lot, yes?"

She shrugged. "Maybe."

"Does it make your pussy wet to think about how good it feels? To sit here and talk about it?"

"It seems to me you're the one doing most of the talking."

He conceded the point with a gesture. "Please. I'm all ears."

"And cock."

He conceded this as well.

She looked around the room again. "I've never seen this place so crowded."

"I thought we were talking about your wet pussy."

"Did I say it was wet?"

"No, in fact you didn't—not yet. Why the delay in imparting this information?"

"You appear to be fairly sure about it without my input."

He reached across the table to take her hand. "Evelyn, there is nothing more important to me than your input on this subject."

She inclined her head graciously. "Thank you."

"So, then, it's wet?"

"Maybe." But she knew she was nodding *yes*.

"And this has something to do with telling me how much you enjoy peeing, correct? You did say you liked it, didn't you? A lot?"

"Oh, for crying out loud. *Yes, yes*, I like to pee, OK?" She laughed.

"A lot. Right?"

She sighed, then burst into another round of laughter. "Well, since it makes you so happy: Yes. A lot."

"I want to hear more about how happy it makes *you*."

"What's to tell? It—um—it's a really good feeling. And, yeah, sort of sexy." She shifted in her seat, and this did not go unnoticed; Horace's face lit up.

"Maybe you have to pee right now, eh? You're imagining what the sensations will be like when you do it: almost like an orgasm.

Am I right? In fact, Evelyn, I propose that you're squeezing your thighs together holding it at this very moment, and that this is turning you on, as well."

He put the napkin he'd been gesturing with back on the table. "But I'm talking too much again—speculating here, without giving you a chance to answer me. I apologize. So, tell me: do you have to pee?" He was speaking softly now, his voice an insinuating velvet.

"I can wait." She felt herself blush.

"Oh, yes, I bet you can," he said, looking more gratified than ever. "Waiting is part of the fun sometimes, isn't it?"

"Damn, Horace, what are you doing to me?"

"Making love to you," he replied instantly.

"I see."

"It's akin to a not-yet-answered sexual urge sometimes, that tickle of water, isn't it? Waiting a bit can be like foreplay … delicious anticipation."

"I never thought of it that way."

"But neither do you deny its aptness, I note. Splendid. And how nice that you're holding your pee right before my eyes. Isn't it exciting that I know what's going on between your legs, Evelyn, dead center in the seam of those flirty slacks you're wearing?"

"You're making me squirm in public."

"Is that a problem?"

She opened her mouth to respond, then hesitated. Then she shook her head *no*.

"I don't blame you for getting aroused, sitting there with a tickle in your panties, squeezing your pussy while I watch your every move. I don't blame you at all."

"I appreciate the vote of confidence."

"Is it like a man's flat fingers strumming slowly, just outside the periphery of your cunt lips? A faint, pulsing tension that lurks vaguely in the vicinity of your taut pussy?

"You're very skilled at describing things."

"Am I? These things? Thank you, Evelyn, that's wonderful to imagine."

He took a bite of focaccia before indicating the ladies' room at the back of the bar. "Just think of it: Out here, me—an erotic sentimentalist. In there, beautiful faces and beautiful bare asses, sitting pretty to pee … soft, round bottoms ennobling toilet seats. Warm, feminine crotches exposed … open … and tingling with the sensuality of release. All right behind that door."

"You're quite the romantic, aren't you?"

"It's true. Alas, they won't let me watch you pee, here."

"You've inquired, I assume."

"But there's a sparkling commode in the bathroom at my place. Its seat would welcome your charming derriere."

"I don't think I've ever received an engraved invitation from a toilet seat before."

He returned her grin. "It would be impolite not to accept—don't you agree?"

"I have no intention of not accepting." She sipped her Chardonnay and shifted in her chair again.

"We're almost there," he said, glancing toward the passenger seat. "Looking forward to it?"

"Perhaps not as much as you are … but yes."

"My pleasure is mere commentary on your own. It all begins with the pleasure between your thighs, Evelyn."

"I'll try not to disappoint you."

"Oh, I don't think there's any risk of that."

"Too bad I didn't know our evening would include a scheduled pissing session. I would have written it on my calendar."

"Next time, I hope you will."

"Mmm," she purred, involuntarily. She had a hand resting lazily in her lap, and her ass jiggled on the vinyl. "You know, I had a weird dream a while ago. I should tell you about it."

"Please," he said with unsuppressed excitement.

"Well, I guess I'd had a beer close to bedtime. So there I am, in the middle of a dream of some kind, and I have to pee. But what happens, while I'm looking for a place to do it—I'm wandering around, you know, seeking the right place—is that all these men are watching me. Everywhere I go, there are men—horny, good-looking men—and they're aware that I have to pee, and I can tell that they're watching to see if I'm going to do it in front of them. Some of them have their dicks out. And I get so turned on by all this that for the moment I forget about pissing and I start rubbing myself like nobody's business, and I have a real live killer orgasm in my sleep."

"Very nice," said Horace with relish. "Very, very nice."

"You're telling me. I woke up all hot and juicy—and immediately dashed to the bathroom, of course. I was in total orgasm afterglow while I peed there in the moonlight."

"You should have shared this dream with me earlier."

She laughed. "When, 'earlier'?"

"Oh, somewhere between 'hello' and 'pleased to meet you.'"

"To be honest, I'd completely forgotten it. Somehow, you managed to prompt the memory. But, OK, I'm glad you did. Whoo-baby. I suppose you've created a bit of a monster tonight."

"You give me far too much credit. I didn't create a thing. You were simply waiting for me to come along."

"Yeah, waiting." Again she laughed. "Waiting with my legs crossed, holding it for you."

She felt the car accelerating under her.

"Show me how you do it."

"You're not going to stand there and tell me you've never seen a girl pee."

"Of course not. But each woman has her own style. Or styles."

"Ah. Don't men?"

"Perhaps. Not my field of expertise."

"So you're an 'expert' in female urination, huh?"

"Erotically speaking? Yes." He sat on the edge of the vanity. "Do you wiggle your bottom while you do it? Tap your feet? Hold the toilet paper at the ready, like you can't wait to stroke your pussy with it? Toilet paper can look so elegant in a peeing woman's grasp, so crisp and fresh."

She had to admit it was an aesthetically pleasing image, as rendered by Horace.

"On the other hand, maybe you're the type of woman who doesn't even want to think about wiping until every sacred drop is out. Maybe you're so in the moment with the pleasure of pissing that all you can think about is how rapturous it feels. Do you squeeze your eyes shut when the pleasure shudders through you, Evelyn?"

She studied his features. "I still can't believe we go for drinks on a Friday night, and you turn out to be obsessed with my peeing."

"After all, what *should* I be obsessed with?"

"You make it sound so logical." She shuffled in place, her hands cupping the front of her slacks. "I'm really going to take my panties down and pee with you watching, eh?"

"That was my thought."

"Come to think of it, I bet you'd look plenty sexy with your cock hanging out of your pants, standing in front of this scintillating toilet of yours."

"Thank you."

"I could get into that, too, you know—watching you do it."

"I don't have to go."

"I may just have to stick around until you do."

She closed her eyes, pressed herself harder, and gave in to the impulse to sway more dramatically from side to side. "Oh, wow, Horace, I have to pee."

"That's why we're here," he sang encouragingly.

She opened her eyes and crossed one leg in front of the other, feeling giddy and daring. "Seriously, I could lose it any second," she giggled.

"Tell me more." He stood up, alert.

"I mean, if I just kept standing here and talking like this, I might ... "

"Yes?"

"OK, Horace, so what would you do if I wet my pants right here?" she heard herself ask, a little breathlessly. "Right here over the bathroom floor, just for kicks."

"What would I do? I'd savor every moment of it, until you dripped to a stunning conclusion."

"Yeah?"

"Then I'd pull your sopping pants off you and lick every inch of you clean. I'd—"

"Oh, Horace—I'm gonna—"

"Yes?" His smooth voice had gone husky.

"Oh! Oh! I'm pissing my pants!" She hadn't anticipated quite how amazing this would feel.

"It's so lovely," Horace whispered.

"Oh, oh, oh … ohhhhhhhhh."

"Feels nice?"

"Holy fuck, yeah. Ho-o-o-ly fuck." She was in ecstasy.

"Aren't you glad you didn't wave that magic wand? Aren't you glad you didn't pee at the restaurant, all by yourself?"

"Uh … y-yeah. I—ooh!—fuck, Horace, I want to see *your* magic wand. Take—ahhhh-hahaha, oh god—take it out. Please."

He did.

"Nnnn," she moaned approvingly. Her legs twitched as she pumped and flooded. She clutched her pussy and rolled back and forth from heel to toe. "Oh-ho-o-ohhhh, oh fuck, oh f—"

He stepped toward her, placing his fingers on her elbows. "*Gorgeous.*"

"Touch me. T—ahhh … a-hahahaha. R-rub my clit. My *clit*, Horace! Oh, god, I'm wetting. I'm wetting …"

He undid her trouser button while she trembled, still flowing.

"Hurry," she squeaked. "Touch my clitty, my cl—"

He quickly found her button of flesh.

"*Ahhh!* Yes, yes, keep—"

"Good?"

"Y—oh-o-o—oh! I'm gonna, I—"

"Yes?"

"*Oh, you fucking horny pervert, I love you, I love you … oh, you fucking fucking piss-my-pants pervert … oh fuck, oh fuck, oh fuck …* "

His laughter was lewd honey in her ear. "*Now* who's doing most of the talking?"

No Blame, No Shame

I'M ON MY WAY TO THE LADIES' ROOM WHEN I SPOT THEM: Jessica and Peter, getting down and dirty in the conference center's little glass-doored library.

And I don't blame them. I'd do Jessica and/or Peter in a second, if I ever got a chance. The next best thing has to be watching them do each other—and it looks like my beneficent bladder has escorted me straight into the path of the next best thing.

The hotel designers have placed one of those ice-machine alcoves directly opposite the diminutive library. And when I instinctively back myself into it, I can tell right away that the angles and lighting would make it difficult for me to be seen.

Whereas Jess and Pete are quite easily seen.

Oh, yes. At the moment, she's kneeling on the couch, and he has her pants down. He's tickling her bottom, and she's giggling lewdly and thrusting her starkly bared ass upward at him—*more, more.*

And I don't blame her. My mind doesn't blame her and my pussy doesn't blame her and my own tickle-loving ass cheeks certainly don't blame her.

I might have thought that my three-drink need to pee would prevent my getting properly turned on by what I'm observing. I find, on the contrary, that it only further encourages the horny electricity that warms my groin.

And the self-indulgent silk panties I've worn to this evening's event feel complicitly cool against my hot cunt, as if my arousal were a beautifully wrapped gift from an admirer.

I'm squirming.

Now he's kissing her—kissing all over the creamy globes of her behind. Gradually he centers in on the crack, which he slowly follows south. I'm riveted, wondering when his lips will make it to her cunt—caring as much as if it were my own.

Her whole body telegraphs a new level of joy when he arrives there. Peter really gets into it, slobbering like an animal.

And I don't blame him.

My hand gets busy in my conference slacks, initiating an oh-so-productive breakaway session with my pussy.

Soon I realize I'm practically on the verge of wetting my silk, because I've refused to cut short my thrills by exiting to the restroom. But no problem—it's feeling sexier than ever to hold it, to jiggle there while I watch them from my makeshift voyeur station, the dull ache of fullness grounding the twin tickles of excitement and urgency. Even while I'm teasing my clit into a frenzy, I clutch my brink-hovering bathroom need like a security blanket.

I'm in a kind of kinky paradise, frankly—who knew how exquisite it could feel to be having vicarious sex and anticipating a killer piss at the same liquid instant?

Pete finally removes his muzzle from Jessica's snatch, and he makes the excellent decision to pull her pants the rest of the way off. When he gets everything past her feet and tosses it all offstage, I'm given a glimpse of pink panties in transit.

And, speaking of panties, I notice I'm actually tinkling in mine a bit now—dribbling trickles of pee through my cunt-slick fingers because, yeah, I'm full of cocktails and so turned on … and it all feels so fucking good, even the maverick drops of piss kissing their way down the smoothness of my thighs.

Jess is now on her back, with Peter eating her tits. She's writhing like crazy, with her legs splayed; and thanks to the generous library lighting, I can see how wet she is. The effect suggests to me, in my present state, that *she* has to pee and it's starting to seep out … but I remind myself that, no, it's not that Jess has to pee, it's that she has to be fucked—and her desire is what's seeping out.

Peter is, to say the least, hip to her desire, and he doesn't let much more time elapse before getting out his gorgeous, tautly swollen cock, and putting it up Jessica's lust-drenched hole.

I'm trembling with arousal, and even the hum of the ice machine sounds libidinous. As for Jess, she's getting pumped so well that their couch is shaking. Jess, who doesn't have to pee just now.

But, sweet fuck, I do, and the sensation of holding most of it back while the hot little trickles continue is almost better than sex. I know that eventually something will have to give—my ass will claim the nearest toilet seat or, so help me, I'll wet my pants gloriously right here—but for the time being I'm in a fabulous steady state, just relishing the warm erotic buoyancy of it all.

Peter's delicious butt is supremely tight and intent, and Jess looks like a beautiful rapture of female flesh, all O-mouth and closed lids and hungry thighs.

Oh, god, they're both coming.

And, yes, now I'm really wetting my pants by the ice machine, having the best goddamn orgasm of my life and pissing relentlessly—totally surrendering control to pleasure, excited to the point where I have no shame and wouldn't dream of relocating to a bathroom stall, even if it weren't so emphatically too late.

Because it's a privilege to wet myself in tribute to them—to have glued myself to this spot until I pissed my freakin' panties, because I couldn't take my eyes off them or get my hand out of my pants.

I guess, after three drinks, I'm what you'd call a romantic.

It's a marathon: a marathon pee and a marathon climax. A double-fucking-decker marathon of ecstasy. And I don't even mind that Jess and Pete have noticed me through the glass, that they're watching me dissolve into a blissful, perversely glamorous mess—leaking my passion all over the floor, staring out at them with my glazed but unflinching eyes … and wondering if they envy me for this moment.

Because I wouldn't blame them.

Man of a Thousand Wet Dreams

MAN OF A THOUSAND WET DREAMS SEEKS IMAGINATIVE WOMEN WHO want to pee for him.

I never ran an ad like that. I would have, but I didn't need to.

I don't know what it was about me, but sooner or later every woman I dated offered to pee for me. Actually, "offered" isn't the right word—they practically implored me to watch them do it. As if there were some concern that I might turn them down, for god's sake.

Janet just wanted to spread her legs for me while she perched on the toilet seat, letting me enjoy her pretty little waterfall. She was an aesthete, and the toilet tissue she left behind her each time she peed seemed to magically rearrange itself into a floral shape in the water, like a napkin at a fancy dinner.

Becky wanted to wet her panties for me in my kitchen—flushed and giggling, clasping the edges of her skirt and looking right at me. Or sometimes she would do it through the leg-hole of her panties, slowly pissing herself dry in little spurts, each spurt accompanied by a whimper of pleasure.

Polly liked to leap into my chair and soak my loins with sweetheart piss, while covering my face with hungry kisses. Polly loved beer, and every Friday night she'd make herself pee to her heart's content—and mine—by drinking two pints, back to back.

Marie-Claire, by contrast, favored wine. On a leisurely Saturday evening, she would sit in my lap and sip until she wet herself, pissing dainty white-wine waters, with a tender natural fury, through her lace onto my wool … straddling me so that I could feel it all with her, a participant in her calculated surrender to the tide. Yes, Marie-Claire had a particular kind of class.

Joan liked to be masturbated into letting go. As I stroked and teased her pussy, she would babble hotly, feeling the irrefutable trickle begin, letting it surprise, arouse, and overwhelm her in waves and bubbles of bliss. Joan was so deliciously vocal: "Oh, yes, unh, I can't, oh, I'm leaking, oh god, oh yeah, ooh, oh no, I can't, ooh! unh, yes, yes, oh god … "

Milly, whose deepest desire was to be gently tickled under the arms with a feather when her bladder was full, was a talker as well. When my free, featherless hand reached into her writhing center to greet her clit, Milly's discourse would invariably climax in something like "oh fuck I'm gonna come I'm gonna pee I'm gonna oh—" and, transmuting indecision into synergy, she would do both, letting her heavy tension dissolve into a wet, mind-melting double ecstasy on our bed.

Gloria taught me to unbutton her blouse and feel her up while she peed. She told me how horny it made her for me to touch her casually bared nipples while she pissed and pissed into the toilet. She would moan that she couldn't wait to be finished, so I could fuck her; and then she would change her story and tell me that she never wanted to stop, because it all felt so good just like that. As I fondled her, Gloria would clutch a thick complement of toilet paper in her hand, knowing how wet she'd be down there when she was finally finished.

Tender slaps on the bottom were Annie's thing. She'd wait till she could hardly hold it and then curl up across my thighs, where my swift, gentle swats would send her into a panty-pissing, knicker-soaking orgasm, while I gripped her body tightly.

Finally, there was Tamara.

Tamara had an amazing instinct for the art of pissing as display. She could use her natural need to release water as a means of showing off her womanhood to full effect, and it never failed to drive me wild. There she would stand, proudly nude in a dry shower, proving her femininity with piss—the delicate anatomy overwhelmed by the copious, uncontrollable rush of water. Tamara was flexible, and sometimes she'd raise a leg, bracing herself against the shower wall and using her fingers to project her stream into a beautiful arc for me.

Her creativity seemed to know no limits. Where erotic pissing was concerned, she was a true artist, whose repertoire included—with no prompting from me—virtually all the variations my previous lovers had embodied, and many more. One night, for example, she carefully composed herself on the couch after we'd been out drinking, facing me across my little coffee table, wiggling and squirming in her long skirt, blowing kisses to me all the while. Finally, a musical "oh" escaped her lips, as she froze in her seat and let the water flow forcefully through her. A sly smile creeping across her face emphasized what was happening under her skirt, as she sat there in evident repose.

On another occasion, I was about to take her doggie-style. She was bent forward, her hands on her knees, her bare snatch exposed beneath a minidress. "Want to see me really flood my flower?" she suddenly asked. Soon I was watching the warm liquid dribble exuberantly out and down. I held my cock under the stream, becoming harder than I already was, and when at last I entered her she was still dribbling onto me. We squelched together in warm euphoria, enjoying an intimacy beyond intimacy.

I became addicted to the erotic attraction of Tamara's manifold displays of urinary sensuality.

This evening, with the summer sun still smiling for us, Tamara and I will strip and face each other in the seclusion of a grove I know. I will stand straight, grip and aim, and gently water her bare feet; she will pose, legs apart, and pour herself voluminously onto the ground beneath her. Man and woman, naked and natural, in elegant harmony. Partners in ecstasy, watching each other thrill to the private pleasure of release. Sharing a ceremonial, but heartily real, lovers' piss.

And I'm so pleased I was able to find a judge who's willing to officiate.

Slightly Ajar

SLIGHTLY AJAR

First, she started to leave the door slightly ajar. More or less closed—but not, technically, shut. Open just enough so that the merry reverberations of her waterfall would squeeze through the crack, creating a subtle soundtrack to accompany the glowing sliver of bathroom fluorescence that I could see from across the dimly lit bedroom.

On the first couple of occasions, I attributed it to carelessness. I assumed that Bernadette had intended to shut the door but hadn't pushed hard enough. But soon a pattern emerged. The narrow stripe of light became a reliable indication that Bernadette was in there peeing. This was the only time the door was slightly ajar, neither really open nor really closed. It was what a statistician would call a one-to-one correlation, and a mathematician an "if and only if" statement. If Bernadette was in there peeing, the door was ajar; if the door was ajar, Bernadette was in there peeing. It was a logically airtight correspondence.

It excited me. I didn't know why it excited me to have two inches of bathroom light bring me closer to my own wife's tinkling, but it did. This was a woman I'd fucked almost every night for three years, whose most intimate areas I'd probed and explored and titillated and feasted upon till I knew every one of her erogenous hot spots better than I knew the back of my own cock. And yet it triggered a novel sort of arousal to hear her peeing with the door slightly ajar.

I became accustomed to this curious new habit of hers, and

I waited to see what, if anything, would develop from it. Was something expected of me?

A few weeks after she had introduced the sliver of bathroom light into our relationship, she began talking to me through the crack. Now, we have a little rule between us that we try not to talk when we can't see each other's faces. We both grew up in homes where family members would shout to each other from the bottom of the stairs, from far corners of the house, or even from outdoors, through the screen windows … and we were determined to be more civilized than that. We'd learned early on how easy it was to mishear content or misconstrue tone in the absence of visual cues. So our rule is that if I have something to say and Bernadette is not in sight, then I will go find her, and vice versa.

Therefore, Bernadette had to know that if she spoke to me from her womanly perch on the toilet when the door was almost-but-not-quite shut, I would instinctively come through the door, so as to better facilitate effective communication. After all, *she* clearly wasn't going anywhere for the time being—so the burden would be on me to come to her.

The first time it happened, this instinct propelled me into the bathroom before I was fully conscious of the implications. But when I gazed on the sight of my wife, poised elegantly on the commode, her panties rolled slightly out of place—aptly analogous to the barely ajar door I'd opened—it hit me that I'd walked into a hitherto unknown space. I felt as if I'd entered a shrine. Though I was, of course, entirely familiar with our bathroom, it had become at this moment a sacred locus of feminine mystery: the place where a woman urinates.

She was asking if there were any mushrooms left. I'd made a stew the night before, and she wondered if I'd used them all up. It was a reasonable thing to ask at 6:00 p.m., with dinner on our minds. But did she really need to know the answer before returning from her brief visit to the bathroom?

As I stared at her bare thighs, which emerged with a jaunty raunchiness from her bunched-up skirt, I became conscious of my erection. And of the fact that I couldn't, for the life of me, recall the status of the mushrooms.

Though Bernadette had actually concluded her pissing before I'd arrived, she didn't appear to be in a hurry to remove her bare ass from the seat. So we stayed where we were, while I muttered something about checking the refrigerator. I noticed that her smile seemed to have a special glow to it.

Finally, she reached behind and under herself to wipe her pussy dry, thus exposing me to a routine gesture of feminine maintenance—one that I naturally knew about, but had never before observed. She did it with such a graceful motion that it was anything but mundane. And it surprised me that she did it from behind, which somehow made it sexier. I felt a vibration in my groin that had an odd, sentimental quality to it. For some reason, this act of hygiene emphasized my wife's softness and put a tender finish on my libido. I reached for the vanity to steady myself.

When we made love later that night, I was thinking about what I'd seen before dinner.

Over time, the crack in the door began to widen. And the unnecessary conversations that Bernadette engineered became a frequent feature of her evening tinkles. These dialogues were always timed so that I'd enter her sanctuary shortly after her activity had trickled to a conclusion, but before she had wiped. I didn't fully understand her motivation, but I knew that the ritual was one that always left me tingling, and Bernadette glowing. And it gradually dawned on me that this, of course, *was* the motivation.

The timing of Bernadette's toilet-seat conversations changed momentously one evening. "Are you going to be able to drive me to work tomorrow?" she inquired. In this instance, she spoke just moments after she'd dashed out of sight. I had returned home only a few minutes earlier, and had found her waiting for me in the bedroom, but evidently ready to head into the bathroom without further ado. I'd noticed that she was already undoing the belt buckle at the waist of her denim skirt as she crossed the threshold.

Upon hearing her voice from beyond the unclosed door, I

looked at the wide shaft of light as if it were a beacon of joy.

I entered.

She had not only dropped her denim skirt and powder-blue panties; she had allowed her feet to step out of them entirely. Her legs were spread generously as she prepared to let go. From her navel on down, I could see everything.

She sat poised, exposed in naked glory. And here, as in the bedroom, she had waited for me. Not a drop had yet emerged to kiss her quivering pussy and journey down into the bowl.

I started to stammer something about tomorrow's car pool, when an impressive roar overtook me. How could I never have ventured in to watch before? How could I have missed such a wonderful, erotic phenomenon? Smooth thighs, sensuous bush, adorable nether lips … frame and backdrop for one of nature's most breathtaking miracles—a woman peeing. A woman spreading her legs and giving in to an insistent private fountain-head. Letting all her senses be overtaken by the aquatic bliss of the flow, and allowing—in effect requesting—that I watch every drop come out of her.

I was enchanted by the fact that it was difficult to see through the rapids to discern the actual source. I was fascinated by the illusion that the water was coming from everywhere at once. It was spectacular.

Bernadette, in her present guise as a urinating woman, seemed to exude a sexuality more potent than anything I'd previously seen her express. This simple biological process, in its feminine incarnation, threw her femaleness into such sharp relief, both anatomically and sensually, that I felt this might be the quintessential context in which to admire her. Bernadette, legs apart, immersed in this all-absorbing task, was perhaps the most beautiful Bernadette I'd ever seen.

Idiotically, I still felt obligated to address the question about who was driving whom to work the next day. I struggled to concentrate, despite the fact that I had my hand in my underwear, stroking hard. "Uh … I have to be in the office a little early, so … "

She interrupted at once. "Shh! Please, Derek. Shut up, honey.

Shut up and watch me," she said rapidly. "Just watch me pee, for goodness' sake." Her face was transfixed, watching me watch her. She attempted to spread her legs even further. It was physically impossible … but she tried, with a symbolic compulsiveness. Her cheeks were flushed and her eyes were half-closed, though still focused on me. She was now squirming, clearly making the most of her intimate sensations. Then she started to laugh—a strange mixture of delight and release. "You're watching. Oh wow, you're watching." She was as turned on as I'd ever seen her.

She grabbed herself. Her eyes closed as she cried my name.

She was still pissing forcefully across her fingers as the orgasm cooked through her. I imagined how the warm waters must feel against her hand. This was when I shot my seed all over her thighs.

Testing the Waters

He didn't know it, but my obsession had begun the night our friends Tammy and Craig came over to sample beers. It was around midnight when they left, and—for the umpteenth time on this lager-laden evening—I had to piss for all I was worth. I ran upstairs, not even waiting till I was in the bathroom to start sliding my panties down. Just as I closed the door behind me, I heard Derek's footsteps on the stairs. By the time I'd settled into place, I knew he was in the bedroom.

The water came out of me quickly at first, then slowly and deliciously. And I realized, as all my muscles relaxed and my nerves oohed and ahhed with the joy of peeing, that I was seriously horny. After three years of marriage, it was suddenly driving me wild to know that Derek was on the other side of the bathroom door while I sat here, exposed and tingling.

I'd had quasi-orgasmic peeing sessions many times in the past, but they'd always existed in isolation. It had never occurred to me to relate them to my larger sexuality, or to link them to my sex life with Derek. But now, as I pissed my pretty ass off, I found myself craving something I'd never craved before—that Derek could be in here watching me, sharing this experience, seeing every pulse of pleasure travel from my crotch to my face

… dipping his hand into my water, touching my nakedness and feeling my two wetnesses.

It struck me that with my legs spread immodestly and my pee flowing freely, I was uninhibited, open, and sensually awake on a level that rivaled or perhaps even surpassed the sharing of myself that occurred during sex. My entire body seemed united in the electric carnality of what was happening between my legs. I was peeing as only a woman could, feeling that special pleasure spread itself through places that only a woman has. I felt primally and holistically in touch with my own femininity. I felt like I wanted to piss forever. And I suddenly had a revelation that, as a sexual being, this was perhaps the ultimate, essential me—the horny, natural woman with water flowing out of her feminine juncture, whose intimate muscles and nerves were dancing euphorically around her stream. And it struck me that this was the woman I now desperately wanted Derek to meet.

I dragged it out as long as I could, until I simply couldn't pee anymore. While the warm, lingering drops still tickled my most sensuous zone, I brought myself off, trembling on the toilet seat with my panties at my ankles. I could hear Derek puttering around in the next room as I came. Afterward, I tenderly licked my fingers dry.

That night in bed, I pounced on Derek even more enthusi-astically than usual. As my cunt pulsated around him, I caught myself fantasizing that I was pissing in his presence.

I knew I had to test the waters. So I started "forgetting" to close the door all the way. I began chattering to him from the toilet, so he'd come into the bathroom just after I'd finished, when I was still cunt-naked on the seat. It made me slippery to play host to him while I sat there.

Then, it was time to take the next step.

I was wearing a short denim skirt that evening, I remember. I felt the slow, lazy beginnings of a need about thirty minutes before he was due to arrive home. Once I'd made the decision to wait for him, it became a pleasant challenge. I turned it into an autoerotic game, nurturing my kinky predilection for the thrill of "holding it"—something it was high time I told Derek about,

I realized. (Would he get off on it?) I turned a reverent focus to the current dammed up inside me, and I paced myself through the passing minutes of anticipation and excitement. The need blossomed, and at moments I felt like I was about to lose it, to wet myself wildly over the bedroom floor—and it further aroused me to fantasize about Derek finding me in such a situation. But then I'd re-cross my legs or wedge a hand into my crotch ... and immediately the impending flood would become tame again, a force that I could control a while longer, and whose pulsing tingle I could continue to revel in lewdly. Like a skillful woman on the brink of an intense orgasm, who prolongs that moment for as long as she can continue to milk her pleasure from the tension, I was as reluctant to release as I was certain that the release would rock me to the heels when I finally permitted it. Every minute, half of me hoped that Derek was about to pull up in the driveway and accompany me to the commode for my cascade. But the other half hoped his arrival would be delayed just a few minutes longer, so I could keep squeezing my thighs and playing with that inner tickle.

He arrived at last, and I lured him into the bathroom by dint of some inane conversation. I roared forth with a piss so glorious that it made some of orgasm's greatest hits pale in comparison. And Derek saw every fluid ounce of it. I was in fucking paradise, sprawling there on the toilet for him. He was very cute, trying to answer my irrelevant question about the car while I showed him what it looks and feels like for a self-actualized lady to piss herself giddy after deliberately playing into thirty minutes of overtime.

It Never Rains but It Pours

After that night, my wife's routine need to urinate gained the status of a featured attraction in our life. Our evenings now often seemed to be structured around Bernadette pissing her heart out while I watched, crouching on the tile floor. She would finger herself, sometimes not even waiting till her stream abated. I would jerk off, usually coming while she was still in full flow. Sometimes it was my hand that caressed her wet pussy, instead of her own. Whatever the details, the sense of intimacy was indescribable.

It had always been common for me to look at Bernadette and think, "She's so very beautiful." These days, this thought was no less common; but it was often followed by the kinky corollary, "Will she have to pee soon?" I might have been troubled by this obsession, were it not for my confidence that Bernadette approved of it, and indeed had deliberately encouraged it. And I was not left alone to wonder when her panties would be coming down. For Bernadette had begun to keep me informed, with blushes and whispers, whenever she felt the liquid tickling up inside her.

When we had wine with dinner, I would watch her as she drank—study her face, her posture. "Is she starting to feel the need yet?" I would wonder. With every ambiguous shift in her position, with every swallow she took from her wine goblet or her water glass, I would anticipate the inevitable. And on the nights on which she opened a beer, I could barely contain myself as I envisioned the fluid consequences.

Imagine that you happened upon the banks of the Niagara River, and that the falls had been magically switched off. And imagine that you never knew that there were supposed to be falls there. You would, I believe, still find it gorgeous. But if you knew about the falls, you'd miss them. At times, now, this was how I felt about my wife's pussy. It was as lovely as it had ever been. But, at certain moments, what I craved most was to see it with her water pouring out of it.

It was when we were dining downtown with Tammy and Craig one Saturday that I realized how absolutely fixated I'd become on Bernadette's waterworks. We were indulging liberally in a selection of marvelous wines—with plenty of lemon-tinged water to accompany them—and I kept wondering when Bernadette would need to excuse herself. My attention wandered, again and again, to her body language—did I detect a pressure, a shifting of weight? I would be heading for the restroom myself before too long, and I was speculating that the rather pleasant sensations I was feeling behind my zipper were analogous to what she was feeling in her panties. As I communed with the familiar presence of my own beckoning reservoir—relishing that mixture of tension and titillation, that impetus to release which could, for a time, be cherished on a comfortable, gently swelling plateau—I imagined her experiencing the same things, in the anatomically female variant.

I was irrationally resentful of the fact that I wouldn't be able to accompany her when she went. And it was a bit of a shock to note that I cared more about my visions of Bernadette piddling voluminously into the restaurant's sparkling toilet than I cared about the excellent wine, the five-star food, or the urbane conversation. What, I wondered, would our friends think if they knew that the better part of my consciousness was now turned toward meditations upon the joys my wife feels when she holds her pee, along with rich conjectures regarding what pleasures travel through her erogenous territories as she releases it? They might be less inclined to pick up the tab, I supposed.

Despite my social qualms, my mind was drifting further and further from the restaurant chitchat. I found myself entertaining the bizarre thought that it would be incredibly erotic for the two of us to eschew the restrooms entirely and simply wet our pants in unison—or, more accurately, in harmony, the alto and tenor ecstasies complementing each other. It had never before crossed my mind to seek sexual gratification through a fantasy of pissing in my clothes. But sitting there at the elegant restaurant table, I had a strong vision of how magical it could be to watch Bernadette quietly piss herself, while feeling a wet warmth in my own groin. I could vividly imagine how my own physical bliss would give dimension to the voyeuristic thrill of studying her face as she sensuously wet. Ah, to hold her hand across the table and watch her features relax as she gave in to her wetness. Ah, to look under the table and see her little knees twitch and her cute trousers darken at their feminine crotch, while I allowed a dedicated, complicit trickle of my own to approximate a shared experience.

Though this train of thought was making me hard, I was reasonable enough to see that this was a blueprint to file away for possible home use, and not one to bring to life in front of our friends in a restaurant. So I reluctantly set this fantasy aside before I came in my pants, peed in my pants, or both. It was then that my eyes met Bernadette's. She must have been observing my peculiarly preoccupied face, for her smile hinted at delight and curiosity.

She got up at last and headed in the appropriate direction for ladies who had been drinking much water and wine. I watched her handsomely trousered ass recede until she was out of sight. Then, while I feigned interest in a discussion of local jazz quartets, I wondered how thick and how forceful Bernadette's piss would be, how long it would continue, and how wide her smile would become as she enjoyed all the associated sensations. Would she touch herself, wishing I were with her? Would there be a woman in an adjoining stall who would hear a faint squeal of pleasure as Bernadette finished up? Would my wife's pelvis bounce as she made her last dribbles, or perhaps gyrate with tiny aftershocks?

My turn to leave the table came soon after Bernadette had reappeared, looking radiant. I had the men's room to myself. And, for the first time in my adult life, I elected to pee sitting down. In a convoluted twist on autoeroticism, I closed my eyes and pretended that I was Bernadette—pissing for me. It felt great; but I knew that we needed to go home and fuck before I drifted any further into an erotic haze.

By the time we arrived at the house, Bernadette was making it clear, with semi-masturbatory explicitness, that her bladder had long since forgotten the trip to the ladies' room. As had become typical, she made an uninhibited display of the enjoyable mixture of urgency and arousal that she experienced while holding on.

Hustling behind her jiggling ass as we traveled up the stairs, I felt that our splurgy evening out with our friends had been a mere prelude.

We entered the bedroom, and I turned on the light.

"Come on," she urged, pulling me forward toward the bathroom.

I stopped. It seemed so ridiculous, but I knew what I wanted. "Wait," I breathed. My heart raced to hear myself say it.

She giggled with a tipsy charm. "Derek, I'll wet my pants if I wait any longer."

"Yes," I said hopefully.

Her eyes widened.

"Unless you don't want to," I wavered.

I waited to see if she would rush for the toilet. But she froze in place. Her eyes lit up the room.

"Oh, Derek," was all she said when she dissolved into sensation. She shivered as she wholeheartedly relinquished control. An instant later, she was clutching frenetically at her pants, celebrating what was happening down there with bold, nurturing strokes.

Now it was my turn to freeze in place, as I watched her intimate waters seep through the crotch seam, rush down each leg, and puddle crazily onto the hardwood floor. It was, for the observer, a transcendent experience.

Bernadette was laughing, dancing, and chanting. She was totally enthralled by her own act of sensual abandon. She was wetting her fucking pants for me, and she was having the time of her life doing it.

Eventually, with the vigorous flow still continuing, she peeled the trousers and clinging panties down so that I could see the inside story. I marveled at nature's sweet, gorgeous cascade. I admired it as it descended from the delirious pink pussy of a lady on the brink of knee-knocking orgasm, into the yearning geography of her woman-soaked clothing below.

It was Niagara Falls, with everything switched on.

Peeosk

SEAN STANDS IN THE WELL-LIT STAINLESS STEEL KIOSK, WHICH opens in an oval at the top—about a foot above his head. Mounted on the wall in front of him is a high-quality monitor, with sound.

The outside of the kiosk is encircled by a utilitarian staircase. The woman who has signed up for tonight's "pleasurable erotic adventure," having arrived as instructed with a reasonably full bladder, downs a glass of beer and mounts the stairs.

Viewed from the outside, the hole at the top of the kiosk is a sparkling toilet seat—mounted on a pedestal complete with cushioned foot rests, so the woman can sit in total comfort. The camera, suspended by a boom, faces her from a few feet away.

She pulls her cute little panties to her knees and lowers her bare bottom to the seat; but she is asked not to release her pee until she can't help it. She smiles for the camera.

Inside, Sean relishes the sight of the volunteer's pussy from below. It looks so sweet and delicate framed by her ass flesh. And he knows how ready it is to pee down for him.

Without further ado, he raises the feather. He watches her face on the monitor as he gives the plump, beautiful outer lips of her vulva the first gentle brush.

The woman's face lights up. "Oh my godddddddd," she giggles. "Someone's tick—he's ti—he's eeeheeeheeeheee." Sean looks up from the screen to watch the pussy squirming delightedly as he titillates it. Then back to the monitor. Her face is a portrait of erotic excitement, moaning between the broken giggles. He continues.

"Oh, my g—I'm gonna … I'm …"

And now, here it comes. The pink, fleshy split, still dancing on his feather, releases its rain, and woman-water pours down, reverberating magically wherever it hits the metal floor.

On the monitor, the woman's face is ecstatic now. She whimpers *yes*es as she writhes on her toilet seat of pleasure.

By keeping his gaze in motion, Sean can almost see both perspectives at once—the near-orgasmic woman and the pee-crazy, tickle-loving pussy—and he grinds his dick into the palm of his free hand while he enjoys every moment of this.

Her piss showers his shoulder; stray drops dot his lips. He licks them up, and kisses her from afar.

Judy Never . . .

My girlfriend Judy never asked me to follow her around so I could watch her pee. On the other hand, she never asked me not to.

She never said, "Get out of here," or even, "May I please have some privacy, Neil?" She never closed the door on me or asked me to close my eyes on her. She never frowned while I listened.

At her office, where she was alone on Wednesday afternoons, I knew that if I appeared at around 3:00, I'd probably be in time for her customary mid-afternoon piddle. She never raised an eyebrow when I followed her into the company's tiny bathroom.

And one week, when I arrived a bit later, I was pleasantly surprised to find that Judy had waited for me. No sooner had I kissed her hello than she scurried into the john, with me close behind. When she quickly pulled her panties down, the raw scent of her pussy hit me in the face like a warm ocean breeze. She didn't tell me she'd gotten turned on, waiting for me to show up so that she could piss on display. She didn't have to tell me.

And all the while, I'd thought of this as *my* kink. Little did I know that sexy Judy could outkink me.

That same Wednesday afternoon, I was invited to fuck Judy over her desk after she'd peed. I licked her pussy for ten minutes first, while I supported her legs on my shoulders and fondled her bare ass. I remember tasting the tartness of a lone drop of pee that she'd missed, which added sass to the sweetness of her juice. While she came in my face, I visualized her pissing pretty on the toilet, sitting up so straight and proud, in a quintessential feminine posture.

A couple of minutes later, she writhed beneath me with particular gusto while I rammed into her. I slapped her butt cheeks lightly and imagined tinkling sounds harmonizing with the real-life pleasure squeals she was making. As I squirted spunk into her pussy, I was crazy with lust for this vixen who had waited to pee in my presence.

When we returned from a pleasant evening of drinking that Friday, I was expecting Judy to head immediately for the bathroom. Instead, she embraced me lingeringly and kissed me deeply.

"I really have to pee," she whispered in my ear.

My cock instantly hardened. "OK," I said. "Let's go."

"No," said Judy. She kissed me again and wriggled into me. I could feel the tension in her body as her mound pressed against my erection. I could tell that she was savoring what she was feeling inside.

I reached under the back of her skirt, slipped a finger under the floss of her lace thong, and teased between her cheeks.

"Yeah," she purred.

I dropped to my knees and crept behind her. I lifted her skirt and studied the clenching of her near-naked ass, knowing she was relishing the pee she held tightly in her crotch—so close to me, so ready to spill out. Just a tickle away.

"Make me wet myself," I heard her say.

This was something she'd never asked of me. But I was more than willing.

I worked a mischievous finger along the edge of her gusset, coaxing her release. As I stroked her there, I nibbled gently on her right bottom cheek.

She soon succumbed to my titillations and lost control, just like she wanted to. Her warmth began to flood sensuously onto my hand, while her derriere wiggled deliciously in my face. "Oh, fuck, wow," she moaned, dancing in ecstasy as her crotch became a magical sea of womanly piss, a juncture of sensuality.

I was in paradise knowing that Judy's clit, vibrating like an electric motor, was throbbing against the white lace as the hot fluid filled every niche inside her panties. I'd rarely seen her this overwhelmed by pleasure, even when we fucked.

I pulled the sopping gusset aside and watched the furious stream hurry down. So much sweet water, rushing thickly out of Judy's little body. I was enchanted, and my cock ached deeply, inside trousers made damp by her cascade. I touched her delicate lips through her fountain, and she gasped erotically.

When she finally finished, I unzipped and welcomed her onto my lap. I shoved my crazed rod into her soggy pussy and bounced her ass on my thighs like a big rubber ball. She had a hand glued to her clit, and she came, howling, even faster than I did.

"Did you like that?" I said softly.

"Mmhuh," she replied weakly. She collapsed in my arms, using what little strength she had left to kiss my neck.

It wasn't Judy's style to tell me what she wanted far in advance. She would unveil her fantasies on very short notice, or she would wait for me to stumble upon them. Sometimes I could guess that a new desire was taking shape in her mind, even though I didn't know what it was. For example, she'd had a strange glimmer in her eye for about three weeks prior to the night she handed me a feather and told me it needed to go up and down, up and down the length of her bottom cleft until she was a millimeter away from an orgasm.

The week after she soaked her white lace for me, Judy didn't ask me to crawl under her desk, when her boss was busy with a phone call in the inner office, and remove her panties. No, she never asked, but she made sure her legs cooperated fully with the maneuver, making my access easy and efficient.

She didn't ask me to kiss and lick her snatch for as long as I could, until she saw the phone light on her console die— meaning that Cynthia might emerge from her office, and I'd better be somewhere other than in between Judy's legs when and if she did.

Judy didn't ask me to occupy Cynthia with small talk while she quietly slipped into the restroom to finish what I'd started. Sometimes, a devoted lover simply knows what to do.

As it turned out, Cynthia was glad to have me alone, because she wanted to enlist my help. Judy had been with the company for about a year, and they were planning a surprise party in her honor. My assignment was to escort her, under some pretext, to the site of the party—a banquet room at a restaurant the company was in bed with, in a business-to-business way. I assured Cynthia that I would make it happen. I had a week and a half to fine-tune my plan.

Accomplishing Cynthia's assignment was a no-brainer. It wasn't unusual for me to spring "I'm taking you out to dinner" surprise dates on Judy, and I would simply present this as one of those. But I decided I wanted to fulfill more than the basic task that had been given to me. I felt there had to be a way to turn the whole thing into a special erotic event for me and Judy.

The idea came to me. It might or might not work out—the timing had to be just right. But, with a little luck ...

It was a fun evening—enough fun that I kept forgetting this was a work party and not a "real" party. Laughter flowed in abundance, and so did the company-sponsored drinks.

As things were winding down and I felt Judy's leg fidgeting against mine, I knew the time was near.

"Excuse me a minute," she said to me, beginning to get up.

"Hold on," I said suavely, placing a hand around her waist. "Suppose you waited till we got home?"

Could she, comfortably, do that? I watched her calculating in her mind. Five minutes to say goodbyes. Ten or fifteen minutes to walk home. I saw her thighs squeeze together and her eyes flicker with interest.

"OK," she said cheerfully. I gave her bottom an inconspicuous pat before she eased back down.

Speaking more loudly now, we casually began to hint at

calling it a night. When we stood up for real, I saw Judy quickly smooth her short skirt down in front, and I could tell that she was feeling her need—and cherishing it.

She walked gracefully around the room with me, shaking hands, hugging shoulders, kissing cheeks. All the while, I knew she was nursing the waiting tide, feeling an insistent tickle in her panties as she stood still or strode along. And I felt a different sort of tickle, the erection that was developing in response to Judy's private sensations.

On the walk home, with no one else in sight, she pressed her palm into her crotch on occasion and giggled.

"I don't know if I'm going to make it," she said when we were just a block from our door. "It's kind of exciting, isn't it?"

Fuck, yes, it was exciting.

Once in the house, she dashed for the bathroom. I was right behind her. She got her panties off in record time, then pulled me into the bathtub and pushed me down onto my back.

And there was my Judy, bare under her miniskirt, poised inches from my face. Her soft pussy, in another instant, pissing tenderly onto my sealed lips … pissing freely, freely onto my quivering chin.

Naked pussy gushing. Peach-hued ass squirming. Horny woman moaning.

"Fuck me, Neil," she growled. She was still pissing hard, but she was so turned on she was yearning to be filled, thinking about that before she'd even finished this.

My Judy, full of party wine, was leaking gorgeously all over me and dying to be fucked. Life was sweet.

Showing amazing restraint, we waited till she had stopped wetting onto me—and until we'd cleaned ourselves up—to deliver the fucking she craved. Her body, fresh from the shower, was hot against our cool sheets, and her cunt gaped open for me while I finished drying myself off.

Judy didn't ask me to jump on her and start pounding away, rather than spending long, delicious minutes teasing her nipples with my tongue or licking gingerly at her pussy lips, as I often did. She didn't ask; but it was clear from the personality of her hungry sprawl that she needed me banging inside her without further ado. She was wildly aroused—and to think, I'd ultimately brought her to this state just by encouraging her to walk home with a bladder full of nature's Chablis.

With my dick between her legs and my hands madly groping her breasts, we quickly wrestled ourselves into a frenzy. Judy, all the while, was holding on to her clit for dear life. Our orgasms arrived in sync, and the flow of my come and the wet contractions of her cunt recalled the motion of her warm rain over my face.

Judy never told me that she expected our hike in the woods to climax with some piss-primed fucking. But I knew where two hours sucking down water under a generous October sun were sure to take us; and I suspected that her enthusiasm for this particular form of weekend recreation had a lot to do with that physiology. There was no doubt by now that pee-drenched sex was Judy's latest obsession.

It was an easy trail—as unrugged as it could be without actually being paved—and Judy was good to go in hiking boots, knee-high bramble-resistant socks, and a denim skirt. Above the waist, she wore a straw sun hat and a lightweight V-neck sweater that flattered her perky breasts.

And with no panties on—as I learned when she pulled me off the trail—she was especially good to go.

While she raised her skirt in the uneven shade of a friendly tree, I unzipped my jeans. "As long as we're stopping," I said.

I began to piss on some dead leaves, but Judy sidestepped in front of me and backed toward me so that my stream arced under the perpendicular arch of her legs. "Oh, yeah, that's sexy," she murmured, shimmying in place as she waited for her gates to open. "Oh, me too," she then said, as she gushed before my eyes, drowning my thin line in her awe-inspiring flood.

Though we were mostly in the shade, a stripe of sunlight nestled in the crack of her bottom, giving it the gleam of a smile.

She sighed as tremors of release ran through her. Her contribution to the party was a sheet of liquid beauty, sparkling like diamonds where unpredictable slivers of light favored it. "I love you," I said as I watched her piss in champion feminine style.

Judy was in a raunchy, outdoor mood, and she didn't bother with any dainty leaf-wiping. Without standing on ceremony, she turned to face the trunk of the tree, bending forward to hug it and putting her ass exactly where I needed it. We were far enough off the trail that she knew no one would disturb us.

Her pussy—slick inside and damp outside, for different reasons—took me with ease. Her warm, wet curls teased my balls as I dicked around within her. I held her middle and pressed myself to her ass, rubbing my belly sensuously across the edge of her hoisted skirt.

The world seemed so fresh as I scraped my desire-plumped shaft this way and that in her cunt. Judy, I'd learned, was at her most fuckable after a good piss, and I felt proud to have pissed with her this time.

The leaves beneath our feet made nice witnesses for our secret quickie—they were picturesque and quiet. Judy wasn't quiet, though. She was in heat, and her heat wasn't something to keep quiet about. She laughed and moaned every step of the way, and she wailed at that tree when she exploded.

Judy didn't tell me, at that moment, that it was time for me to come into her pussy like an animal, grinding every last drop out of my groin and into the soft, churning flesh that ground back at me.

But she didn't have to tell me, now did she?

Her Sensuous Secret

"OH, YES," SAID CAROLYN, "I'M ALMOST THERE."

"Let go for me, you sexy creature," said Oliver. "Go ahead and give in."

Carolyn gave in.

"Oh, wow, that feels good," she said, as her body quivered in his arms.

"I know, baby," said Oliver, gently kissing her neck. "You really had to pee, didn't you?"

"Um-hmm," said Carolyn, still in full stream. Her eyes were closed as she savored the sensation. Oliver fondled her breasts, and she squirmed pleasantly on the seat.

Pleasure pulsed between Carolyn's thighs. It had been building for a while, and she had been making it last as long as she could. Now, with the fantasy sizzling in her mind, she knew she couldn't eke it out any longer, and she let herself slide into the ecstasy of release.

She peed so forcefully that her eyes closed as if she were in a trance. What else could feel so good? she wondered.

She was no stranger to orgasms. But her best orgasms were triggered by pissing, and the orgasms were almost like afterthoughts. It was the pissing that really made Carolyn tremble, made her stuff her fingers into her mouth, made her glad to be alive.

This was her sensuous secret. It made her feel like a freak. A lucky freak, able to reach nirvana whenever her bladder was full.

"Tell your boyfriend," Anne kept urging. "*Tell him.*"

"I will," Carolyn promised her friend. "Eventually."

In her fantasies, Oliver watched her, sharing and reveling in her private quirk. In real life, Carolyn wondered when she would actually work up the nerve to let him in on her secret.

She'd been dropping hints, trying to safely plant the idea. "I have to *pee*," she would say before leaving a restaurant booth for the ladies' room, emphasizing the word, making brief eye contact with Oliver, and wondering if the idea excited him. Was that a flicker of interest she saw each time, or just a projection of her own enthusiasm?

In general conversation, she chose her words in a calculating manner, using colorful images like "I was so excited I was wetting my pants," and "It was so funny, I nearly peed my jeans."

Peed my jeans. The phrase, with its breezy sounds and startling imagery, was magical to Carolyn, and it made her panties a little moist with arousal to hear herself say it. She wondered what effect it had on Oliver. Was it just a figure of speech to him, or did it titillate him to imagine her cheerfully wetting herself?

She was aware of how noisily she pissed after they fucked. Her furious cascade seemed to reverberate more loudly in the still of the night, while Oliver lay in bed, drifting off, just a few feet beyond the bathroom door. She had to assume he heard every drop, and this excited her immensely.

"I hope I didn't disturb your sleep with my loud pissing," she said one night, deliberately drawing attention to it.

How long would she dance around it? she repeatedly asked herself—only to become immediately aroused, as she imagined herself dancing around Oliver, holding herself, about to do it for him.

She had discovered her sexual quirk early in her adult life, and it was a manifold kink. She relished the fluid, sensual act of emptying, with much more than the typical "relief feels good" attitude of most people. Carolyn's attitude while she peed was more like "Oh, *baby*, that feels good." Sometimes she even said things to herself in her head while it was happening: "*Do it. Yeah. Do it.*" Pissing away, she was like the sound track to her own private porn flick. She would have been embarrassed by this, if it hadn't felt so hot to hear these words resonating in her mind.

Once she had emptied, she relished the sensations of having done it. It was a luscious state of relaxation that, paradoxically, went hand in hand with a tingling ache in her clit and a slippery urgency in her pussy. After a hearty piss, Carolyn rarely left the seat without first doing justice to her arousal.

And how she relished the sweet sensations of holding it in, of taking herself to the edge of wetting her panties, with clenching thighs and jiggling ass, before finally giving it up. The ticklish pressure of those final moments, before she decided she absolutely had to let go, was indescribably delicious to her. If she gave herself a one-minute margin, she could let the urgency of her arousal trump the other urgency, and she'd hit the loo with fingers in her crotch, not simply to hold on, but to bring forth the orgasm she needed now, first … a quickie that would then inaugurate a free fall of post-climactic piss that became, in turn, its own climax.

Life could be sweet, when you knew how to get the most out of your own body.

Carolyn had a secret fondness for public restrooms, when they were empty and shiny and grand. What better place to recognize and celebrate herself as a woman than behind a door marked WOMEN, where she would expose the most female part of herself and utilize her feminine logistics? In this room, Carolyn reasoned, women proved their womanliness, no matter how little thought they might give to their gender in the course of their lives outside the door. With her panties lowered in some spotless stall, she always enjoyed feeling her feminine rain of pleasure come splashing down.

Rain. Like the real rain of rain-pelting days when she'd stride along the sidewalk, full of hot tea that raced to her bladder, until she felt she was ready to melt into a warm, autoerotic puddle.

Sometimes, when the circumstances were just right, she indulged herself fully, by actually wetting her panties. The feeling of saturated, clinging fabric caressing her pussy with her own warm wetness was heaven to Carolyn. When she was alone, Carolyn treated herself to panty wettings the way some women treated themselves to chocolate-chip cookies.

"How did you get up the nerve to tell that other guy?" Anne asked, over pizza and coffee.

"I didn't exactly have to tell Bert," Carolyn explained.

She told Anne the story of the one time she had wet herself accidentally, taking her "hold it" game too far in public, miscalculating during an evening of pub hopping with a group of friends. Carolyn deliberately left one of the pubs without visiting the restroom; and, in the course of hopping to the next, she soon found herself almost *literally* hopping. It didn't feel bad—in fact, it felt exquisite—but she recognized that she was really on the verge of losing control. Ultimately, she stopped and stood on the sidewalk, telling her friends she'd catch up with them. Bert, a friend of her roommate's whom Carolyn barely knew, looked back from the corner to see her soaking her jeans. Carolyn knew that her face looked pink under the street lamp—not from embarrassment, but from excitement.

Two days after the incident, she received a phone call from Bert.

"It's Bert. You know, Liza's friend."

"Sure. Hi, Bert." She was surprised to hear from him.

"I don't know how to tell you this, but … I've been thinking about the other night."

Carolyn felt a tingle begin to run through her. "Yes," she said cautiously, "that was a fun evening, wasn't it?"

"Yeah. You … uh … I hope you didn't mind too much what happened to you … on the sidewalk."

"No big deal," Carolyn said quickly, feeling flushed all over again.

"It sort of seemed like … well … like you enjoyed it."

At that point, Carolyn didn't know what to say. She felt a

rush of emotions at being found out—and she recognized that the primary feeling in the mix was a strong sexual thrill.

"I keep thinking about it," Bert confessed.

Bert had understood. And, during the semester that they dated, Carolyn had made the most of it.

"I have to pee," she'd whispered shyly the second time they were alone in his room, pressing her vibrating body against his belt buckle. "Let's fuck right now."

Bert was stroking her ass. "Will you be able to relax for it, baby?"

"I don't want to relax," she replied, pulling him onto the bed. "I want to jiggle and squirm and feel you tickling inside me till I come."

Soon she became comfortable enough with Bert to stage repeat performances of what had happened between pubs that first night—the difference being that these performances were intentional. She couldn't remember how many times Bert had chased her home to a bed of passionate fucking, after watching her piss her jeans or knickers for him.

But there was more to a relationship than wet panties, and they'd eventually drifted apart. Nevertheless, memories of squirming under him with her bladder full could still make her come in a jiffy.

It had been a long time since she'd shared her special delights with a man. But every morning, afternoon, and evening, she treated her flowing water like a lover, delighting in the way it touched her in places that only a lover would touch. The warm fluid licked and caressed her between her legs, aroused her, and, with the help of her horny fingers, brought her off.

As for Oliver … apart from the hints, she'd been biding her time. He was sensitive and kind, and the relationship was a very solid one; but it had built itself up slowly. Everything in its time, Carolyn told herself.

At 7:00, Carolyn cut short her dinner with Anne, because Oliver was scheduled to perform for her at 8:00. Technically, he was performing for an entire audience—but Carolyn liked pretending it was just for her.

While a backing track cranked his compositions, Oliver filled the club with his delicate voice and magnetic stage presence. He looked especially appetizing up there to Carolyn. He was wearing a silk shirt in a handsome burgundy, and tight black jeans that she wanted to peel off with her teeth. The spotlight caught his face in a way that seemed to capture every detail of the kindness that she could always read there.

Watching his captivating performance, she was getting hornier and hornier … and she also realized that she had to pee, thanks to her two cups of coffee with Anne. This realization quickly moved from the back of her mind to the forefront, where she took the usual kinky pleasure in savoring the feeling and anticipating its release. She was reluctant to leave the room while her hunger for Oliver was surging so magically in her cunt, so this was a good opportunity to indulge her fondness for holding on. The desire and the piss welled up in harmony until she could no longer tell them apart, and the intimate hand she pressed against herself, hidden under the nightclub table, was there both to help her contain her water and to give some satisfaction to her wide-awake clit.

She couldn't sit still. In the dark, invisible even to Oliver, she became a kinetic masterpiece of arousal and containment. At last, she absolutely had to dash to the bathroom. As the hot piss rushed out of her, she felt that her entire body was consumed with the heat of her passion for him. Empty, she trembled on the toilet, wishing his cock could be rammed up inside her at that very moment.

She resolved that she would one day tell him every detail of this evening.

She fucked his head off that night, and in the days that followed she could think of nothing but the fact that she wanted desperately to share her secret.

"I have to pee," she said with her now-customary emphasis, as they strolled through the park.

"I think the restrooms are that way," said Oliver, pointing ahead and to the right.

As they walked in the direction of the facilities, Carolyn's mind zoomed off in a different direction.

"I'm not in the mood for a restroom," she explained, a hand darting to her crotch. "Come here." She grabbed his hand and pulled him off the path.

Still clutching his hand, she led him down a hill and onto an empty chunk of grass, out of sight of the path. He sat down to watch her bare her ass and water the lawn.

He was surprised when, instead, she climbed upon him, her sun-kissed cutoffs dry and warm against his lap. Her hair brushed his nose as she took his arms and pulled them around her.

She turned her head and whispered, "Tickle me."

He gently titillated under the hem of her jersey, then snuck a couple of fingers up into her right armpit. She giggled prettily.

Suddenly, his lap felt pleasantly warmer. And wet.

Anne continued to be her confidante on this topic, as on so many topics.

"When we're having sex, or even when we're just doing any old thing, I keep visualizing these scenes. Scenes of pissing for him. On him. With him."

Anne nodded. "Very sexy," she said.

"*You* think it's sexy?"

"Don't act so surprised," said her friend. "You don't have a monopoly on thinking that peeing is sexy. I can just picture you, you know, doing it. Nice."

"Oh, come on." Carolyn waved Anne's remarks aside.

"What? I've told you that I like girls, and I've even told you that I'm sort of infatuated with you, despite your tiresome straightness. Or weren't you paying attention?"

"No," Carolyn smiled, "I was paying attention. Thanks, Anne."

"You've got to tell him these stories, babe." Anne's cheeks looked warm.

"I know I should. I know."

"You've been living with the guy for three months. What are

you waiting for?"

"I know."

"Here," said Anne on the next occasion they met, handing Carolyn a microcassette recorder.

"What's this?"

"A tape recorder, obviously. Now that classes are out for the summer, I won't be needing it for a while. I've even put a blank tape in there for you."

"But what am I supposed to do with this?"

"Tell it every one of your fantasies. Then play the tape for Oliver."

Carolyn felt herself blushing.

"And you just let me know if you need more tapes," said Anne. "Or if you need someone to preview them."

Carolyn reasoned that it couldn't hurt to record her fantasies. She could always decide later whether or not to play the tape for Oliver.

That night, while Oliver was out of the house, she switched on the recorder.

"I'm on a stage, in a grand old auditorium. The stage is black, and a warm spotlight illuminates me. I am dressed only in lingerie, and I need to pee. This is what these thousands of people have come to see, and this is what I have come here to give them. You, of course, are in the front row.

"I strut, I touch myself, I tease by pulling my knickers down and then up again. I cross and uncross my legs, I stand and dance and squat and rise. Then, when I can't hold off any longer, I stand with my legs apart and my arms extended, fingertips sparkling like a jazz dancer, and I wet my lovely panties for the whole auditorium, for the whole world … and for you."

Her right hand was deep inside her underwear as her left switched off the machine. She wasn't sure she would ever play it for Oliver, but it had made her incredibly hot to speak it aloud for the inanimate audience of the magnetic tape.

She hit "rewind," then listened to her own narration while her pussy danced around her fingers and her clit sang over the melody line strummed by her thumb. Her voice sounded meek, but impassioned and compelling. Though the story on the tape was a short one, Carolyn was coming like a teakettle before it was over.

It was becoming an obsession, and Oliver realized he had to tell her. Even if he risked shocking her.

It was laughable to think that she'd actually apologized for the noise of her water music through the bathroom door. He'd reassured her, of course, that it was nothing to apologize for. What he hadn't told her—not yet—was that the sound was an incredible turn-on, always leaving him fixated on the image of her sitting there, panties absent or at her feet, tinkling beautifully. On the occasion she'd apologized, it was amazing she hadn't notice how hard he was after her return from the bathroom.

Oliver thought about how predictable a man's pissing was— always that thin, tight line. With a woman, the breadth and shape and force could span such a variety of fascinating patterns, depending on the urgency and her position and what she did or didn't do with her hands … and on the infinite possibilities afforded by physics. You never knew what the show would be.

He remembered his times with Peggy, the woman who liked to water him like a garden.

He had asked Peggy to share her deepest fantasy; and, in the due course of events, he lay naked for her as she made long-legged strides toward him, her legs conveying a beautiful tension. When she stood directly above his lap, she bubbled forth an eager, uncontainable stream, soon followed by a hissing rush.

"Thank you, thank you," she said fervently as she gushed down onto his middle, dipping her fingers into her own stream to masturbate. Only later did Peggy learn that the experience had been as thrilling for Oliver as it had been for her.

Oliver and Peggy had had some pretty wild times—such

as the party where, at Peggy's request, he and her best friend hoisted her up, each holding one leg, and gave her a ride around the room while she peed ecstatically and uncontrollably through her pink underwear, making a trail on the floor. He could still remember the taste of her freshly wet panties as he kissed her crotch, before setting her back down.

What would Carolyn think of a story like that? Oliver honestly didn't know. But he thought perhaps he could teach her to appreciate the erotic potential of her private fountain, if he could persuade her to approach it with an open mind.

In his own mind, he'd developed various scenarios for bringing the matter into focus. Were these strategies, he wondered, or merely fantasies?

"I have to pee," she said with a smirk.

He saw something in her eyes that looked like an open door, read something in her smile that might spell an opportunity. His voice was husky as he grabbed her by the waist. "You like that feeling, don't you?"

Her laughter became instantly more erotic as she wriggled joyously in his arms. In that moment, he knew that she knew what was going to happen, and that it was what both of them wanted.

She broke free of him and began to scamper giddily around the room, her ass wiggling in her aqua panties. Soon she let him catch her again, knowing full well that he would coax her into pissing her drawers. His hands roved over her.

"You realize if you so much as touch my nipple again," she said breathily, "I'll be pumping hot piss into my boy shorts. You realize that, right?"

"You're not wearing boy shorts," he said softly. "You're wearing little bikini-cut panties."

"I forgot," she answered, dancing in his arms.

He ran a feather-light hand over her delicious midriff. "Do it, angel. Wet those little bikini panties for me."

"I can't hold it any longer," she said between giggles, and it seemed to him like the sexiest statement he'd ever heard. He felt her panties begin to turn warm and moist against his jeans, the beginning of a slowly spreading wetness.

She twisted so that her bottom pressed against his denim-clad cock, and she gyrated across him. He bent with her, giving her a lap to anoint.

"Tell me how you can't stop," he urged.

"Oh, god, no," she breathed, "I can't stop. I can't stop and I wouldn't want to, because it feels too—oh!" She clutched her crotch and shuddered in his arms.

When she had finished soaking herself for him, he stripped her wet panties off her and unzipped his jeans. She reached a hand behind her ass and guided him into her slippery chasm. She ground around him in a juicy, restless ecstasy.

Carolyn hoped, on whatever night she finally sprang it on him, that it would stop the evening in its tracks, turning it from a mere date into an historic event. She could visualize his expression—the expression she hoped he'd have, anyway—when, sitting in their bathroom, she kicked her panties off, pivoted her legs, and lifted her skirt to give him a good view. Only when she was sure he was looking right there, right at her pussy, would she let the water flow.

After he'd seen that, she hoped that perhaps dessert could stay in the fridge and the rented movie could be saved for another night. She imagined being carried to the bedroom, her intimate muscles still tingling, and then feeling his face explore between her legs. She imagined his huge appetite for her after he'd enjoyed the voyeuristic after-dinner treat.

On the Saturday she chose, her mind was fantasizing overtime, hours before they were scheduled to leave for the restaurant.

"Do you need to pee before we go out?"

She laughed, moving close to him. "Would you like that, kinky boy?" She took his hand and brought it up to her crotch for a moment. "Does it feel like I need to? Do you want to watch?" She pulled her panties halfway down her thighs, brought her own hand to where his had been, and squeezed it against the juncture of her legs. "Mmm ...

I guess I do need to." She shimmied in place.

"Oh, yes, nurse it," *he groaned.* "Nurse it between your legs till you start to dribble into your hand."

Carolyn had planned for a strategic display of after-dinner pissing. As it happened, however, events before dinner overtook her plans.

They were chatting affectionately while Carolyn applied her makeup, standing at the bathroom vanity in the lacy white underwear she liked to wear under her elegant summer date clothes. Oliver leaned against the doorway.

"OK, I have to pee now, babe," she said, after she was satisfied with her face.

In the mirror, she saw that his eyes were moving left to right to follow the motion of her ass, which swayed a bit as she held her water.

"So I guess I should leave," he said, without moving. His eyes looked very bright.

"I guess so," said Carolyn. She could hear that she sounded unconvinced—and unconvincing.

She turned to face him, without moving away from the vanity. She placed a hand over the front of her panties. After a pregnant silence, she smiled. "You haven't left."

"I guess I haven't." He returned the smile.

Before either of them could overthink it, she slid her knickers down and plunked herself onto the toilet. It amazed Carolyn to find that it was as simple as that.

Oliver instinctively averted his eyes.

"Hey—over here," Carolyn cooed, drawing his gaze back her way. "Enjoy," she said, spreading her knees for him.

As the water flowed, she couldn't believe it was finally happening. Her pussy was slick with excitement, and her clit was buzzing; and when Oliver stepped forward and reached between her legs, not even waiting for her to finish, she twisted in ecstasy. The combination of his touches and the brazen intimacy of what she was doing for him drove her wild, and she jiggled on the toilet seat in an uncontrollable frenzy of pleasure.

When she was finally done pissing and coming, he kissed

her pee-drizzled thighs tenderly, working his way up to her hot, raunchy slit. He caressed her with toilet paper and then escorted her to the bedroom, without his hand ever leaving her throbbing groin. So much for dinner, thought Carolyn happily.

Oliver took in the sight and the sound. It was all so beautiful, from the fuzzy little flowing pussy to the glow in Carolyn's eyes.

The waterfall between her legs was intoxicating, and it represented what could only be called a watershed. The unarticulated obsession that had, to some extent, divided them had now emerged as something to further unite them.

On the bed, he took the top position, so as to devour her with wild kisses and plunge in and out of her randy hole, with a tool made extra stiff by the thrill she'd just given him. Under these circumstances, his libido was as beyond control as the heartiest session of urination, and he soon erupted into her.

When he withdrew, he continued to hold her legs open. He tasted the complex flavors, relishing the tiny hint of fresh, feminine pee that lingered in the cocktail of their combined juices. Slowly, he licked and teased her toward, and then over, the brink of her second orgasm.

As she climaxed on Oliver's face, Carolyn replayed her bathroom exhibitionism in her mind. She couldn't wait till she had to pee again.

When the time came, she whispered her need to him, and invited him into the bathtub.

She'd slipped into a tank top and thong after they'd fucked. Now, before lowering herself onto his lap in the tub, she yanked the panties down and off.

She sighed, and, almost immediately, she knew that he was feeling her first warm wavelet. He stiffened in response, and he began to press against her tenderness, even as the stream continued to build.

"Yes, rub your dick against me," she urged. "Rub it and then fuck me while I pee." As he complied, the uncontrollable dribbling picked up force, and her warmth bathed him.

She loved feeling some of her piss caressing their skin while she was simultaneously feeling more of it flow out, and still more of it tease inside her. The flow of her water linked them together, touching both of them at once and pleasuring each of them in different ways.

The mixture of sensations was almost too much for her, and she orgasmed around him while still wetting his lap. Her warmth and wetness and wildness, in turn, took Oliver over the edge, and he added his sticky fluid to the mix.

They sat nested in the tub, and he kissed her breasts and shoulders. "Hmm," he said after a while, "I have to piss now, too."

"All over my belly. Please." She took hold of his spout and invited his stream up onto her tummy, rubbing his piss onto her skin. "Mmm … so warm."

Sitting half in and half out of his lap, her ass in their warm, intimate puddle and her cunt pulsing with an animal satisfaction, Carolyn couldn't remember ever being so happy. She thought of the tape in Anne's cassette recorder, which she had filled with private fantasies. Whether she and Oliver would listen to them together or skip ahead to acting them out was a matter for conjecture.

She shuddered as another little offering of piss tinkled out of her and onto Oliver's toes. She closed her eyes as he kissed her, and she felt gratitude and love flowing from his lips to her own.

Volume 2

Phone Support

THE ART-DEPARTMENT MANAGER HAD A TYPICAL SET OF GOALS for this retreat—a glorified camping trip for the art staff. And Alec, always a good sport about corporate nonsense, had resolved to show the proper team spirit.

But much more important to Alec was the personal goal that he'd set.

Alec's goal was to take things as far as he could with Iris, without crossing the line. No, he couldn't cross the line—that was of paramount importance—but he was also intent on not leaving any thrills untasted on this side of the line. In the coming days, it was desperately important to him to make the most of the magic of flirtation and the sparkle of play.

Paulette, waiting back home, would expect no less of him.

Iris would have been his favorite workmate even if he hadn't found her sexy as hell. She was someone he could gripe to, kid around with, and get good advice from. Meanwhile, the fact of the matter was that her teasing eyes, her quirky nose, and her cute, compact arse gave him a hearty response in the turn-on department, which complemented the feelings of camaraderie quite nicely.

"So, they're sleeping in their underwear out here," Alec related into the phone the first night. "At bedtime they wander around, tent to tent, socializing—mostly just in briefs, panties, and bras. Do you want me to opt out of all that?"

"Don't you dare," said Paulette.

This is what he'd known she would say. Alec and Paulette had always been enthusiastic supporters of each other's innocuous little adventures outside their own bedroom.

He kissed the phone goodnight; then he stripped to his own underwear and left his tent, in search of a midnight beer. Iris, scrumptious in a tee and tight blue panties, was near the cooler.

"I like your pajamas," he said.

She slowly rotated a full 360 degrees, showing off her "pajamas." "These are my summer pajamas," she said with a witty lilt. "In the winter, I add a pair of socks."

Alec grinned, and his erection bobbed in his briefs.

"I like what *you're* wearing with your pajama bottoms," Iris quipped, nodding toward his crotch.

He shrugged, affecting nonchalance. "Thanks. In winter, I put a sock over it."

She chortled into her beer and slapped him affectionately on the shoulder.

Paulette had a dinner to attend the next night, so Alec phoned her at lunchtime.

"Everyone pees in front of everyone else out on the trails— the guys, the women … There's no standing on ceremony, no ducking behind trees, no hands over eyes."

"Uh-huh."

"So it's bare asses when the ladies squat out there to piss."

"I understand, Alec. I've done it." There was an undercurrent of laughter in his wife's voice.

"Sometimes I see a little bush." He cleared his throat. "You know, for example, Iris's bush."

"Bound to happen," Paulette's voice shrugged.

"I could skip the hikes, if you want."

"Hiking is good exercise." Did he detect a note of excitement behind this mundane statement? "Enjoy yourself, and keep your eyes open."

"Even when Iris is peeing?"

"*Especially* when Iris is peeing."

Iris didn't have to pee during the afternoon hike; but she and Alec did hang back from the rest of the group, and Alec got to enjoy the music of her conversation, the jauntiness of her jersey-cuddled breasts, and the muscular sassiness of her long, trail-trudging thighs, all without distraction. Finally, when they saw how far behind they'd fallen, she remarked that they'd better hustle. She smacked his butt, for emphasis. Alec only hesitated an instant before returning the compliment, adding a slight squeeze to his smack.

"Sorry," he feinted. "Reflex reaction." Another hard-on was developing. Her bottom had felt so warm and erogenous, even through her shorts.

"Ho ho ho," Iris returned. And she grabbed his hairy thigh, right where it protruded from his hiking shorts, tickling him momentarily before letting go. "Reflex reaction," she explained.

Then she dashed ahead, giggling, looking over her shoulder to make sure he was jogging after her.

Following a late-afternoon swim session with the group, Iris and Alec gravitated to a Ping-Pong table by the lake. Soon they were enmeshed in an endless game, with no one keeping score beyond the most recent point. Iris beamed after each volley, regardless of who had won it. And despite her focus on placing her shots, it was obvious that the eye contact she made with Alec when she served had nothing to do with table tennis.

On the rare occasions that her shots went wild, Iris laughed out a "Fuck!" The uninhibited language made her even more appealing—just as the crotch-clinging bikini made her even more appealing. The suit dripped precious drops of lake water from the apex of her legs now and again, and Alec pretended to himself that it was sweet sips of her juice filtering through.

"What are you thinking about?" She said it as she served, with the result that both the ball and the question caught him unawares.

"Well, since you asked … I was noticing that you look sexy in your bikini." He wondered if he'd sounded gallant or lascivious—and which she would prefer.

He bent down to locate the ball, which had bounced off the table. He found it and tossed it back to her. "I hope you don't mind my saying that."

"Why do you think I wore it?" She served again, hard and

fast, while he tried to imagine every detail of how it felt to Iris to squeeze her own legs together when she served, with her sex perhaps tingling between her thighs as he admired her.

The next day, they were only five minutes into their hike when Iris held him back from the group, whispering that she had to pee. "Will you wait for me?"

Watching her step off the trail and cheerfully drop her shorts and panties, he surmised with glee that she must have deliberately held it, so as to indulge in this flirtatious game.

Her flow came instantly, pale and full—yes, Alec affirmed, she'd been waiting for this opportunity. Her pretty ass swayed while she emptied, and Alec's cock grew fitfully down into the breezy gap of his hiking-shorts leg.

"What a lovely day for a hike," said Iris, still pissing.

"Yes," said Alec. "Lovely."

She burst out laughing. Then she bounced contentedly in place while she wiped up with some leaves.

The first thing Alec did when the hike was finished was pull his cock as hard as he could in the privacy of his tent, replaying the trailside scene.

After he'd showered, he was very surprised to find Paulette in the tent, reading a novel. She answered the happy perplexity on his face: "I realized I could drive out and be with you for the last day."

He joined her on the sleeping bag and kissed her, squeezing a breast. "Tell the truth," he said, making a circle around her nipple through the cotton of her dress. "Are you here to make sure I don't cross the line with Iris?"

"No," said Paulette. "To tell the truth, I'm here to make sure that you *do*."

Pausing only for a moment while his brain fell off its stand, Alec reached up his wife's skirt, noting at once her lack of panties and her deliciously wet condition. This, he decided, was no time to reflect on the strange erotic reality that Paulette had created.

She purred and wriggled as he stroked her, but then she quickly wrestled herself atop him and lunged for his cock. Within seconds, she was working herself up and down, riding his lap with vigor.

"Oh, yes," she panted, each syllable punctuated by a bump. "You—*bump*—like—*bump*—Iris." Paulette groaned, clenching Alec with every jot of strength in her cunt. "Don't—*bump*—you?" Her speed increased, and her ass cheeks slapped manically against his legs.

Alec was thrown into high gear by the name of his alluring friend on the lips of his fuck-hungry wife, and he felt his come rising. With Paulette straddling him, he was in a paradise of passivity, and he trembled libidinously in her grip until he couldn't hold back any longer.

Paulette wailed, fingering her own clit as she lingered with a few final, exquisitely slow plunges, and the couple exploded together in a sloppy afternoon frenzy.

"Iris," Alec said with a false calm that evening, "you know Paulette, of course." With a generous gesture of his hand, he indicated that he hoped Iris would join them at the picnic table they'd claimed, near the edge of the eating area—out of earshot of the other tables. Iris accepted the invitation, and settled in with her plate and her beer.

"I hope you've been keeping my husband entertained," said Paulette with evident sincerity, giving full voice to her own form of generosity. "I think you're the only one in the department that he likes."

Iris smiled shyly, yet held her own. "Is it true, Alec? Do you like me?" She reached across the table to poke his arm, playfully.

"Oh, dear," said Paulette slyly. "I think we're making the poor boy blush."

Alec couldn't deny it—Paulette's bold eloquence, in conjunction with Iris's charisma, had left him tongue-tied.

"But, never fear, *I* know what—and whom—my Alec likes. And, yes, I think he likes you very much, Iris. And I can't say that I blame him."

Now Iris was blushing, too. "Oh, you're sweet."

"He talks about you, you know," Paulette continued. "And who can blame anyone for liking the kind of disposition you have, and the kind of wit you have, and the kind of smile you have …"

"Gosh, thank—"

"Not to mention the kind of breasts you have, the kind of legs, the kind of ass …"

"I—"

"Yes, you have quite the smart little arse, don't you, Iris?" Paulette shifted in place. "I bet Alec has been enjoying seeing your smart little arse in your smart little knickers—haven't you, Alec?"

Alec's throat was burning with a strange new variety of lust. "Holy fuck, Paulette," was all he could articulate.

Paulette went on: "Or maybe he likes you—and your little arse—best *out* of your knickers, eh? On the trail, when you pull them down to pee?" She reached for the other woman's wrist, gently but persuasively. "You've almost finished your beer, honey. Wouldn't you like to pee for Alec, right now?"

"Holy fuck," echoed Iris softly. She was squirming on the bench, her eyes brilliant with possibility.

No further answer seemed to be required. As if in a trance, they followed Paulette to a secluded area over the nearest rise. Well lit by the moon, it was the ideal private playground.

"Why don't you help Iris with her shorts?"

His cock throbbed as Iris steadied herself against his shoulders and he fumbled with the snap. While he did so she pushed her mound against his palm, seeking stimulation. He smelled the sweetness of fresh beer on her breath.

"I think Alec's cock is getting hard, Iris," Paulette said from a distance of three feet away. "Would you be a dear and check it for me?"

Iris nearly sobbed with arousal as she complied, clutching him through his shorts, and Alec bellowed. He scooted Iris's clothing down her thighs, grabbing for her bush.

"Oh fuck, oh fuck!" Iris chanted the phrase in her heat, while dancing against Alec's fevered fingers.

She managed, without losing the rhythm of her excitement, to unzip his shorts, and soon he knew the kiss of the evening air on the tip of his cock—and the sweaty, horny grip of his coworker around its girth.

"Maybe peeing can wait, hmm?" Paulette suggested.

Almost immediately, Alec had found his fingers covered in the fragrant nectar from Iris's pussy. She was trembling, her strong hiker's legs turning weak as her cunt opened for him. Each stroke along her lips, each titillation just inside with his fingertip, elicited throaty, sensual noises that he'd never heard from anyone but Paulette—and even some that his wife had never made.

Paulette's breath was on his neck now. "I imagine Iris would like her clit touched," she advised. "Here." And a feminine thumb joined the masculine fingers running rampant over Iris's pussy.

The pleasured woman's cries became half-laugh, half-shriek, and they began to alternate with iterations of the half sentence, "I'm gonna c—." She cycled through these elements until she screamed for real into the night.

Paulette removed her hand from Iris's crotch, leaving Alec to clutch the mound in its afterglow. She brought a cunt-seasoned thumb to her husband's lips.

The air reverberated with a sultry, female sigh. And suddenly Alec realized that Iris was peeing for him … wetting his hand, as well as the shorts and knickers at her knees. He watched, fascinated, while she soaked it all with a post-orgasmic orgasm of release, letting herself lose control to celebrate the moment—and taking herself into a fresh, whimpering climax by doing so. As she pissed away, she ground her right heel into the soil, in a spasmodic expression of ecstasy that resonated in Alec's balls.

"Piss, pretty pussy, piss for my man."

He caught Paulette in his peripheral vision, and he saw that she had her skirt lifted high and a hand in her panties. She was rubbing herself furiously, eyes blazing like lecherous campfires, while she watched him watch Iris.

Then he saw Iris's gaze move from his face to Paulette's and back, and her own face break into an expression of serene bliss.

He found that he'd been so absorbed in everything that had

transpired, he'd practically forgotten his own erection. But Iris hadn't forgotten. She now gave her full attention to stroking him, repaying the attention he'd given her own most sensitive flesh. Alec's hips began to shimmy, and Iris's face lit up in yet another way, this time with reflected pleasure.

"*Dance, my baby*," said Paulette, who was doing lewd knee bends while she fucked herself. In another beat she lost it, chuckling freakishly the way Alec loved, letting her orgasm ripple through her like a wave of tickles.

And he lost it, too, spurting into Iris's hand, and getting an extra thrill when Iris mouthed "Wow" to him.

He bent to kiss her knee, and she mussed his hair with her clean hand. He could see a tremor running through her leg.

"I like your wife very much," said Iris dreamily.

Seduction with a Splash

KARA HAD TO PISS LIKE NOBODY'S BUSINESS. THIS COULD WORK out perfectly, she thought. She had discovered long ago that flooding her panties was the best way at her disposal to seduce a certain kind of man. And she had also discovered, long ago, that she very much enjoyed doing it—so much that she often did it when there was no one around to seduce. Alone. Hot and dripping over her kitchen floor. Maybe it was kinky—OK, she had to admit it was *definitely* kinky—but Kara was making no apologies. It was a kink that repaid her in orgasms, time and again.

Now she was especially glad that she was headed toward Daniel's office, to drop in unexpectedly.

She shifted sensually in the driver's seat.

She knew that one type of guy would run screaming from a woman who was unabashedly pissing herself and expecting him to like it. But Kara had discovered, long ago, that she could easily live without that type of guy.

Come here and wet upon me, beautiful lady. Contain yourself just long enough to walk briskly across this room and straddle my zippered lap. Mount me and wiggle into position . . . your ass, in sassy panties, pressing on my summer trousers, your short skirt draping down to tease my legs with its crisp edges. Then let your womanly ocean hiss, trickle, spurt, and gush onto me. Yes, flood my lap, you gorgeous creature, let me feel your wild ecstasy of release washing over me. Let me know the sensation of your soaked knickers clinging to my hardening fly. Let me memorize the charismatic, fluid texture of your

*warm piss as it creeps saucily between your clenching thighs and my
bony hips. Come wet me, darling.*

Driving toward Daniel's building, Kara wondered if she was
the only woman on earth who wrote flowery but crazy-lewd
love letters to herself in her head—in the voice of a refined,
imaginary man who lived to watch her urinate. Though the topic
of her fantasies might have caused many jaws to drop, it was the
voice rather than the content that puzzled Kara herself. Where
the hell did that vaguely old-fashioned, literary tone even come
from? English One-Fucking-Ten, way back in freshman year?

But she recognized that she wanted, someday, to have a man
like that—a man whose soft, soothing voice would fuck her with
its eloquence. A man who would convince her, with earfuls of
beautiful words, that the sight of Kara Rebecca Wallace taking
a leak was positively sublime. That's why the fantasies were so
powerful, she realized. They represented exactly what she craved.
She wanted to be someone's pissing paragon of loveliness.
Paragon—now there, thought Kara, was a nice leftover word
from college. She wished she remembered more words like that.

With aching reluctance, she resolved to put her fantasies
aside for the moment, lest she end up losing it—and seducing
the seat of her car with her fresh piss, rather than Daniel.

Right where the street skirted the park, she hit a red light.
She looked around at the scenery while her knees twitched
together, and she saw a young man lying on his back along a
thick stone wall. His girlfriend stood above him, her feet positioned on either side of his waist. Her knees were bent enough to
allow her to reach down and clasp both his hands. Kara noticed
that the young woman was weaving gently from side to side,
as if she were peeing lovingly onto her boyfriend. She realized
that she was projecting her own obsessions, that this was almost
certainly not what was happening; but, symbolically, the feeling
Kara got from the scene was of that kind of intimacy, that kind
of tender anointment (as the voice in her head might say). Her
hand fluttered down from the steering wheel and pressed tightly
against her underwear.

The green light snapped her out of it. So much for keeping

her mind off her favorite topics. She was still managing not to dribble pee into her panties, but they were getting damp enough from girl juice that it almost didn't matter. With a masturbatory laugh, she acknowledged that, however you sliced it, Kara R. Wallace was all about wet panties this afternoon.

A few minutes later, she had parked her car and was heading up the stairs of a nondescript downtown office building. Daniel, who wrote content for various local websites and dabbled in tech support, inhabited a tiny space—a desk, a filing cabinet, a phone, a bathroom. He'd be alone there, as always, and it would be the perfect setting.

She walked through the office door, ready to make a big splash for …

A man she'd never seen before?

"Oh, hi," Kara said, at a loss, her crotch pulsating with all kinds of insistence. "I was looking for Daniel."

"I think he'll be out the rest of the day," said the stranger. "He had a meeting with a client. I'm just here to work on his quarterly taxes till I take off at five." The man instinctively looked at his watch.

Ah, Kara thought. The occasional accountant needed by every small business.

But she had not come here to piss herself for an occasional accountant.

"Gotcha," she said. "Do you mind if I use the restroom before I leave?"

Sitting on the toilet, she almost felt like crying. This pee should have been for *him*, damn it. But she quickly saw that a sulky, defeatist attitude was stupid—and unnecessary. There would always be more pee. It was her birthright.

Let me watch you in the morning, when you tiptoe into your bathroom, only to eschew the seat awhile. Let me enjoy the sight of you brushing your teeth or combing your hair, while your body twists and shimmies in a manner that I know feels as delectable to you as it looks to me. Let me see you wriggle as you sit on the bed, pulling up your beige stockings. Let me silently observe you as you stand, jiggling before the dresser, slowly donning bra, blouse … even earrings. Allow me to study you while you study yourself in the full-length mirror, so satisfied with the lascivious elegance of your bare-bottom, bare-cunt ensemble. You are dressed everywhere, delicious woman, except across your intimate turf. Permit me to follow you as you walk back to the bathroom, which you do as if you were crossing the lobby of some stately building. You have confident, businesslike strides, as though your readiness to pee were your most discreetly kept secret. Then spread your legs, like a sex-hungry lover, and I will watch you lower your naked ass onto the seat, to finally give yourself over to the sea that rises within.

Even with her bladder empty, the fantasies made her squirm. As she switched the engine off in her driveway, one hand was already active inside her moist panties.

She had the rest of the day free, and she had a pretty good idea of what she was going to do with it.

Come drink wine with me, and let loose your brazen torrents in my bathroom, your breath ripe with a tipsy vitality. Then we shall continue to drink together, until, at last, you release yourself over me. Yes, I long to share tangibly in your sensuality, to come alive with erotic fever beneath a private rainstorm of urgent, splashing fluid from your dancing body. Teach my hands to tickle at your nipples and surprise you under your arms, while you soak my loins with the poetry of your urination, my special one.

As horny as she was, Kara giggled at these fanciful words—words of her own creation. But hey, she thought, why the hell shouldn't she be poetry in motion, pissing down magic for the right observer?

I will visit you on your quiet nights, when you drink a pot of tea and curl up in smooth pajamas, when you read from a hand-written journal of your own erotic whispers until you can't sit still. Those nights upon which you escort yourself into an empty bathtub, ensconced all the while in your sleek silk. Those nights you clutch your knees and play private films in your head ... until you're luxuriating, from throbbing pussy to delicate ass cheeks, in your own warm puddle.

Lying on her bed and petting herself between orgasms, she remembered how it had all started. The college party at which the guy she'd been hot for all semester had shown up—on the arm of one of her friends. She recalled, in her mind and in her panties, how she'd become so excited, watching from across the room as he nibbled her friend's ear and stroked her friend's ass, that she had literally wet her pants. And how fiercely it had turned her on to feel herself losing control between her legs, under such sexy circumstances.

Kneel and dance above my face, holding your water precisely as long as you like, mesmerizing me with your gyrations, inviting me to lick you from moist to uncontrollably wet. Let me bring your source to my lips, to communicate and commune with the powerful river that flows from between your soft legs.

Her mind raced while her fingers worked in her panties. Finally, even the seductive voice in her head was drowned out by her shrieks.

Following an afternoon of slow- and fast-cooking mastur-bation, Kara showered and dressed for a friendly dinner with Daniel—which she knew it would be premature to describe as a date. But despite the sexually noncommittal stance that Daniel had taken thus far, Kara had high hopes. She felt sure that he was the type who would stare transfixed, rather than turning away, when she stood before him and suddenly, studiously, watered her panties, looking him in the eye so there could be no mistaking the deliberateness of her act.

How you like being dressed to the nines, my vixen—heels, stockings, skirt, blazer, and blouse—but pussy and upper thigh in the raw, crouching over me and slowly pissing, pissing, pissing. Pissing freely, then stopping abruptly, to dwell in a no-man's-land where the pleasure of letting go and the pleasure of holding it in can coexist … only to let go again when the moment calls for it, dribbling lazily over me while time stands still. A woman's time is her own while she pees; the world will wait for you, my flower. How rapt you hold me each time you hesitate, as I watch you relishing your moistened wriggles, each so pregnant with anticipation. Then, each time you resume, you once again have me writhing in masculine ecstasy beneath your feminine faucet.

She made a mental note to drink plenty of wine, and plenty of water, at the restaurant. If she could just get him back to his place, or her place, with a full bladder rocking inside her body …

Tonight, lovely one, I have your water upon my flesh before, during, and after our sensuous fucking. Before—when you're so eager to have me that you're subtly leaking, and I stroke your knickers just where you drip preciously down; before, when you piss hurriedly, impatiently over my caressing hand and into the bowl, taking care not to empty entirely. Then, during—as we fuck upon a dark, luscious towel, knowing that you've saved some, so that when I make you come hard enough, you will bathe me. And after, when I hold your chest close against my waist while you empty at last into the commode, your liquid kissing my fingertips, the fluorescent light humming to our heartbeats while the orgasmic kineticism of your act pulses through you. I feel you relax, by stages, in my arms, and your body becomes heavy with a grand, sensual contentment. And yet the flow has barely stopped when I feel the relaxation across your pussy begin to blossom into fresh arousal.

Daniel was late for dinner, and Kara decided to get a head start on the wine and the water. She sipped the two in alternation, enjoying the chill-out music that was piped in over the restaurant's speakers … and wondering where he was.

He was sincerely apologetic when he phoned her, fifteen minutes after he should have been there. He explained that he'd been stuck in a monster traffic jam, with no reception. And that when he'd finally been able to connect, he'd found a frantic message from a client whose computer had crashed—one hour before vital spreadsheets were due on the desks of some bigwigs. He bowed out of dinner but suggested she call him in a little while. Maybe they could catch a movie.

After her solitary dinner, Kara profited from the summer-eve sunlight to take a leisurely stroll around the immediate neighborhood—a quiet section of the city. As she did so, she began to feel the effects of the wine and water she had diligently consumed.

This wasn't one of those times when it came over her suddenly and made her rush for a bathroom. No, she recognized it as one of the slower-building needs, when the reservoir would inch gradually upward over the course of an hour or so. This was something to be savored, as she would savor the sensation of ice cream melting reluctantly against her tongue. She continued her stroll, nurturing the sweet, arousing ache in her groin. The scents of countless trees wafted through the air, and even that felt arousing to her.

Lying in your room with my eyes closed, I hear you bounce lightly out of bed. I doze off to the distant, charming music of your waters, as your stream cascades merrily into the porcelain.

As the voice resonated from her mind to her pussy, Kara was surprised to find that she had miscalculated, and that she really had to pee now. Perhaps, she belatedly realized, it was because she had failed to account for the accelerating effect of being so aroused.

She could scurry back to the restaurant and apologetically avail herself of their facilities. Or she could hustle to her car and head for a nearby supermarket, convenience store, or fast-food joint. And yet … she was by herself on a secluded, residential block. Her eyes widened and her clit tingled when she realized she had an excuse to do something she'd always wanted to do.

Twice today, she had been cheated out of wetting her panties for Daniel. The least she could do for herself, Kara reasoned, was grab the consolation prize of peeing on the sidewalk. Her hands began to tremble with excitement.

There was a specific way she needed to do this, as it had been rehearsed in her mind countless times. Her panties came off. All the way off.

She closed her eyes as she began, and she let the gentle voice in her mind describe what he would have seen:

How beautiful you look in the evening light, panty free, making your personal puddle on this deserted stretch of walkway. Let me admire you face on as you stand spread-eagled, your skirt hiked to your waist and held in place by your cheeky elbows. My eyes are drawn to your dainty fingers, which pry your private lips apart while you sway softly into your business. Let me walk around you and stare unblinkingly as you descend into a feminine squat, your summer-sweet ass hovering proudly above the darkening pavement.

As the sun began to set, she walked jauntily back to the

restaurant parking lot, a woman who had just pissed on the sidewalk and wouldn't have missed it for the world.

Sitting in her car, nude and damp under her skirt, she fingered her slick lips with one hand while dialing Daniel with the other.

Does the dampness excite you, knowing that what's tickling your thighs is the remnant of the fountain you poured onto public cement? While you wiggle in your car, do you feel the clinging wetness merging with fresh, fragrant juice from your fruit?

Her orgasm arrived before the second ring. Daniel picked up on the third.

She told him she was tired, and suggested they call it a night. They arranged to have dinner the following Friday. That was what she wanted, Kara affirmed to herself as she disconnected. Wetting herself for Daniel some other time. Because tonight, she was to be not the seducer but the seduced. Tonight, she had a date at home with a very articulate voice in her head.

She took a large gulp from her water bottle and started the engine.

A Day with Audrey

Audrey always wakes up horny. Horny, and tingly-full of pee. So she lies there and makes herself hornier still by squeezing her thighs closed and open, wiggling in place under the bedsheet. She loves starting her day this way, with her jiggling anticipation a sexy wake-up call between her legs, and her forthcoming release a treat to relish while she defers it.

She knows the vibrations of her autoerotic squirming will soon wake me—and that it's my favorite way to be awoken. My eyes creak open to see her lusty smile.

I kneel at her feet in the dry shower. The first slow drag of my tongue up her slit makes her lose it, just like she wants, and the inaugural drizzle of pee trickles out, while her feet do a sensuous shuffle. My tongue returns to blot her sex lips. She's crazy for its warm, velvety wetness, and her hips shudder with delight as she pees some more.

My tongue grazes her clit, and now she can't stop tinkling. Nothing, *nothing*, has ever felt so good, she tells me, as this combined release and arousal she's experiencing. It feels so good she doesn't know what to do, she says; but what she does is tangle my hair, twist her own nipples, and moan. And pee, and pee. And, finally, come fireworks in my face.

The feeling of having emptied is evidently luxurious: every muscle in Audrey's crotch has relaxed, and she wriggles hedonistically. I lick up the drops of piss … from her thighs, from the undercurve of her bottom, and from the tender, pouting lips of her pussy. I can tell that the slow, lingering stimulation makes a seductive cocktail with the relaxation. Her wriggles turn to writhings—and she's coming again. As for me, I can't hold back anymore. While still licking her, I jerk my cock in a frenzy.

10:00 A.M.

Audrey has had coffee at her workplace, and for the past half hour she's been enjoying a "gotta pee" fidget under her desk while she deliberately lingers over this or that task. Finally she goes to the loo, scurrying efficiently across the office on the wings of her now urgent need to bare her ass and spring a leak. Her alert clit throbs in her underwear with every hurried step.

I can visualize her there in the ladies' room, wholly absorbed by the sensuality of the voluminous piss she's built up to … her panties at her ankles and her head thrown back in the kind of pleasure that feels so intense as to prompt disbelief even as it's experienced. As she sits atop her toilet seat of ecstasy, awash in sensation, her shoes anchor her. She's told me how she loves the feeling of peeing while wearing shoes, of being so dressed at the feet while so open and naked between her thighs.

She phones me while she's pissing away, holding the cell over her crotch rather than speaking, letting me hear how prettily her body hisses out its cascade.

1:00 P.M.

Audrey walks home from her office at lunchtime. She dashes up the stairs and arrives, knees together, at the door of my study.

"I held it all the way home," she tells me. It is not always so; sometimes she likes to pee in an alley, or indulge herself in a mid-walk panty wetting, perhaps under a cloaking skirt—proudly displaying to me, upon her arrival, piss-darkened undies that complement her calf-high boots.

But, no, today is one of those where she shows up needing to pee, and turns herself on by holding it in my presence, giggling in the doorway with her hand at her crotch, swaying flirtatiously on the edge of soaking her form-fitting print slacks for me …

putting her gotta-pee self completely on display and getting herself more aroused with each moment she draws this out.

I usher her into the bathroom, where the commode awaits in its "lady" position. "I saved a seat for you," I quip.

She stands well clear of the toilet as she wiggles out of her pants, inviting me to intercept her ass as she begins to lower herself. I squeeze in, drop once again to my knees, and kiss her underside while she squeals merrily. When she tells me she can't wait another second, I get out of the way so her bottom can hit the seat. She's watering into the bowl before she's even settled in. She giggles again, in harmony with the melodious liquid.

5:00 P.M.

As the workday ends, Audrey visits the bathroom—but skipping the toilet, opting instead to squeeze herself shut while she uses her stall merely to change into shorts and a tank top.

Her coworker Anne, whom Audrey finds seriously attractive, is in the other stall, and Audrey hears Anne's pee gracing the water beneath Anne's gorgeous derriere. It makes Audrey deliciously aware both of her own unreleased water and the libidinous butterflies that Anne always gives her.

Anne gives out an involuntary sigh of satisfaction as she empties, and Audrey almost wets her little shorts right there, inches from the unused toilet, as a tremor of excitement jolts through her. Does Annie feel sexy when she pees, too? Audrey wonders. When she hears the rustle of toilet paper against Anne's soft pussy, Audrey almost comes against the fingers she holds tight to her quivering crotch.

Having left the restroom while still cherishing her afternoon's worth of coffee in her bladder, Audrey hops on her bike, and she rides to the park with a delicious tickle in her groin. She gets increasingly hot as her cunt smooches the saddle through the thin fabric of her shorts.

By arrangement, I am standing by in the privacy of a little-used corner of the park. She wheels to a stop mere inches away from me; and, as I watch with fascination, she humps her clit against the bike saddle until she comes with a shriek, drenching her cute shorts in her surrender to multifaceted pleasure and lost control. She looks lovingly at me as the piss runs down her legs.

8:00 P.M.

The dinner date begins at our favorite bar. As we stand there drinking our beers, I admire Audrey's long, slim legs, which are in black all the way down—tapered slacks and Beatle boots. We chat and kiss our way into our second round, and eventually she starts to do that lovely pre-peeing thing where she lifts her foot and subtly stamps down to dissipate the tension in her groin—punctuating the rhythm of our conversation with this elegant mini-dance. A hand slides into her front pocket so she can pull her panties tight across her pussy, to contain her water and indulge in a bit of mild masturbation.

After a while she whispers those magic words, "Gotta pee," in my ear, because it turns her on to say it—and me to hear it; then she puts down her beer and bops back to where the ladies' room is, her ass churning voluptuously in the course of the brisk walk.

The ladies' is occupied—but she has factored that in, knowing she'll get a kick out of holding it a smidgen longer. From the bar I can see her waiting happily by the back wall, rocking a bit, subtly resting a hand on the front of her slacks and blowing me kisses.

When she rejoins me, refreshed after her turn in the loo and smiling with post-release radiance, she gives me her hand. Her fingers taste of pee and pussy juice.

10:00 P.M.

After those beers, and the glasses of water she always chases them with, Audrey's waterworks are on an accelerated schedule—just the way we like it on a Friday night. By the time we're halfway home, we're both lurching along, Audrey cheerfully hobbled by being within an inch of losing control, and my own walking hampered by the rectilinear encumbrance of a raging hard-on. Finally, she stops in her tracks—shaking with laughter, leaning on my shoulder, and secretly wetting. It's really no secret, of course: I've guessed right away that the first drops are already tickling down her legs. Her tight but lightweight trousers crinkle in the crotch when she dips, and I clutch her round bottom, so excited that she's wetting her pants.

By chance, I notice the mannequin in the shop window behind Audrey. The stance of its creamy thighs, which are sheathed in a tight miniskirt, strongly suggests to me that she, too, is poised to piss for her lover, that at any moment her elixir will pour generously down to grace the ground beneath her.

Now I release Audrey, to watch her luxuriate in earnest as a delicious wetness spreads along the seam of her crotch, then backward, down, and up, saturating the seat of her pants and bathing her thong-naked ass cheeks. As the converted beer spills heartily from between her legs, she basks in the warm, pissy kiss of her fabric, tapping the heels of her Beatle boots while she fills every cozy crevice with pee.

Thinking quickly, I film her beautiful spectacle with my phone. I lick my lips as I take in her after-twitches of satisfaction, then watch them morph into a lewd grind. I record the orgasm she gives herself, zooming in on the hand that rubs frantically in her piss-soaked pants in celebration of the visceral joy of tension's release.

I zoom back out as Audrey's lower body enacts contortions of kinky, dripping-trousered ecstasy. It's a lovely night.

11:00 P.M.

This time, Audrey wants the pee to be tickled right out of her.

I've stripped her out of her soggy pants and we've fucked on the floor. She's showered and changed, and opened a beer from the fridge. Now she sits on our vinyl couch in a spaghetti-strap slip, crossing and uncrossing her legs, giving me glimpses of the fresh panties that she may be just a sip or two away from spilling herself into. With each recrossing, I wonder if perhaps a diminutive splash will already have decorated the seam of her white knickers.

She gestures for me to join her on the couch, and she

climbs onto me for a squirmy, tickly, on-my-lap wetting. As she bounces up and down, giggling like an angel in her spaghetti-strap, I tickle her and watch her crotch for the first evidence, which comes soon—a modest circle that widens before my eyes. Within moments she's pissing her love all over my dark trousers. I squeeze the globes of her derriere, so warm in the clingy underpants.

No sooner has she finished than she peels her knickers and unzips me for a desperate shag. She wrestles her own clit while she rides me, and her juicy contractions milk the come out of me as my ass vibrates into the couch cushions.

MIDNIGHT

"Now," says Audrey, shimmying down onto her knees, her raspberry panties—her only garment—in my face.

I run my finger down the fabric, finding the yield of her slit. "Ohhh," she says.

I stroke the cloth, and she moans more deeply, delighting in my touch and the game of containing her pee.

She elevates her arse so that I can shove my nose right into the core of her panties—so that if I were to tickle her midriff, I would make her piss right in my face, squirming, drenching the cotton and me with it.

I do it. She sighs and shivers; and now she's peeing, pumping her hotness into my face, the dampening panties acting like a warm compress against my muzzle.

I yank the panties down to rest snugly around her thighs, as she continues to piss. Her pee now kisses my face in sassy squirts. I poke my tongue into her slickening hole, then dab it against her clit, repeating the series of moves until she's coming like hell in my face—and peeing still, thanks to those beers. I clutch her tightly around the waist, pressing her soft hind cheeks against me, letting all her juices trickle onto my lips.

"Fuck me while I'm still pissing!" she urges. "Quick!"

So I get into position and penetrate her under the downpour. I grind into her, and she roars with erotic laughter. I slip a fingertip into her anus; her bum crack is slick with pee. She comes again when I spurt into her, and cute little afterthoughts of feminine pee sprinkle my balls.

1:00 A.M.

Audrey has cleaned up again, and now she meets me in the bedroom. She's lacy and silky, respectively, in a plum camisole and panties. Grinning, she holds her pussy and nods, indicating that the beer is making itself known yet again.

I've placed a thick towel on the bed, and she situates herself there for the upcoming game—the one where she tries to keep her thighs squeezed shut, and I try to pry them open. We both know I will prevail—faster if I tickle—and that when I do, her eager pee hole will have no choice but to leak, then spurt—just like she wants.

But she somehow holds back awhile, even after I've splayed her legs open and have my face at her juncture. She holds on while I service her gusset with dedication; even through the knickers I'm hitting the right places to make her come. Meanwhile, I start scissoring her legs, thrilled at the idea that she could lose it at any moment. Will she pee first, or come first? It's win-win, and the adventure interests me enormously.

She bucks in my face, giving herself over to whatever will happen. And what happens, I'm delighted to see, is that she pisses and comes all at once, a rushing, ecstatic waterfall of woman.

Then I kiss the inside of her knee, and pee and orgasm come even harder.

Now she lies there soaked with bliss … eyes hazy, panties saturated … wearing the large, damp stain across her crotch like a badge of honor. Completely happy and beautiful, Audrey is satisfied as only a full-fledged panty-pissing orgasm can really make her.

And I must say I'm pretty damn satisfied myself.

Uninhibited

"MAY I HELP YOU?" ASKED THE PRETTY, ROUND-FACED WOMAN behind the cash register.

"Just checking you out," said Desmond. "Er—the shop, I mean."

"Of course." She flickered a smile at him, then resumed looking over her paperwork.

He browsed the bookshelves for several minutes, then checked his watch. "Thanks—see you later," he said to the clerk. They made eye contact briefly when he nodded in her direction.

As he made his way out the door, another woman hurried in. "Sorry I'm late!" she called to her coworker.

Desmond had been sitting with his still-too-hot-to-eat pizza slice for only a moment when the cute woman from the bookstore entered the eatery and headed for the counter. He watched her as she purchased a slice of her own, admiring her scrumptious nose whenever she happened to turn her head in profile.

When she began walking back toward the tables, he waved to her. And as she came within earshot, he spoke.

"Hello again. You're welcome to join me." The eatery wasn't full, but he'd calculated that there was enough of a lunchtime crowd that offering to share a table with a new acquaintance of sorts wouldn't seem too shocking.

"Oh." She looked around. "OK. Thank you." She took her seat across from him.

"Nice bookshop you folks have. I'll have to go back when I

have more time."

"Glad you like it. What kind of books do you enjoy reading?"

And thus began Desmond and Kerry's first date, after a fashion. His visits to the bookshop became regular, and it became a tradition for the two of them to have lunch together when mutually convenient.

"How was life in the book business this morning?"

"All right," she yawned. "But I'd rather be home in bed."

"Hmm ... Doing what?"

They were gently flirtatious with each other, but the nature of the friendship was comfortably ambiguous for a few weeks. Meanwhile, Desmond relished Kerry's seductive laughter, the way her slacks fit her, and the whiffs of her hair that he sometimes got when they stood side by side ordering their wraps or sandwiches.

It was Kerry who first kicked the seduction into a higher gear one day, as she returned to their table after getting up for more napkins. Des was smiling at her fondly, and when she smiled back she surprised him with a direct question.

"Were you looking at my ass?"

"No," he answered truthfully. "But I wish I had been."

She laughed.

"The people at that table over there were blocking my view, you see. But don't worry—I have, um, had a better view on previous occasions."

The ice thus broken, Kerry asked Des if he'd like to go out on the upcoming Friday night. And so ended the ambiguity.

After drinks and dinner on Friday, she invited him up to her flat. As they walked along a quiet street, he tried to take her hand; but Kerry pulled it away.

"Later," she said quickly.

A few minutes afterward, while Kerry maneuvered her key into the building's downstairs lock, Desmond tried to kiss her on the neck. But she shook her head *no*.

"Not here," she said apologetically.

She got the door open, and led him upstairs.

"Now?" asked Desmond hopefully, standing with his arms spread wide just inside Kerry's apartment.

"I have to explain something to you," she answered. "Let's go in the kitchen."

It was a spacious kitchen, with plenty of floor space and a breakfast table. Kerry gestured for Desmond to sit. She remained standing.

"OK," she began, breathing deeply. "Here's the thing: I'm sort of … *inhibited* about sex."

Desmond was confused. "Really? You don't seem like it. I mean … you weren't inhibited, for instance, about asking if I was watching your ass the other day. That was delightfully cheeky. As is your ass itself."

"Ah, but that was just talk," she replied. "When it comes to the physical, the inhibitions kick in. Even for kissing, even for hand holding. I've always been this way, I'm afraid."

"Oh," said Desmond, trying not to look too disappointed. The last thing he wanted to do was be selfish or appear insensitive.

But Kerry brightened. "So that's the problem. However, there is a solution to hand. I've used it before, and it works like a charm. You just have to be OK with it."

"Oh, naturally I'm OK with it." He nearly shouted his relief. "Bring on the solution!"

"Let me tell you about it first. It's a little odd."

She sat down at the table with him.

"Here's how I can break through my inhibitions and become physically intimate with you, Desmond: I'll … "

She hesitated.

"Yes?"

She looked him in the eye as she completed the thought. "I'll wee myself for you."

Desmond swallowed. "You'll—"

"Yes. It never fails as a method of overcoming my inhibitions. That's why I ordered that second pint of beer toward the end of our meal." She winked. "So what do you say, Des?"

The incipient erection in Desmond's pants responded even before he did. "Please … go right ahead," were the words that finally came out of his mouth.

Kerry looked much more relaxed now that this crossroads had been negotiated. And Desmond never would have thought of it before … but as Kerry stood up again, he noted that she was dressed very suitably for a staged panty wetting—not that he'd previously heard of such a thing. Her skirt was quite short—he was fairly certain her knickers would become visible if she squatted or bent over—and her colorful, striped thigh highs were sure to add a jolly, festive touch to the proceedings.

He fingered the buttons of his fly, and he spoke with a shiver of excitement. "I'm ready to watch you … do it, whenever you're ready to … do it."

"Not so fast, sir," she chuckled. "You see, for the strategy to be complete, I need to start by letting you watch me while I hold it, while the need grows stronger. Don't worry, I won't be uncomfortable—to tell you the truth, I *love* the way it feels, holding back until I'm twisting my legs into a pretzel. That's part of the whole point: I get immensely turned on this way. *And I hope you'll enjoy it as much as I do,*" she added in a whisper. It was the sexiest tone of voice he'd ever heard her employ.

"You sit there and watch the show. Once you've seen me clutch myself between the legs, and seen me groove around to hang on that much longer … once you've seen me soak my knickers when I just can't hold it anymore—pissing myself silly right in front of your eyes—well, after that, trust me, you'll be a stranger to my body no more. In fact, I'll be so ready for it I'll have you up my snatch before you know what's happened. Assuming that's all right with you." She put her hands on her hips, to underscore her carnal intentions.

Desmond wondered if the other men to whom Kerry had given the outrageous, deeply private performance she now had in store for him had been instantly aroused by the prospect, as he was. She couldn't have known it, but he had sometimes found it titillating when a woman confessed that she had to pee—if she acted, for instance, a little flirty and jiggly about it, hinting that she was savoring the anticipation and basking in the attention her announcement drew to the juncture of her legs.

And so what was about to occur here was not merely Kerry's method of loosening her inhibitions; it was also the fulfillment of a dormant fantasy that Desmond hadn't even fully conceptualized. Whatever he had observed in the past in this area, she was about to take to an astounding new level.

"I've already been holding it since we left the restaurant," Kerry continued. Mmm." She pressed a hand against the front of her skirt. "If I were by myself, I might very well have my sweet arse poised on the toilet seat by now, my pussy ready to tinkle away. But tonight is special."

"Yes," agreed Desmond passionately. He squirmed in his chair.

"Ooh, yeah, I have to go," giggled Kerry. She swayed with her hands between her thighs. "Just think, I downed that extra pint of beer instead of having dessert! Every drop." She closed her eyes briefly, and Desmond thought he saw her stroking herself for an instant.

As the minutes ticked by on Kerry's large, cheerful kitchen clock, the radiant woman clasped her hem, intertwined her striped-stocking legs, bent a bit from the waist—revealing peach panties—all the while smiling saucily at Desmond as she progressed from one posture to another. "I have to pee, I have to *pee*," she said every so often, emphasizing with her words what her body was saying loud and clear. Her physical presence became increasingly sexual as she coaxed her body through its display, with her hands now rarely leaving her crotch and her nipples turning visibly hard beneath her top.

Any off-topic conversation was unnecessary, with Kerry's wee-holding antics dominating the scene. Eventually she was traveling back and forth across the breadth of the floor, stepping nimbly like a dancer in what her boyfriend recognized must be her final stages of holding on.

Suddenly she held herself still and sighed. She pried her hands away from her pussy and lifted her skirt, fully exposing her peach-panty crotch. Then she gingerly separated her legs, letting her knees bend slightly and her toes point inward.

"Look, Desmond, look! I'm pissing, pissing my knickers!" Her laughter was a wild, erotic howl.

He was, of course, looking. And as Desmond watched, the flimsy gusset became a sopping, spongy paradise of pee, raining deliciously onto the floor as Kerry indulged in sensuous knee bends.

"Ohhhh," she moaned blissfully.

As she continued to wet and wet, Kerry started parading the floor for Desmond—twirling, gliding, and even curtsying lewdly for him once or twice. Then she paused, lifting her hem once again to show off the darkened, dripping knickers framed by her widely spread thighs—which she then squeezed playfully shut, to eke her river out. "Slow feels yummy, too," she commented. She opened her thighs again a crack and trickled lusciously, her body sinuous with pleasure. Desmond marveled at her control.

"Oh-ohhhhhhh!" Kerry cried, letting the full power of her flow resume. "It feels so good, it feels *so fucking good*." Her feet virtually tap-danced in ecstasy as she gave herself over once more to the evidently magnificent sensations of furiously pissing away an evening's worth of liquid refreshment.

By this point, Desmond had his trousers unbuttoned and his hand on his cock. His gaze, naturally, remained on Kerry.

When she'd finished peeing at last, she stood grinning at him, her cheeks flushed from the near orgasm. She was still rubbing herself in the after-twitches of release.

And her promise came true. Now that she had danced before him with the unrestrained kineticism of a woman who needs to pee soon and doesn't care who knows it … now that she had wet her cotton for him, shrieking in giddy rapture as a torrent of water splashed to her floor … after all this, her inhibitions were indeed gone. Where once she had evaded a simple kiss, she now pounced on him with vigor, straddling him and lunging for his prick without the slightest reserve.

Together they wrestled the sopping knickers off her. Desmond held them to his face for a moment, relishing the sweet aroma of her still-fresh floodwaters, mixed with the unmistakable perfume of her arousal.

The condom came out of his pocket, and they got it in place. Then Kerry took possession of his engorged cock and fucked him right there on his chair, bouncing and humping, holding him by the shoulders and letting her clit delight in the friction she generated against his abdomen. He could tell that her exhibitionistic, inhibition-negating floor show had left her in such a state of peak excitement that she would soon come.

And, sure enough, she did, banging her knees against his hips and kissing him all over his face while her hot pussy twitched manically around him. He exploded in the grip of her cunt, and Kerry writhed joyously in the wake of his tremors.

"There," she said a minute later. "Everything is as it should be, and I won't even have to wet myself for you ever again."

"No?"

"No, I won't *have* to." She kissed him. "But, if you don't mind, I *will*."

"I was hoping you'd say that," said Desmond, slapping Kerry affectionately on the cheekiest part of her cheeky self.

The Water-Cooler Routine

IF YOU'D NEVER WORKED AT CYNTHIA SYSTEMS, YOU PROBABLY wouldn't get it.

As far as most of the town was concerned, CS was just an office on the second floor of that corner building next to the bagel place. A pleasant office, to be sure, because by all accounts Cynthia Sysek, the owner and brains of the small company, was a very congenial person to work for. Most people found Cynthia to be fairly stunning, too, with her brilliant smile, her dancer's body, and her "touch me"-soft hair.

But unless you were actually employed by Cynthia, you wouldn't be conversant with the whole water-cooler routine. No one ever said much about it outside the workplace, except to hint that it was a sort of company ritual—something kind of special that everybody appreciated.

So the rest of the town didn't know that the ritual had to do with the boss's exhibitionistic passion for letting the men and women on her staff watch her when she needed to pee.

You could always tell when the late morning water-cooler break was approaching, because Cynthia would start saying—as if to herself but loud enough for everyone in the little office to hear—"I have to pee."

And if you'd been there longer than half a day, you knew this was not a cue for the CEO to excuse herself to the restroom. Rather, it was the beginning of a much more exotic—and much more communal—experience.

After a few repetitions, spaced out over about fifteen minutes,

"I have to pee" would eventually morph into "Wow, I really have to pee." At that point Cynthia would stand up and head, not to the bathroom, but to the water cooler.

There she would fill her cup and drink. And there she would stand, beginning to jiggle, as her employees gradually gathered around her. She would smile at them all, greeting them with a faux-shy aversion of her eyes and a murmured, giggled reminder that their gorgeous boss *had to pee.*

As the gathering swelled to the entire staff, generic water-cooler chitchat would ensue, but with a sensual subtext: the physical poetry of Cynthia's erotic display of her bladder's fullness. As she shimmied left and right, continuing to refresh herself with spring water while surfing the ocean clasped between her legs, she would dart a neatly manicured hand into the juncture of her thighs, with an ever-increasing frequency.

A mere ten feet behind her, the door to the single-occupancy restroom would gape wide at water-cooler time ... a gleaming toilet beckoning its proprietor, its seat at the ready for her warm, feminine ass. Cynthia would glance its way now and again, smirking, and clutch her crotch a little harder.

Eventually, she would be not only clutching but rubbing. Her long, black-trouser-clad legs would snake over each other; and the fruit-perfect round of her ass would dip rhythmically down and up, as if practicing for its imminent descent onto the welcoming seat. Occasionally a sexy CEO foot would stamp the carpet, punctuating the performance.

And by the time she at last shoved her drinking cup into the hand of her nearest colleague and dashed toward release, panting with anticipation on the verge of wetting her panties, most of the staff of Cynthia Systems would be rubbing in unison, fingering their own excitement right through their slacks or jeans or skirts.

Cynthia Sysek would pee with the door open, her narrow-cut trousers clinging to her shins, her knickers peeled askew in her beautiful haste, her clever shoes clicking irrepressibly on the bathroom floor ... her face beaming at her employees in ecstasy.

Her fingers wedged deep, bringing herself off while she pissed and pissed.

But if you didn't work there, you probably wouldn't get it.

Jenna's Gambit

THERE WAS NO DOUBT THAT JENNA LIKED THE WAY THIS FELT. The dully aching clench in her groin was pleasurable rather than painful, and the tickle of not-quite-urgent need felt downright delicious when she squeezed her thighs together.

In fact, poised here on her bar stool, Jenna found that her only discomfort was psychological: would she have the nerve to go through with this?

She'd planned the entire evening around it, she told herself, glancing at the two empty beer bottles in front of her. By focusing on her emotional investment in tonight's gambit, she managed to provoke a surge of confidence. A shiver of erotic anticipation came in tow.

She was wise enough to act at this juncture, while the confidence was surging. In any event, it wasn't the only thing that was surging; she couldn't wait much longer.

"Can we go home now?" She put her hand on Eric's knee. "I'm horny," she whispered. It was the truth, if not the whole truth.

Eric grinned. And, without articulating an answer, he stood up and reclaimed his denim jacket from the back of his stool. For an instant, Jenna thought she noticed his eyes drifting toward the rear of the restaurant, where two restroom doors straddled a "staff only" passageway.

She dismounted and insinuated herself into the crook of his arm, letting her chest warm his frame. The smell of his skin reminded her that this was a man who had long ago accepted her, 100 percent, for who she was. He was crazy about 90 percent of it and OK with the other 10.

Nothing bad was going to happen tonight.

"I love you," she murmured into his throat. Her pelvis gyrated in slow motion.

Just nine blocks more, she told herself as they walked, hand in hand. *Just seven more blocks … six …* For a second or two around block 5, she thought she might not make it—not because of miscalculation, but because of arousal. But she reasserted control, and the tickle felt better than ever. Soon the fence was in sight.

They'd stopped at this safe little neighborhood park before, on other nights when they'd been out for drinks. Eric would always wait at the gate while Jenna dashed in to water the ground.

On one occasion it had been Eric who'd requested a moment among the trees; and Jenna had stood on the sidewalk watching a crescent moon sail in and out of clouds, while she strained her ears for the distant sound of her lover's tight, male stream of release. Her pussy had sweetened with slickness as she listened.

"I need to stop at the park," she said tonight, as they approached it. She could detect the tremble of excitement—and nervousness—in her own voice. She observed with approval that dusk still lingered on this lazy June evening, offering reasonably good visibility for anyone who had something bold and compelling to look at. She'd counted on this.

"See you in a minute," said Eric, pulling her toward him for what he obviously expected to be a quick, affectionate peck on the lips.

But Jenna didn't let go. Instead, she pressed herself against the front of Eric's jeans, and kept her mouth as close to his as she could without impairing speech. Her clit buzzed as the friction from Eric's crotch complemented the giddy tease of holding on just a little longer.

"I want you to watch me."

The admission, though softly spoken, resonated deeply in the quiet of the night.

She was heartened to note—proud, even—that at this critical moment it was not her anxiety that came to the fore, but her joy: her sensuous relishing of an act that for her held no shame, except insofar as it had always seemed a "shame" not to share such an intense and intimate area of pleasure with the man she loved.

In the instant that she waited for his response, a tide of memories welled up—like the water inside her. Memories of the times she'd brought herself off on the seat while she did it, imagining that she had an eager male audience.

She recalled the workdays where she'd kept herself right on the edge as long as possible at her desk, fidgeting and fantasizing, until she was an inch away from rubbing her pussy in a frenzy—and a breath away from soaking herself.

She remembered those nature hikes with women friends during college—how the other gals had perennially been concerned that some guy might come along just when they were squatting, bare-bottomed, to make their girly rivulets … and how Jenna, by contrast, had secretly hoped for such an eventuality.

Eric's eyes were alive with interest, beneath asymmetrically cocked brows. "Well then," he said with a reassuring jauntiness. "Lead the way."

Jenna sighed, basking in the good vibes of his complicity. It was really happening. She pressed a hand to where her body readied for release.

They shuffled together shyly, like virgins, to the dense bank of trees. When they arrived, she hugged him again.

He laughed. "I thought you had to go."

She ground into him. "I do, I do. Fuck, I'm nearly wetting my panties." It thrilled her to say it aloud—*wetting my panties*—and once again she wondered if he had any idea how raunchy she was, deep inside her private world, on this hitherto unbroached subject. "But I'm so turned on knowing that I'm going to"— she hesitated only a fraction of a second over the word—"pee in front of you." She savored the magic of the situation before finally breaking away from him to lift her skirt.

She held the miniskirt in folds just above crotch level, clutching fabric and self in one handful, pushing her mound against manic fingers while she feasted on the exhilaration of display. She was almost reluctant to stop fondling herself long enough to get her pussy out in the open.

Eric was staring at her with fascination, a hand grazing a ridge in his jeans.

"Well?" he prompted sweetly, but with an undercurrent of urgency. "Let's see you take those panties down and make a pretty puddle, gorgeous."

She hadn't been prepared for the possibility that Eric would be so wrapped up in the show she was staging, right away. The sense of gratification that washed through her was overpowering.

As she hooked the fingers of her free hand into the waistband of her lime bikini briefs, "pretty puddle" rang like the sexiest poetry.

"You're going to do it right from between your legs, aren't you?" he asked rhetorically. "Nothing like how a boy does it, eh?" He seemed to know exactly what she wanted to hear—as if she'd tape-recorded the fantasies in her head, and he'd been rehearsing from the transcripts.

She moaned in lieu of a reply, and Eric licked his lips while she scrunched her panties out of the way and bent her knees. She saw his gaze go appreciatively to the smooth roundness of her exposed ass.

"Come on," he said, with gentle insistence. "Show me what a woman you are. Show me how you pee, Jenn."

The words might have looked silly on paper, but in the night air they pinged Jenna's nipples and made her clit throb. As she felt the first tentative drizzle of piss blazing a trail down her slit, she couldn't recall ever being so turned on.

She ached with visceral bliss as her muscles creaked open and the hot trickle kissed her pussy lips on its way to lower ground. She used her hand to coax the engorged lips farther apart, while the knowledge that Eric was watching her every action thundered in her consciousness.

Oh, yes, she'd gotten herself exquisitely aroused by curating those beers all this while. But letting go of them at last was positively heavenly. It felt so good that her eyes blinked closed and her shoulder blades quivered. And when the flood began in earnest as her muscles twanged back into relaxation and freedom, Jenna squealed with raw delight.

Oh, it felt so good, so good. She let her fingers brave the downpour to skitter along her sex.

She opened her eyes to find Eric's attention locked on the feminine wall of water that rushed from her underside, cascading to earth with all the ecstatic turmoil of an impassioned lover. She fantasized, without even meaning to, that the whole neighborhood could hear her pissing—and she embraced the image.

She felt so lewd and fulfilled and desirable and honest, peeing her heart out for her man. She felt she was a living expression of natural womanliness and lust, with a river of love and libido pouring from between her thighs.

Her forefinger was riding her clit, and now she was coming. Her legs were twitching and all her nerves were crackling, each neuron individually intoxicated and euphoric. Her pussy was the center of the universe, and the muscles she peed with spasmed in satisfaction as the final drips and drops luxuriated out of her.

Jenna and Eric remained silent, in a kinky afterglow, while she reached in her skirt pocket for tissues. Eric stroked his fly as he watched her wipe her pussy, thigh flesh, and fingers. It was quickly done, and yet she didn't change positions when the task was accomplished.

Except to step out of her panties.

Her eyes met his.

He was behind her with unzipped jeans in a heartbeat, encircling her waist and aligning their bodies.

"That was magnificent," he slurred in her ear, as if drunk on her spectacle. He slapped her right ass cheek lightly, then groped her there until she jiggled. He teased the soft pout of her vulva, and she widened her stance further, elevating her derriere and leaning forward to brace herself on a tree trunk.

The collegial horniness of his bloated cock, sliding lusciously into her, underscored the fact that she had made Eric wild by peeing for him. Inside her fuck-hungry cunt, this evidence of her effect on him sparked a network of sensations that spread in all directions to delight her—just as the orchestrated paradise of orgasmic, exhibitionistic release had rocked her body a few minutes earlier.

He began pounding in and out. Each inward thrust, like an accented syllable, hammered home what she'd done here tonight. "I *peed*, I *peed*, I *peed*," sang her inner voice, in time with the rhythm. "I fucking *peeeeeeeeed*," said her new orgasm, the *e*'s trickling out like more pee, to be heard as a beautiful shriek in the twilight. The sound made Eric wiggle inside her like an out-of-control screwdriver. He came with a carnal sob.

"I have to piss like a son of a bitch now," he informed her after he had pulled out and she'd danced back into the panties. He touched her elbow. "Does that make you excited, you little tinkle-angel? To think about my warm cock all set to piss and piss while you look?" He chuckled when she nodded through hot blushes.

She watched him take his semi-flaccid pink flesh in hand; she got an excellent view when he turned in profile to aim at a tree.

She shoved two fingers into her mouth as she admired Eric's stately arc. When she sucked, rocking in place, she tasted the salty tang of a stray, lingering drop of her own.

Still leaking, Eric growled, a satisfied animal—"*Ahhh*"—and Jenna tried to imagine precisely what it felt like for him to let pleasure stream and stream through his dick while he emptied. Her own groin muscles flexed idly in sympathy, and the delectable wetness of renewed want licked into her clinging panties.

He winked at her as he zipped up. The night was turning pleasantly breezy, and Jenna heard the wide-open park gate knocking against the fence: gate and fence banged like a pair of happy fuckers.

Eric took her hand. "I don't know about you, but I'll be ready for another beer when we get home."

His palm, squeezed against hers, was solid like a promise.

Give the Customer a Choice

"Excuse me," said a perky young woman in a green dress.

Sander looked up from the shelf he was rearranging in the empty-as-usual hat department. "Yes, madam?"

She smiled shyly, her eyes flickering as she fidgeted with her purse. "Where do I go to … pee?"

"Ah." He put down the hats that were in his hands. "You have a choice, madam." Sander knew that customers liked to be given a choice.

"A choice?"

"Yes. There's a ladies' room right over there." He pointed beyond the dressing rooms that lined the southern wall of the department store. "Or …"

"Or?"

"Or, you could choose to stay right where you are, and wet your panties."

"What?" She looked more amused than shocked. "Now, why would I want to do *that*?"

Sander spoke softly, professionally, persuasively. "Well, madam, some ladies find it pleasant to wet their panties in front of an appreciative observer," he explained. "They find it … exciting."

"You're kidding," she said, her mouth agape.

"No, madam. But, as I said, the ladies' room is just over there."

She didn't move. He had, as usual, chosen wisely, spotting the wild playfulness in the eyes of this woman in green. Picking up on her comfortable use of the word *pee*, selected over something more euphemistic.

"Or perhaps you'd like to think about it," he said.

She stood there, her thighs pressed together, contemplating him.

"What type of panties are you wearing?—if I may ask."

"Green cotton," she said without hesitation. "Why?"

He smiled knowingly. "Of course, to match your pretty green frock. May I suggest, madam, that they would darken handsomely. And cotton does cling so nicely when it's warm and wet."

She seemed to shiver in place, making no sign of moving. "I'd—I'd have to change afterward."

"This store is full of new, clean panties, madam."

"And your carpet … "

"Is easily cleaned."

"I … don't … know."

"I notice that you are squeezing your thighs together. Perhaps you'd like to relax them, just a little?"

"But I'll—you know … "

"Yes, I know. You'll wet yourself. Standing beautifully here, in front of me." He looked her in the eye. "Isn't that what you want?" he said soothingly.

She studied him again, her face a mixture of confusion, curiosity, and erotic anticipation. Then she looked around them, taking in their forgotten corner of the store.

"We're quite alone, madam."

Apart from a subtle rocking of her hips, she didn't budge.

"Oh god," she said at last, letting her legs separate ever so slightly from their compression, in slow motion, as if a seal were being gently broken.

"Ohhhh god," she said again, lusciously, as she lifted the hem of her skirt, so that he could see just an inch of the green panties … darkening, darkening.

The Last Dry Lady

PUDDLES IS A SPECIALIZED COMEDY CLUB CATERING TO A FEMALE clientele. Women show up here to fulfill a specific desire—to be mentally tickled into peeing in their panties, in a suitably arranged environment. The thirty-dollar cover charge includes unlimited beer, and a complimentary change of underwear. The floor is hosed down after every show. There's a huge, well-maintained restroom at the back; but it's used primarily by ladies who have already peed gloriously on the floor and now want some privacy to wash up—and maybe finger themselves quickly to climax.

On a good night, many of the women are already crowding the stage, in various states of jiggling and leg crossing, when the comic comes out. Other ladies lounge in booths, with knees pressed together and discreet hands shoved up under their skirts. A few straddle bar stools that the management has outfitted with special saddle horns that a girl can press her mound into while she holds it. Along with the pleasurable throb of the piss welling up inside her, the rider can feel her clit tingling while she lets her ass jiggle on the seat, waiting for her cup to runneth over.

As his thirty-minute routine rolls out, the comic loves watching the early gushers, the hangers-on, and the diehards go through their parade of delicious anticipation. While they titter and guffaw at his stories and one-liners, they dance in place, and they bite their lips. They squeeze their thighs together grace-fully, or they explicitly hold themselves. Some of them stroke their panties with an obvious eroticism. Suitably primed with beer, each of them knows she can wet whenever she wants to, and each knows she eventually will. This, after all, is why they are here. There is no anguish, no humiliation, no struggling to conceal their condition. This is a room full of uninhibited women who relish the teasing, arousing sensations of holding it, their tense bodies assiduously retaining control as the pee tickles inside their crotches … until they finally let the ecstasy of release wash over them, while they create beautiful puddles for the man who makes them laugh, whose gentle patter coaxes them into wetting themselves like they want to.

What these determined wetters crave is not a garden-variety, unrehearsed, beer-driven panty soaking. These ladies have come here seeking the special seduction of being transported into the embrace of wetness and warmth by the erotic magic of unre-strained laughter. Blissfully they stand, they sit, they gyrate in front of the funnyman, legs crossed, hands wedged, each awaiting the punch line that will trigger her personal waterfall.

When each woman wets, the comic studies her laughter-glowing face. Here he witnesses the transformation of the tense, anticipatory ecstasies of maintaining equilibrium into the orgasmic watershed of letting go. He has learned to recognize, in the subtleties of her expression, the precise moment at which an audience member's lower muscles have relaxed. He can see it all in her eyes, even before the hiss begins and the flood emerges. The comic loves that moment, loves the feeling of having gently led a stranger into her intimate female joys. He also loves the shrieks and whoops of delight that his customers emit in the moments that follow, as they wallow in their wetness and rejoice in their loss of control. Their frenzied sounds of release tickle the hairs on the back of his neck. Nor does he neglect to appreci-ate the quiet ones, the ones who sit almost motionless as their tides wash through them, bobbing ever so gently like scattered bathers in warm coastal waters, their faces rigid with rapture.

Usually, the last one left dry is a woman who's been dragged along by a friend, who has eschewed the beer or taken advantage of the empty restroom—in short, someone who isn't into it. The comic respects her lack of interest; he has nothing to prove. No one has to wet herself. No one should do it if she doesn't want to. No one even has to laugh. He does not resent the presence of video games in the outer bar for those who favor more conventional recreation and don't even care for his jokes.

But one night, the last dry lady is not a blasé tag-along. She has been watching the comic intently, making the most erotic "need to pee" moves he's ever seen. From the angular to the fluid, the moves combine into sensual dances of grace and tension and pleasure. And yet, she does not even smile at his jokes. She smiles, all right—but strictly at her sensations, with a rhythm independent of the comic's buildups and punch lines. She is different from the other women, for whom the inner, physical ticklings and his own verbal ticklings work in concert. And when he delivers a gag, the Last Dry Lady's face greets his with a serene, tolerant, but unamused gaze that is so intense he begins to feel awkward. Meanwhile, her body gyrates, her hands dart back and forth to and from her crotch, and her thighs pulsate. The comic notices everything about her—her pale white skin, her fine black hair, her delicate torso that flows beneath a skin-tight aqua jersey . . . her shapely but athletic legs that press significantly together beneath a denim miniskirt. He especially notices her eyes, which are a green so vibrant he risks losing his rhythm when they meet his own.

Now all the other women have gushed their puddles. They have retreated to the lobby and restroom in giggling groups and quivering solos. A few of them stand by the bar at the back, topping off their ecstasy with a little more beer. No one is paying attention to the comic now. No one except the Last Dry Lady, who hovers directly in front of the stage, just a few feet away from him.

The comic pauses in his routine. "I'm sorry," he says softly to the Last Dry Lady. "I don't seem to be able to make you laugh. And I'm almost out of material."

"Look," she says, hopping like a ballerina from foot to foot. Her voice is hoarse but velvety, and it augments the hard-on she has already given him with her dance and her eyes. "I'll make this easy. I want to soak these panties in about another thirty seconds flat, and I want to do it laughing. So I'm going to direct you to a riddle that always gets me. The one about the butter."

His mind races. He's on it. "How can you tell when an elephant's been in your refrigerator?" Even as he says it he is dubious, slow to believe that this is really what she wants.

"Tell me!" she shrieks.

Her reaction has left no doubt, and his confidence returns. "Footprints in the butter," he states with perfect, musical precision.

Her face dissolves into mirth, her knees buckle, and a beautiful waterfall tumbles down. Beside herself in ecstasy, she squats lewdly and tugs at the hem of her mini-skirt. Her saturated aqua panties are just visible at the source of the broad cascade. "Oh, w-wow," she stutters between phrases of laughter, "I'm pissing so hard I'm coming." Her eyes close and her body shakes as she forges on, her pee unabating and her sensations climaxing, a hand pressed fervently into the core of the flooded underwear.

Her crotch still drips prettily when her eyes blink open in post-orgasmic sweetness.

She straightens up, wrings herself out, and wipes her hands on a dry part of her skirt. She blows a kiss toward the comic, then leaves the building, not even stopping to clean herself up.

The comic makes a mental note to add more corny riddles to his repertoire. He feels a sticky patch in his briefs where his cock has acknowledged the beauty of the Last Dry Lady. Then he becomes aware of something that has never happened before. He is gently pissing his pants, his body leaking rapturously in homage to the erotic power of what he has just witnessed.

As he soaks himself in warm, transcendent comfort, his only regret is that she is not there to see.

Wet Vignettes

ONE

My girlfriend had trained herself to have roaring orgasms when she peed.

On a typical Saturday afternoon, she'd drink her pot of tea and disappear into the bathroom, and soon I'd hear her absolutely screaming in ecstasy as she emptied her reservoir. Sometimes she'd even text me a selfie from the toilet, showing her face contorted with the pleasure of release.

Eventually, I asked if she might like me to be there in the bathroom with her. She nodded eagerly.

The following Saturday, she counted the minutes till her regular tea time. Finally, the moment arrived. As I followed her to the toilet, I admired the delicate steps she took across the room, knowing they were to be followed by a fierce torrent that would contrast with them splendidly.

She peeled her panties down methodically, and let her pee-tense pussy greet the air and hold itself ready over the toilet water. Before my eyes, she used her fingertips to part her lips. The elegance with which she infused these actions—elegant peeing!—only added to my arousal.

At first she released herself slowly, evidently savoring the sophisticated joy of peeing in brief shudders, interspersing the release with the tension. I could vividly imagine the waves of titillating pressure, punctuated by velvety moments of letting go. My cock responded with its own jolts of excitement, and I found myself sharing her desire to prolong this phase of things.

"Oh, wow," my lover sighed, looking delectable with her panties at her knees and her crew socks pressing into the floor. "I'm always so happy when I'm peeing." Then she gasped; and down came the full force of her cascade, and out came the beautiful, rounded scream.

When she'd finished, she reached between her legs with her bare fingers, then rose up from the seat just far enough to touch the front of my boxers, which she deliberately streaked with two fingertips' worth of her warm urine. I tented into her hand, and she stroked my calf with one of her sexy socks.

Two

Trudy has just mentioned that she has to pee.

And Helen wants to strip her down, pinch her imploring nipples, and see Trudy water the bathroom floor like a faucet as the pressure from her fingers runs straight to Trudy's juncture.

She wants to see Trudy's gaze dissolve in the pseudo-surprise of ecstasy when she lets go ... hear Trudy groan deep in her throat at that instant of release, when the first hot splash pours from her grateful pussy ... watch Trudy continue to gyrate in her "I need to pee" dance even as the liquid runs down her thighs.

Or she wants to work Trudy's beautiful legs like levers while she pees and pees, lying in the bathtub with her head against the plastic cushion, no water under her bottom but her own, her pissing crotch wild with arousal.

Or tickle Trudy while she sits on the toilet with her bladder deliciously full, so that the benign mischief of her hands all over Trudy's middle will make her pee rush out in even more of a frenzy than it otherwise would ... and Trudy will giggle there on the seat while her busy little pussy tinkles into the bowl, the music of her precipitation echoing her erotic laughter as it tickles the water's surface.

Or hold Trudy lovingly from behind in her clothing, pull her skirt up at the rear, and watch her soak her thin panties. And yank the panties down to Trudy's knees and lick her sopping pussy clean ... and lick her and kiss her and lave her, moving her lips and tongue all over Trudy's most sensitive spots—her innermost thighs, the flesh immediately surrounding her clit—until Trudy can't take any more pleasure, and comes in her face.

Trudy has just mentioned that she has to pee.

THREE

Alan pulled the car over.

He was the only one of their team of grad students who didn't need to urinate here at the side of this little-used byway, but Joyce encouraged him to get out of the car anyway.

"The other women and I talked it over while you were asking directions back there," she said, "and we thought it might be fun if you watched us all pee."

"We can all demonstrate different positions!" Cindy said enthusiastically.

"Assuming you *want* to watch," Amy added thoughtfully.

"But make up your mind fast," Vi giggled. "Because I, for one, am *sooo* ready to go."

But Alan's mind was already made up, and he followed his friends over the slight privacy-enhancing rise that had attracted them to this particular spot.

Apparently, they'd discussed their plans in full detail while he was asking directions, for they now very efficiently lined up and assumed four distinct postures.

Joyce, standing at the far left from Alan's point of view, unbuttoned her stonewashed jeans but took them down only as far as her thighs, along with the soft, pale blue panties that Alan admired from his observation point ten feet away. She quickly adjusted her intimate anatomy with her fingers, and soon she was pissing a thin, male-style arc off into the wings. She turned her head to wink at Alan.

Meanwhile, Amy, standing stage left of Joyce, had slipped off her sandals and thong, kicking these articles toward Alan. She now bunched her calico print skirt into her fists and lifted it all the way to her belly, letting the brown fur of her pubis shine in the sunlight. She parted her legs and poured straight down like a spigot, with no hint of the shyness he'd sometimes seen in her personality.

Next over was Vi, the traditionalist. She'd pulled her pants all the way to her ankles and was squatting into action—facing away from Alan so he could watch the broad, ragged sheet of her heavy rainfall originate under her happy moon of an ass and spray hither and yon as she pissed hands-free.

Finally, all the way at Alan's right, there was Cindy. Cindy had unzipped and removed her denim skirt, and she bent her knees slightly to pee through the leg hole of her purple bikini panties, holding the gusset askew and pissing in hearty spurts while she shimmied her hips and mouthed flirty kisses at Alan.

"Are you sure you don't need to take your equipment out and piss with us, Alan?" said Joyce, licking her lips hopefully—and still pissing gorgeously.

With difficulty, Alan unzipped his trousers. "No, I don't need to *pee*," he replied. "But if no one minds … I think I do need to take it out, at this point."

The four women laughed their approval.

Four

"It's ridiculously simple," she explained. "I have to pee—I *have* to—and just my doing it, just its happening naturally, turns him on. And just his seeing it turns *me* on."

"And … the grass skirt?"

"Yes, exactly. The grass skirt." She wiggled in her chair. "I mean, there I am standing topless on our private patio, with my pussy naked underneath that short grass skirt I save for just such occasions … and it's a fact that this bare pussy of mine *will* pee—it's only a matter of time. In fact, after a couple of cocktails, I'm going to need to do it sooner rather than later.

"Right."

"So, you see, it's a given: I'm going to piss right there in the open, and John's going to see it, and the mere idea makes me cream with excitement. Can't you just visualize it? I'm naked and my thighs are open and I'm going to pee *right there* where my nude pussy is on display. No panties, remember—the piss is just going to travel right along my naked flesh."

"Yes."

"The pee is just going to flow right out of my pussy, while he watches. It just is."

"So true."

"And can you imagine how wet my pussy will be afterward, from all that peeing? And maybe my thighs, and way back under my bottom cheeks?"

"I think I can, yes."

"So?"

"So … what time do you want me there?"

Five

The first time you stay in a hotel with your fiancée, she's in an especially playful mood. Especially frisky, too. Even at home, she's usually the one to initiate sex; but here she initiates it in the morning, not just the evening.

Today, she's already fucked you twice between Continental breakfast and shower time. Now she's done with her shower, and she steps into the outer part of the bathroom wearing only a smallish towel—one of those towels that's absurdly white, white to a degree that only hotel towels can be white.

She pulls it tighter around her torso and rolls back and forth on the balls of her feet, while she glances in the mirror. "Mm. I really have to pee," she comments.

She looks straight at you, smiling, then back at the mirror—remaining where she is, now shuffling sensuously from foot to foot.

It takes you only a second to digest the fact that she specifically *wants* you to enjoy the sight of her this way—thighs practically crossing under the towel, her lovely rear end jutting out. "Really having" to pee, as she has indicated.

She bends down momentarily to straighten the stiff white hotel bath mat, and you see the tense pout of her pussy peeking out behind, so ready to piss. Yes, she wants you to see her barely holding back from leaking right there, see her relishing the way it feels.

And when she scampers back into the inner bathroom, leaving the door wide open behind her, you understand that she wants you to follow her.

Yes, she wants you right here, watching her trickling into the toilet with her thighs apart.

After the initial intoxicating eyeful, you let your gaze travel briefly to her face, just long enough for her eyes to meet yours as she melts fully into relieving herself. She squints in ecstasy, and her mouth opens orgasmically. "Ohhhhh," she says. "Ohhhhhhh…"

Your gaze returns to the spectacle at her crotch. You remain riveted by the sight of her humble, slow, but steady stream. After a long while, she dribbles to a conclusion and her pussy muscles twitch in spasms of relaxation.

And when your eyes meet hers again, the lust on her face tells you that she wants you to stay there—facing the toilet, still naked, unshaved, and unshowered after the morning romp—so that instead of using toilet paper to blot her pee-sprinkled flesh, she can stand up, clasp your erection, and rub her wet pussy up and down your thigh, sensually wiping herself on your skin.

Like that.

Yes, she wants you to feel the place from which she's peed warm and close against your skin while she luxuriates, her refreshment singing through every muscle in her groin.

And she wants you to remain right there, streaked with her kinky lemonade, as she begins to caress herself, as she lets her sensuality complete its transition into arousal.

She wants you to see how open and glistening she is, when she stands now with one foot on the tub, her towel hiked up past her waist and her fingers teasing her clit.

She wants you to notice that forgotten trickle of pee that runs along her thigh, and the sweeter, stickier fluid from her cunt that now begins to shimmer on her labia.

Six

She loved pissing outdoors, of course: panty-free under her skirt, tissues in her purse … just lift the flap, make your puddle, and wipe. Why shut herself up in a dull restroom when she could find a quiet area of the park, let her ass out in the sun, and hiss her sweet water onto the ground?

But peeing outside had nothing on peeing backstage, Kirsten had discovered.

It was the third week of rehearsals, and now that they were running the show without stopping they'd understood she needed a place backstage to pee. Kirsten was the only performer who exited into an alcove that did not communicate with the wings, the dressing rooms, and the facilities; and since, apart from her twenty minutes in the alcove, she was onstage for the entire ninety minutes of the play, she'd requested special arrangements.

Luckily, Kirsten had an exhibitionistic streak, and the idea of pissing into a chamber pot with only a heavy curtain separating her from her colleagues positively thrilled her.

She had privacy in the alcove—and yet she could hear the well-projected voices from the stage, and she loved the luxurious jouissance of quietly leaking while her castmates were so close by. Perhaps they were oblivious to what she was doing, or perhaps they could hear a hint of her gentle rainfall (though the audience certainly would not) … or perhaps, knowing about the arrangements, they might automatically visualize her doing it while she was in there. And the possibility that they might especially appreciate hearing it, or visualizing it, excited her all the more.

That's what Kirsten always thought about, rehearsal after rehearsal, when she stretched her thong to the side and let the high-pressure liquid trickle out as gradually as possible, for maximum quiet. Each time it felt like a slow-motion orgasm, lasting and lasting.

SEVEN

The woman poses in front of the mantel with her arse out, her skirt hiked up to display herself. She braces her palms against the brick.

The man crouches behind her, her naked ass in his face. It wriggles while she waits to pee—waits for the ass-tickling she craves, to put her over the edge.

He begins tickling her bare behind with her feather-duster—the rounds and the soft crevice between them—not neglecting to dust her vulva as well.

Within seconds, she is wetting the floor magnificently.

Her erogenous bottom vibrates in his face as the waterfall rushes, as she pisses down from the sweet spot nestled up beyond where luscious thighs and splendid derriere cheeks meet. Moaning, she brings one hand down and jams it deep between her legs, to stroke her heated clit.

"Oh, yes, my ass," she hisses to the mantel. "My tickled, tickled ass."

Eight

He adored the way she downed her tea right before hopping in the shower ... so that by the time she hopped out five minutes later, she was hopping with the need to pee.

Without breaking stride, she'd hit the bath mat, throw a towel around her shoulders, and lewdly straddle the toilet bowl—standing, not sitting—letting go robustly, beautifully, with a forceful cascade of hot, womanly piss. Liquid lightning.

Once in a while, though, she'd linger in the tub and—when she was on the verge of leaking—beckon him to strip and join her.

While she steadied herself on the towel bar and her bottom wiggled under the caress of the warm shower jets, he'd lift her leg off the floor, and her fountain of piss would spurt uncontrollably onto him. For a wonderfully extended time she would relieve herself copiously onto his skin, her mouth open in an equally extended moan. He would pivot his hips self-indulgently to bathe his cock in her flow.

Then he'd watch the stray droplets of shower water flick down onto his lover's nipples, as she rocketed into the orgasm that always capped the rapture of this release.

Nine

"How soon does the bar close?"

Kate got that mischievous look on her face.

She glanced around quickly to verify that it was all friends tonight, just us regulars.

She locked the door, then turned back and smiled knowingly at us.

"The bar stays open until the barmaid wets her shorts," she announced.

Some of us had played this game before, some not. But we all applauded as Kate took a preliminary bow.

She strode back behind the bar, grabbed one of the tallest glasses she owned, and slowly drew herself a brimming portion of pale yellow lager. She raised it in a toast to all of us.

"Drink up, mates, 'cause I've a feeling it may not be long now."

TEN

Janet squeezes her knees together as she sips her coffee.

"In the dream," she tells me, "I'm surrounded by a group of close friends, male and female. 'You've told us what you enjoy the most,' they say, 'and now it's up to you to judge how much pleasure you can stand at one time. Because if you want it all at once, we can give it to you all at once: there are enough of us that you can have your underarms tickled and your bottom slapped and your clit rubbed while you pee yourself.'"

She spreads her legs now, and I watch her as she finds the weakest point in the crotch of her stretchy old tights. She deliberately rends the fabric, and she purrs as she opens her legs even further, slips a finger past the flimsy gusset of her panties, and inserts it into herself.

While she continues talking, she masturbates right there on the sofa, her thighs fully spread, her shoulders tensed against the couch back, her ass restless on the cushions. Her violet tights still enclose her legs, her hips, and her mound, but pink wet flesh winks at me where her busy finger has breached the fabric.

"So," she says, "I say yes, yes to all of it. And instantly I find that two friends are holding my arms up, one apiece, gently opening me up for all the pleasure. They each use the other hand to tickle my armpits—so lightly—while other people's fingers and tongues indulge my breasts, my nipples. And there's a procession of soft slaps stimulating my buttocks, thanks to yet another pal."

She's writhing with arousal now, but the narrative keeps coming.

"Then someone holds a beer glass to my lips, and soon I'm pissing my heart out down below. It feels so delicious, my whole pussy is tingling. And … and, oh god, someone else is licking my clit and my cunt all the while, distributing the pleasure along my puffy pussy lips and my hard little button, while I piss myself freely. It's all happening at once, and it's more pleasure than I can even imagine when I'm awake. I become nothing but a huge orgasm in my sleep. I wake up soaked in my own come and still laughing—oh god—like I'm still being tickled, even though I'm awake and by myself."

Janet looks at me, continuing to play furiously with her vulva, her face flushed, her whole body ready to come soon. She's wondering what I think of her dream.

The erection in my sweats feels like iron, lying almost horizontally across my lap like a chin-up bar.

Eleven

Michael's new housemate smiled at him, all high-boots-and-belted-minidress sexy as she hastily stumbled in with her shopping bags.

Moments later, he very clearly heard the sound of her peeing vigorously into their powder-room toilet, accompanied by a fluid murmur of fevered words and sensuous laughter: *A-haha, oh yeah, oh yes … ah-hahaha.*

Evidently, the pleasure Michael's new housemate felt in emptying was too intense to keep quiet about. It felt exquisite, apparently.

And Michael's new housemate wanted Michael to know.

Twelve

From the kitchen, I can see Molly and Albert frolicking on the couch here in our shared apartment. They've never been shy about this, and they don't mind that I like to watch.

This afternoon, Molly is in a tank top, and she has her knickers rolled down just enough to expose her marvelous buttocks.

With her knees digging into the sofa cushions, she rides Albert's lap with her back to him so that he can tickle her softly—her bare underarms and, especially, her exposed ass crack. From my vantage point, I can watch her derriere jiggle gloriously as he pleasures it.

"If you keep that up you'll make me pee!" she notes merrily between murmured giggles. But it's pretty clear from her body language that, in fact, she wants him to keep it up.

She lowers her panties a little further and parts her legs a bit. Albert's tickle hand moves into her crotch, and I see Molly slam her thighs closed around his wrist to keep his fingers tickling right, exactly there as she repeats, with even more obvious sexual excitement, "You're gonna make me pee!"

Albert answers her *hee-hee-hee*s with his own throaty chuckles, grabs one of her ankles, and adds a bit more bounce to the tickling routine. Molly shrieks with glee as she falls forward.

With her ass aloft, I can see everything when she loses control and the pretty flood comes.

Thirteen

The two women—best friends, bedroom playmates, and tennis partners—whoop and giggle as they hurry from the court to the park's bathrooms ... both of them practically dribbling in their white panties, both of them titillated rather than alarmed by the recognition that they might not make it in time ... both of them euphorically flustered and giddy with the preoccupation of holding onto their imminent floods.

Inside the restroom, these two women in white tennis dresses dash into the two stalls. Two pairs of panties slide down, and two friends pee—simultaneously, symmetrically. Two trimmed, furry pussies, blonde and brunette, sizzle with the joy of weeping voluminously into emptiness.

Ahhhhhhhhhh.

Intimate water rushes in stereo, then there is quiet. They have both finished, but neither of them moves.

"Oh, god, that felt good," Anne chuckles. They can tell each other anything.

"You want to know something?" says Jill.

"What?"

"Sometimes I get turned on when I really have to pee like that."

"Oh, I hear you. Me too. It's that incredible tingle, you know?"

"Yeah, like you just have to yank your panties down right that second and water something—but then again holding it feels so tickly good. Sexy."

"Oh, yeah, squirmy and hot. Like you can't stand still, and all you can think about is peeing, and how good it's going to feel, but the anticipation is amazing ... like being nine-tenths of the way to an orgasm and you just want to stretch that teasy tension out as long as you can." Anne laughs at her own impassioned description. "Whoo!"

Jill lowers her voice a hair. "I ... well, sometimes at home I even hold it till I wet my panties. I mean, like, on purpose."

"Well, you know what? I sometimes pee myself for Dan in the backyard—on one of those plastic lawn chairs. I wait till I totally have to go, then I strip nude and squirm there on the chair, and he fondles my tits and I just wet my naked old pussy."

"Mmm. Sounds nice."

"Hey, Jill?"

"Yeah?"

"You didn't ... um ... wipe your pussy yet, did you?"

"No, I—sometimes I just don't."

"Yeah, same here."

They flush, leave their stalls, and meet up at the sinks.

"So ... what're you doing after our match today?" Jill asks.

"Sniffing your sexy pee-stained panties," Anne laughs. "How about you?"

"Peeing in your pretty face," Jill promises.

Volume 3

Water Nymph

WHEN I FIRST SAW ANNA, SHE WAS LUXURIATING ALONGSIDE A public fountain in the center of the city, late on a summer Friday night. Her long blonde hair exuded a wild vitality in the light of the moon, and her personal energy seemed to resonate with the flowing water.

I had planned to stop by the fountain even before I knew there was a beautiful, sensual woman sprawled there. It would have been as false of me to bypass the fountain in an effort not to crowd her as it would have been false of me to pretend that I was oblivious to her captivating presence.

"Good evening," I said, in a voice smoothed by a recent glass of whiskey.

"Good evening," she replied, as if from somewhere far away.

We enjoyed the fountain, separately, for a few minutes.

"Peaceful, isn't it?" I finally said. "Peaceful … and yet full of life."

"I love the water," she returned with vigor, to herself more than to me. "Our planet is mostly water. We are mostly water."

I thought about this. "True," I said. "We even spend the first nine months of life immersed in water, don't we?"

Her eyes met mine for the first time. "Yes. That's a good insight."

"Speaking of fluids," I segued, "may I buy you a drink? My name is Tim. And though I don't know much, I do know a rather agreeable bar in this neighborhood."

"I'm Anna," she told me as we headed in that direction.

I ordered my second whiskey of the evening, and she chose a pint of beer. As we made ourselves comfortable, Anna noticed that a lovely seascape print hung above our table.

"Ah yes," I said, the art critic in me rising to the surface. "Here again, the fascination of water."

"Water is not only beautiful, but it can bring such pleasure, don't you think?" she asked.

"Oh, definitely. A nice warm shower … a Jacuzzi. Very sensuous."

"And sexual," she insisted.

I laughed. "OK, I'll go along with that."

"I hoped you might," she said alluringly.

Sometimes, when I'm in the presence of an intensely attractive woman, I start to ramble about my childhood, just from sheer nervous energy. I did so now. "Some of my favorite times, when I was a kid, were spent in neighborhood swimming pools. Every summer, my buddies and I would stay in the water for hours at a time, just splashing around and playing games."

Anna smiled enigmatically. "I'll tell you a secret, Tim." She leaned in and touched my hand for a moment. "I like to play special games with my own water."

I didn't know what she meant. I imagined her tossing a bottle of Evian into the air and catching it.

While we enjoyed our drinks, the conversation drifted into small talk, peppered with more reminiscences from me about youthful, idyllic summers.

Eventually, Anna stood up. "I need to pee," she informed me, with a frankness I found sexy. But instead of heading toward the toilets, she took my hand and said, "Let's go."

"I thought you had to pee," I said as we exited the bar.

"Mmm-hmm," Anna said. "Follow me." And she darted into a nearby alley. So I followed her.

There she stood, dancing in the moonlight, clutching herself like a woman who did indeed need to pee … and who was thoroughly enjoying the sensation. Now I understood what she had meant by playing games with her own water. As the erotic beauty of what I was observing sank in, I felt myself going hard in my trousers.

"Ooh, it tickles," she confided with a magic ripple of laughter. While she stroked her groin with one hand through the front of her miniskirt, she used her free hand to blow me a kiss. My heart fluttered and my cock continued to throb.

Suddenly, with a delectable moan, Anna yanked her tights and knickers down, spun around, and squatted, her smooth ass pointed toward me as it peeked out from the skirt. She turned her head briefly to give me a conspiratorial grin over her shoulder. Then, after a breathless moment, I saw her water begin to dribble out of her, shy little trickles at first that kissed her pussy and dotted her legs and meandered downward. Then the floodgates opened in earnest, and her stream poured thickly as if from a faucet, a powerful, womanly piss that hissed swiftly out and formed an impressive pool, while Anna's thighs quivered with vitality. Her personal fountain, glimmering in the moonlight and artistically juxtaposed with her delicious ass cheeks, made the large, public fountain we'd admired earlier look humdrum by comparison.

"I love being a woman," said Anna, turning her head toward me again as her flow began to subside. "I love the feeling of being so full of liquid that it just has to pour out of a little hole between my legs. It makes me feel so feminine to sense it rushing out of me down there."

I had to admit that the sight of Anna with pee flowing out of her was an exquisitely feminine, achingly sexual tableau.

She took me home with her, and by the time we arrived she whispered that she was already "full of water" again. This time I felt myself in a similar state, I told her.

She invited me to join her in her spacious bathroom. "Let's be naked together," she said as we entered.

I wasn't sure what to expect, but I was charmed, intrigued, and aroused by her, and I was content to do whatever she suggested. So we stripped and met in the middle of the room, where we joined together as if on a tiled dance floor and engaged in a kinky, erotic waltz, grabbing our own groins and stroking one another's, smilingly. As I shifted my bladder-enhanced weight from one foot to the other, Anna mirrored my movements. The effect of watching her soft, nude body in motion was mesmerizing, and her feminine scent seemed to envelop me.

She pulled affectionately at my piss-ready cock, and I insinuated a finger into her slick pussy, which I hoped would make it tingle with pleasurable tension as the dam just to the north prepared to seep and gush. All the while, we danced. Then we both spilled, dancing still, and shared our waters in a crazy puddle.

No sooner had we cleaned up, than we adjourned nakedly to her bed, where the offbeat intimacy we had shared in the bathroom blossomed into the most relaxed sexual mingling I'd ever experienced on a first encounter. Our bodies seemed to tingle as one from the erotic release of our waters together, and Anna was on the threshold of orgasm almost before my lips began to explore her sex. As her pussy trembled beneath my mouth, she seemed to melt into a pool of sensation.

By the time my cock was stroking her inner walls a few minutes later, she was whimpering to her second climax. This time we shuddered together, and the orgasm felt like a sweet, wet, powerful echo of the watery bliss she'd shown me earlier.

I was easily convinced to stay the weekend. As I was gradually introduced to the various rooms in her house, I noticed that all her decor had an aquatic theme. Artistic renditions of oceans, rivers, waves, boats, sea horses, and waterfalls met me at every turn.

On Saturday afternoon, she drove me to a deserted, picturesque park along the lake. It was a beautiful, sunny day, with just enough of a breeze to give some motion to the water. We sat on our blanket and enjoyed the scenery, and I soon noticed that Anna was squirming a little. Before long she was holding herself, and again I saw that enigmatic smile. But it was no longer enigmatic to *me*, and I waited with anticipation to see what Anna would do next.

For a few minutes, she relished the squirmy knot of titillating sensation, holding it in. Then she suddenly stopped jiggling and sprawled back on the welcoming blanket, letting her water claim her, sighing as it washed exquisitely through her. Second by second, her body transformed itself from a tightly wound tapestry of erotic tension into a vision of relaxed gratification. As the dampness spread through the crotch of her tight jeans, release likewise traveled from nerve to nerve, spreading all the way to her flushed, ecstatic face and her trembling fingertips, which clutched the edges of the blanket.

"Oh, sweet paradise, that felt good," she moaned when her after-shudders had subsided.

As after every such display, I found myself wild with desire for her, which she gratified expertly, fucking us both into dizzy heavens with the determined clenchings of her soaked pussy.

Back at her house, Anna performed a sensuous bathtub ritual for me, soaping herself with slow strokes and letting me see every inch of her flesh delight in the nurturing warmth of the oil-infused bathwater.

Later that evening, wearing the sexy "fuck me" skirt-and-stockings outfit that she'd donned after her bath, Anna turned her next bladderful into a striptease with a twist. Having primed herself with lager, she invited me once again into her elegant bathroom. We entered the room in haste, with Anna's hand pressed dramatically against her sex. And yet, as soon as we arrived, she went into slow motion. With erotic finesse, she removed all her garments, her body shimmering all the while in a delicious dance of anticipation. Even her stockings, her blouse, and her bra came off, though their presence would not have obstructed her from doing what she needed to do. There was obviously something intensely arousing to her about wiggling these irrelevant articles of clothing off of herself while her crotch throbbed patiently with impending release.

She had incredible control, and her blissed-out face made it obvious that she was enjoying every minute of letting her piss build to a head while she dawdled over undressing. With full consciousness that her performance was as intoxicating to me as it was to her, she made an exquisite sexual display of both her stripping and her thigh-clamping bodily need.

Only when every shred of clothing had been artfully removed

and carefully set aside did she lower her gorgeous self onto the toilet. Here she posed with open-legged frankness and showed me, so vividly, exactly how much she had to pee. "Just look at me," she prompted—unnecessarily. "Look between my legs and tell me this isn't female anatomy at its best. I'm pissing like a water nymph, and I feel like I never want to stop," she laughed.

When she was finally empty, we spread a thick towel and fucked on her bathroom floor.

On Sunday afternoon, Anna took me behind the house into her garden, which abutted on a babbling brook. She held my hand as we stood watching the vigorous, rushing water.

I was not surprised to learn that Anna's visit to the garden could not be considered complete until she had sprinkled the ground. With her shorts and knickers lowered to embrace her bare ankles, she pretended to be particular about precisely what part of the earth she would rain on. She shimmied this way and that in her sneakers, waddling backward and forward in a lewd semi-squat, until she found the perfect spot. There, she finally went into a full squat. She pulled her top up, baring her saucy breasts.

"Touch them while I water," she suggested, using her favorite noun as a poetic verb. I titillated her sensitive chest with one hand while sending the other into her stream, to let a sample of her fresh pee run between my fingers. I stole a quick, tactile encounter with the slippery tingle of her piss-busy pussy. Then I brought this hand up to her breasts as well. The feel of my digits, wet with her warm fluid, across her nipples made her wiggle and coo.

Pissing. She told me she'd come to think of it as her "other bliss"—thereby putting it alongside orgasm. The simple, intimate joy of urination, cherished between her legs and parceled out to both of us like sweets.

I thought about fountains and ocean currents as I squatted on the bathroom floor with her on Sunday evening. Though Anna remained semi-clothed in crisp knickers and a jersey, I had undressed, and she was clutching my indecisive cock, which luxuriated ambiguously between erection and urination. I felt a certain type of wave rise up, and I decided it was time to piss, to express my own liquid humanity in front of my lover, my water nymph. So I let my cock flop in her hand, and she directed my flow onto the floor, while tickling my balls. I pumped happily, and soon I saw that her knickers were darkening. Anna was leaking, giving in to her beautiful female tide, wetting the floor while she held my hose. We were watering together, two creatures of water sharing the special ecstasies of a watery planet.

Touching Base

<small>Though Cornelia and I work in different departments,</small> I like to check in with her every day, just to touch base.

<small>Monday</small>
"Come in."
I enter.
"Oh, hi, Lance. I'm just getting my nipples licked."
Paul, Cornelia's officemate, tongues one crystal-rigid candy nub, then the other. Cornelia moans.
"Do you need anything from the copy center?" she asks me. "I'm heading down there in a little while."

<small>Tuesday</small>
"Come on in. I'm just getting my bottom slapped."
And so she is. Paul obviously knows how to give her bare cheeks exactly the stimulation she craves.
"Ooh!" says Cornelia, in a shrieking laugh. "Ooh-hoo!"
She queries me during an inter-slap hiatus: "Do you want a ride to the train station today, Lance?"

<small>Wednesday</small>
"Make yourself at home, Lance. I'm just wetting my panties."
Cornelia's skirt is hiked up, and her flirty peach hipsters are dark at their apex. Her finger is inside the waistband, and her water flows freely into a basin on the carpet. "Oh, god, that feels

good."

"Paul off today?" I ask by way of small talk.

Thursday

"Hey, Lance. What's up? I'm just getting my pussy tickled."

Her panties are at her ankles, and Paul is dusting between her thighs with an enormous feather.

"Hee-hee," says Cornelia, "moremoremore, hee-hee-hee-hee ..."

Friday

E-mail from Cornelia. Paul is leaving the company to go back to school. They're asking her if she knows anyone who might want to take over his half of the double office ...

Rest Rumors

THE TWO TRAVELERS WALKED INTO THE HITHERTO EMPTY restroom.

"I am *so* ready to pee," said Alexandra.

They hunkered into position in neighboring stalls.

"On the count of 3," suggested Kelly, and the women laughed as they teased themselves by waiting three seconds more.

"Three" arrived, and the space around them echoed with their furious tinkling.

"*Ahhh.*"

"*Yesss.*"

Alexandra felt as if she would never empty, no matter how hard and fast she pissed. It was a blissful state indeed.

Finally, all was quiet.

"I wish you were wiping me, and I were wiping you," said Kelly.

It was a lucky break for Evan that the ambient noise level in the busy I-95 service area happened to ebb just at that moment. Otherwise, he would have been unlikely to overhear the tidbit of conversation that floated his way when the two cute women glided past him at the road-map display, on their way from the restroom to the coffee stand.

"Fuck, that felt good," was what the first silvery voice said, with a giggle. "I had, like, an orgasm, I was peeing so hard."

"I *know*," the other woman giggled in reply, just as they disappeared into the crowd of travelers. It was clear to Evan that "I know," in this context, meant "me too."

He would never see them again. But, oh, he'd remember them.

A fresh string of self-pleasure sessions now stretched to his horizon, like a densely plotted series of highway exits. He would imagine them in side-by-side stalls, their beauty synchronized, invisible to each other but within mutual earshot. "Yesss," one might hiss, in the ecstasy of release, while her traveling companion sighed an "Ahhh" over her own squirming pleasure. From his imagined vantage point above—or facing them through magically transparent stall doors—he saw everything: the panties off their hips, the smiles on their faces.

In his mind, they stayed there as long as he needed them to, pissing and pissing, wiggling and laughing … their fun lasting and lasting, as long as he could last.

Involuntarily

WILL YOU BELIEVE ME WHEN I TELL YOU THAT I DIDN'T GO looking for the secret voyeur's perch? I'm good with boundaries, actually, and I like to think I respect people's privacy.

But I couldn't help the fact that I was observant. And I couldn't help that when I sat at my desk, in the small apartment that doubled as my office, I saw directly out my window into the window of the travel agency. I found myself watching that window like it was a television with the sound turned all the way down. Involuntarily. I made sure not to stare, but I looked and I saw.

What was I supposed to do—close the blinds and deprive myself of daylight? I certainly wasn't going to move my desk. I'm a decent person, but there are limits.

Anyway, I never saw anything that was specifically intended to be screened from public view. What I saw was G-rated, and the X-rated effect it happened to have on me didn't violate anyone's space. It was a private matter between me and my supply of handkerchiefs.

So, being observant, I became familiar with the wardrobes, routines, and body language of the three women who worked at the agency—and even with some elements of their personalities. If you think you can't learn anything about someone's personality by watching her through a window, then you're not watching right. You can't tell me that the particular way the short, sunny blonde's mouth curled up when she was on the phone wasn't studied flirting. Or that the willowy redhead's eyes constantly drifting toward a stuffed hedgehog on her desk didn't reveal a sentimental heart.

Since I didn't know their names, I eventually made up my own names for each of them. This wasn't something I did in a conscious way. I don't think I would have indulged in that level of linguistic masturbation. No, it just sort of happened. Involuntarily. For example, one day I realized that I had come to think of the fast-typing ace with dark hair and glasses as "Paula." Evidently, on some level she looked like a Paula to me, and that was that. I also realized that she was my favorite. You have to have a favorite, right? To tell you the truth, though, she would have been my favorite even if I didn't have to have one.

Paula, I had observed, was the quiet one. Easy, yes? Lips that don't move much means quiet. But she liked to hum to herself —and, yes, you can tell the difference between singing and humming from across the street, through a window. She looked particularly sexy when she was humming, which was usually during the afternoon. (Her heavy eyelids earlier in the day suggested that Paula wasn't a morning person, and that she was practically typing in her sleep.)

I'll do my best to explain this next part. You see, being observant, I learned, without making any effort, how often each of them needed a pee break. Their habits were predictable, from the redhead ("Lynne," in my mind) who could hold it all morning to the blonde ("Frannie") who punctuated frequent cups of coffee with equally frequent visits to the little room whose door was just at the edge of my field of vision. I knew this was the bathroom and not a supply closet because they never entered more than one at a time; they always closed the door when they went in (but not when they came out); and they consistently failed to produce folders or printer paper or boxes of rubber bands upon their return. Observant—see?

I would watch each of them, on her own schedule, go through that door. And I couldn't help focusing on the fact—a *fact*—that beyond that door, skirts were raised and panties were lowered. When one of them emerged after I'd stared, involuntarily, at the closed door for the duration of her private minute (I reasoned that it *was* acceptable to stare at an inanimate object such as a door), all I could think about was that I was looking at a woman who'd had her panties down just moments before.

That closed door, with its implications of displaced panties, bunched skirts, and bared asses, drew my attention like a magnet. Think of it this way: There they all were each day, so businesslike as they bustled around the office in their smart, stylish outfits, from Lynne's conservative business suits to Frannie's color-splashed dresses to Paula's retro-chic skirts and sweaters. And I was sure that they were, indeed, professional and intelligent and efficient. But I also knew that each of them, x or y or z number of times a day, was ass-naked for a minute behind that door. I had all but seen it.

Mind you, this did not detract from their dignity, in my eyes. It wasn't an audience-in-its-underwear phenomenon. If anything, it was the opposite: I revered these beautiful women for being so businesslike *and* for routinely pulling down their panties, for expressing both these facets of themselves under the same roof.

I knew, of course, that women everywhere did this all day long. But it made it different to see it happen—well, almost see it happen—right out my window, day after day, as a matter of routine. And to know that I had, more or less, been as close to their private ass-baring moments as decency allowed.

I loved the way they would all unconsciously smooth their skirts back into place as they exited the restroom. If they had nothing else in common, they had this.

Eventually, I figured out that if I timed things right—if I got my jeans unzipped a few minutes before one of them was due for a bathroom break, and eased myself along with steady strokes—I could make myself come while staring at the closed door ... thinking about the descended panties of whichever beauty was in there ... visualizing those panties clinging around her knees. Clinging passionately to my own exposure below my desk.

Yes, though I wasn't out to become a habitual voyeur, I developed a habit of jerking off while I contemplated the travel agency's closed restroom door. I couldn't help seeing them walk into that room. I couldn't help knowing about the nakedness that occurred within. And I couldn't help the fact that it made me want to touch myself. Perhaps I could have waited and touched myself later, after they'd all gone home and their office was dark. But I didn't see why, ethically speaking, it really mattered whether I stroked while one of them was in there or I stroked a few hours later, imagining one of them in there. So I elected to stroke while the iron was hot.

And because my body couldn't generate enough orgasms to keep up with the bathroom visits of three women, I had to choose which travel agent's break I would climax to on a given morning or afternoon. I included them all, to some degree; but, as I said, I liked Paula best.

Summer was in full flower on the day I saw a plumber arrive at the travel agency. Through the window, I saw him head straight for their bathroom.

It was 2:15, and I happened to know that Paula was already behind schedule for the bathroom break predicted by my cumulative data. I calculated that she probably wouldn't be waiting till the plumber left.

Sure enough, she stepped outside the office and onto the pavement, at a time when she would normally not leave the building. She looked around. Then she crossed the street.

I was at the door almost before she knocked.

I guess I tipped my hand when I opened the door and, without even waiting for her to speak, gestured toward my bathroom. "It's in there," I said, helpfully but prematurely.

Her eyes flickered momentarily with surprise. But she needed what I was offering, and she didn't stop to sort out any mysteries.

I could have stared at the bathroom door—my bathroom door—while she was behind it. But in such close quarters, that now seemed inappropriate. So I deliberately retreated to the kitchen. As a host, Paula's privacy was my responsibility, I reflected. I felt so fucking virtuous, rinsing a few dishes while harboring a hard-on, telling myself I would wait till she left to begin visualizing her pulling her panties down in my bathroom.

"Thank you."

I'd been so absorbed in my self-satisfied bout of virtuous dish-washing that her voice took me by surprise. I switched off the water and turned toward her. "No problem, Paula. Anytime."

Again, a puzzled expression crossed her intelligent face. "It's May."

It was July. "What's May?"

"I am. Not Paula."

A sense of my own foolishness snapped into place. "Oh! Of course. Hi, May." I shook the excess water from my hands and approached her, extending one of them. "I'm Alec."

She accepted the handshake and smiled. "Why did you call me Paula?"

"It must be that you look like a Paula," I said.

She frowned.

"That's a compliment," I added.

She now studied me through her nerdy-cool glasses with a mixture of amusement and, I hoped, fondness. It suddenly mattered very much to me that she not only accept me but like me.

"Would you like coffee or anything? Water? Juice?" I caught myself before offering iced tea, which always sounds appealing but which I never actually have on hand, making it an impractical thing to suggest.

"Thanks, no. I have to get back to work. Alec." She had added my name as a separate sentence, as though sharing in a private joke. Then she made her way to the door.

She was almost beyond the threshold when she turned. "I have to work till 4:30." And she left me with this single piece of information. Well, that and the fact that her name was May and not Paula.

Standing at my desk, I looked through the window to see her glance toward my building before re-entering her office.

I hesitated before sitting down. Now that May was part of my real world, it didn't feel like I should be watching her. And, at that moment, I realized that I would have to move. If she never interacted with me again, I would have to move. If she and I became lovers, I would have to move. Even if she moved in *with* me, we would have to move. Because if we became a couple, I would inevitably meet her co-workers, and I could then no longer in good conscience observe Lynne and Frannie, or whatever their real names were, with my hungry, anonymous eyes. It was funny how you could sometimes risk violating the privacy of friends more easily than that of strangers. One of life's little paradoxes, I noted as I shut the blinds.

May's knock came promptly at 4:35. I ushered her in, and she seemed to notice right away that the side of the room by my desk was unnaturally dim.

"You closed the blinds," she remarked. She did something with her eyebrows, and I realized at once that she had put two and two together.

"Yeah, I thought I ... I'm—I'm sorry ... ," I fumbled.

Her smile was as strong as it was reassuring. "Don't be. I probably would have done the same thing you've been doing. I mean, what were you supposed to do—shut out the daylight just so as not to spy on us?"

"Earlier today, I—you know—happened to notice the plumber's truck, and I—"

"Oh yes, the plumber's truck," she laughed. "Today. But I'm guessing you've seen a lot more, day in and day out. You and your desk and your open blinds."

I shrugged sheepishly, knowing any further excuses would be futile. And unnecessary.

May continued: "After I went back to the office this afternoon, I was thinking about you here, watching us. It was definitely bizarre to think that you could sit at your desk and keep track of all our routines and habits." She blushed. "But, strangely enough, it made me ... hot."

Her voice had suddenly gone soft and husky, and she stepped forward. She gave me an earnest, inquiring look through her thick lenses.

"*Did it turn you on to look at us?*" she whispered urgently.

As I pulled her into an embrace, I wondered how moist her panties were. Yes, a universe of bliss was opening up before me, but my mind was only large enough to hold that one little unspoken question.

They were moist, all right. And soon they were gone. As were the glasses. And whatever the hell else she and I had been wearing.

That very morning, I'd been intensely horny just from knowing that May's ass was bare while she peed behind a closed door across the street. Now, miraculously, she lay naked and aroused on my bed, and I didn't even know where to look. My eyes roved across her, and it seemed like every cell of her flesh wanted me. Her cunt, her nipples, her underarms, her tummy. All of it yearned to be taken, fucked, brought to a boil. All I had to do was slide into her and give, give, give her what she craved.

And it hit me that the giving was what *I* craved. It was the supreme privilege that I'd been missing when I'd been quietly watching and privately jerking off. So I slid into her and gave, gave, gave, and I watched her body soak up my physical attention until she was so immersed in delirium that she was incapable of absorbing any more pleasure.

When she went over the brink, my keen powers of observation allowed me to become a partner in her ecstasy. And I felt myself giving her just one more gift, in the form of my eruption. Then our bodies stuttered together in involuntary aftershocks, and I closed my eyes.

As I floated in peaceful, self-imposed darkness, the sound of May's postcoital humming reverberated around me. Her humming was bolder and more tuneful than I'd imagined through my window, with more definition and tone.

I had so much to observe and learn now.

I'm Told I Make Good Coffee

"YOU MAKE THE BEST COFFEE, LAWRENCE," CLAUDINE SAID with an emphatic resonance of sincerity in her voice. I knew she was no stranger to the many java boutiques in the neighborhood, so I was especially appreciative of this compliment.

"But speaking of drinking coffee ... " Her cute little bottom hopped off the wooden stool behind the counter, and she shuttled briskly toward the bathroom. I walked around to take her place at the cash register, prepared for the unlikely event of a customer visiting the little record store at the hour of 11:20 a.m.

"Uh-oh," said Claudine from the end of the short hall that led to the bathroom. "The door is stuck again." I bounced over to help her, having myself mastered the "trick" to getting the door to unjam.

As I approached, I noticed that Claudine's ass was jiggling a bit. I remembered how once, in idle conversation about our sexual proclivities, she had mentioned to me that she enjoyed the erotic sensations of "holding it" awhile before peeing. I hadn't given it much thought at the time; but now my breath went short as I speculated that she was relishing the present moment. I noticed how the tight pin-striped fabric of her handsome retro slacks danced seductively with her movements.

"Thanks. I have to pee!" she giggled as I reached for the doorknob. Something about the manner in which she stated the obvious seemed to confirm my guess that she was enjoying herself.

From my position behind her, I pushed my weight forward

while turning the knob. As the door suddenly gave, I lost my balance slightly, and I unintentionally pressed against her.

"Sorry!" I reddened.

Claudine turned and gave me the warmest of knowing smiles. "Lawrence—are you a little hard?"

More than a little, I thought. She was dancing in place now, openly holding her crotch, but she was grinning happily and showed no signs of moving along.

"I guess so." I returned her smile.

"Oh, you sexy boy. This is the kind of thing that can make a grown girl wet her pants," she laughed, with a suggestion in her voice that though it might be a bit of an inconvenience to wet her pants here and now, the scenario otherwise held an attraction for her.

And where she was allowing herself to hover on the brink of wetting her pants, I was now on the verge of pollinating my jeans.

She darted into the bathroom, leaving the door ajar. I began to turn away as she peeled her slacks and panties and backed onto the commode ... but suddenly she called, "It's OK—you don't have to leave."

The next thing I heard was an angelic sigh of release.

As the hiss and roar of her pissing began, I stumbled in without further hesitation, secure in the knowledge that the bell above the front door of the shop would give me plenty of time to return to the counter to serve any hypothetical forenoon customers.

Hypothetical and improbable, I noted cheerfully.

Short Squirts

ONE

It was my mistake. I thought the bathroom was empty, that Karen had left me alone in the apartment. But when I walked through the door, she was sitting on the toilet.

To be more specific: She was sitting on the toilet, nude from the waist up but with pink, boy-cut panties on. Panties that were darkened, and were ever darkening more, with pee; panties that dripped heavily into the toilet like clothes on a washing line drip into a puddle after it's rained.

Her hand was wedged down the front of her piss-soaked knickers, and great motion was visible in her wrist. When my entrance surprised her, her face popped up and her mouth made an O; but the hand did not stop. The O widened, as did her eyes, which fixed me with a look of intimacy and passion as Karen came—as if my presence had put her over the edge, finishing what her autoerotic panty wetting had begun.

Two

She strides busily around her flat this morning, all long legs and round, bare ass … holding her pee until she's ready to make time.

She loves being nude when she has to pee: it's *right there*, the water waiting patiently just inside her exposed lips, all but ready to spurt forth.

Finally, when she's at a good stopping point with her various tasks, she slams herself onto the seat, still a picture of efficiency.

Only the mad rush of water gives an auditory clue that there's a veritable luxury of pissing pleasure concealed by her all-business attitude.

Three

What a day it's been.

The launch party was magical, and we've indulged ourselves in the manner we reserve for special occasions.

Now Julia warms my body in the backseat of the limo, her breath like fresh champagne. She lies arse up across my lap. And, content to let her hardworking bladder have its way, she gently wets her thong while I kiss the insides of her thighs.

What a day.

Four

She tells him she has to pee, and she pulls a basin to the middle of the floor. She hands him a feather. "You know what to do, I hope."

She strips off her skirt and panties, leaving her long-sleeved blouse on. She turns her back to him and straddles the basin. As she slowly sinks into a squat, he relishes how generous and round her bottom is, despite her slight frame. It looks so naked, feminine, and intimate—the ripe, exposed bottom of a woman who needs to pee.

As he slowly tickles up and down her crack with the feather, he hears the piss tinkling out. Her upper body sways a bit; her laughter is sensuous and gentle.

Five

Her lover has fallen asleep by the pool. She's stretched out, facedown in bikini bottoms only, on a thick towel she's laid over the cement. She's entirely in the shade, but it's plenty warm—a perfect situation for her nap.

Milly undresses entirely and silently approaches Jean. She manages not to rouse Jean as she peels Jean's bottoms off her ass, rolling them up and taking them a few inches down her thighs.

She straddles her lover and crouches directly over Jean's smooth, round derriere.

She pees. First it's an incipient trickle, but soon it's a hearty flood.

She rubs her warm pee all over Jean's bottom, massaging her exquisite cheeks, running piss-wetted fingers up and down her crack.

Jean wakes up smiling.

SIX

"I'm afraid I made a puddle on your kitchen floor while you were gone," said Pamela sweetly.

Freddy smiled kindly. "Did *you* do that?"

"Yes." She lifted her skirt to reveal a naked, pee-slick pussy. Droplets dotted her upper thighs. "See? Your bathroom door wouldn't open, and, well, I really had to go."

"Sorry about that door."

"Well, sorry about the mess. I won't pretend I didn't enjoy it, though. It felt sort of—I don't know—*liberating* to just stand with my feet apart and pee right here. It felt sexy." She gave a little erotic shudder. She was still holding her skirt aloft.

Freddy looked at the glistening puddle. "It's beautiful." Then he looked back at Pamela, gazing at her lewd bareness. "And so are you."

SEVEN

The pee-pleasure booth was like a voting station: opaque curtains concealed most of the woman's body.

What one saw from the outside were her legs, which inevitably danced in delight astride the porcelain column. At the curtain's hem, the thighs and porcelain disappeared from view; above this border, the lucky woman half stood and half sat, mounted on a cushioned lip, situated comfortably so her water would flow into the hollow column and her pussy lips and clit would rest, much more than comfortably, against apparatus designed to provide warmth and vibrations—all controlled by the inhabitant through a handheld remote.

The effect, as one could imagine, was a session of intense ecstasy, as bladder emptied and vulva quivered to orgasm. And it was the echo of this ecstasy that one saw in the legs, which danced exquisitely before the outside observer's eyes.

EIGHT

She dials Richard's number.

"Hello?"

"Hello. It's just me."

"*Hi!*"

"Yeah, it's just me, alone with my pee."

"Yes?"

"Alone in the house in my lingerie. Crouched in the bathtub, my petite body so full of pee. I'm parceling it out in little spurts and squirts."

"Ohhh ... "

"It's my private treasure—you know? So I'm making it last."

"Oh, yeah."

"Come over, will you?" She ends the call, knowing that when Richard arrives in a few minutes, he'll find her sitting there in a warm puddle of her piss, masturbating furiously in her lace panties.

NINE

When Harriet excused herself to the ladies' room, Tabitha set down her drink as well. She'd been hoping the timing would work out right, just like this.

As she'd also hoped, it was just the two of them in there; the stall adjacent to the one Harriet was gracing was open.

Tabitha settled in, wiggling her arse as she got into position. The rainfall next door began.

The knowledge that the woman she adored was right in the next stall, ass bared and pussy freely pissing, made Tabitha squirm on her own toilet seat. She imagined Harriet's face, radiant with release, and Harriet's smooth, soft derriere cheeks, warm and cozy and naked.

Tabitha had intentionally held her pee till she was almost wetting her panties. Now she sat jiggling on the loo, bladder still welling and knickers at her ankles, while she diddled herself toward a mind-blowing, pissing orgasm.

Ten

Julene had only just arrived, and she was asking if she could pop into Bob's bathroom for a second.

"It's premeditated, isn't it?" said Bob agreeably. "The way you tend to show up here right when you have to pee. I bet you deliberately hold it when you know you're coming over."

She grinned knowingly.

"Because you want a chance to display it in front of me—like you're doing right now—bending forward a bit and squeezing your knees together ... touching the front of your skirt suggestively as you inform me with a wink and a smile that you need to use my bathroom."

"Well ... ," said Julene.

"Knowing it will make me hard," he continued. "Knowing that I'll be stroking myself through my jeans while I hear you tinkling away through the thin door of that bathroom. Oh, yes, you know it makes me horny as hell to visualize you pulling down your panties—those satin boxers I know you like—so your tense little naked slit can pee urgently into my toilet."

Julene was blushing, giggling, and holding herself tightly between the legs.

"You do it knowing I'll want to fuck you as soon as you're done." He didn't even state it as a question.

Eleven

The woman sits on a gym mat at the edge of the room, her shoulders pressed against another mat that's affixed to the wall. She wears nothing but boy shorts, in white, which are displayed proudly between the V of her extended legs.

She caresses her breasts sensuously for a minute before the wet spot first appears at the apex of her underpants. Then, while she writhes under her own caresses, her hips jerk splendidly. The center of her panties grows increasingly damp as she masturbates by peeing herself.

Finally, she transfers one hand from her chest into her boy shorts. Her face contorts in climax when she sets off her clit, while still peeing away. Her legs spasm with pleasure; her heels bounce against the floor.

TWELVE

"Pee break!" the star called when the director cut.

"*Another* pee break?" kidded her leading man. "We should just keep a chamber pot handy for you, like in antique bedrooms."

"Yes," she laughed, "that *would* be convenient."

"And then we'd get to watch."

All she could think about, as she peed privately in the backstage stall, were those words: *And then we'd get to watch.* She imagined him watching while she tinkled now, and when she was done she quickly rubbed herself off to that story line.

THIRTEEN

Roberta scampers along the beach in a tank top and shorts. Her crotch, happily heavy with unshed pee, seeks a place—or a face—to lovingly water, something worthy of baring her ass.

She won't stop and squat until she finds the perfect rock to anoint—or a man who looks as if he might enjoy having her bottom over him while she lets her floodgates open.

Rock or man? The beach is scenic in both respects, and she knows she'll find the perfect venue soon.

FOURTEEN

Justin sits in the outer office. One by one, he sees the women go by in bras and panties with full bladders, blushing and smiling at him on their way in to see the pleasure therapist.

One by one, he sees them exit, hair mussed and bras unclasped, eyes blissed out and panties soaked with fresh pee.

When things aren't too busy at his own desk, Justin gets to

sit in.

"Just get comfortable there on the couch," Dr. Sanders tells her client, "and I'll place this little vibrator on the outside of your panties. You can adjust its position and control its settings. We'll turn it on when you're ready, and I guarantee you'll be coming—and wetting your panties—within minutes … and that it will feel better than anything you've previously experienced."

Dr. Sanders is never wrong.

FIFTEEN

I could see her hands trembling while she held her skirt up, and she kept looking around, though I was sure we were alone in the alley. She had her legs crossed, holding her water in with the powerful clasp of her smooth, Amazonian thighs.

I didn't want her to be embarrassed. "It's OK," I kept saying, even after she'd uncrossed her legs to let her pee begin dribbling out. I probably sounded like an idiot repeating it, but it felt like the right thing to do. I thought if she could get past the embarrassment, she'd like what was happening. At least I hoped so. Nothing to lose by trying, anyway, because clearly there was no turning back for her now. The only question was whether she'd let herself enjoy it—and let me enjoy it with her.

I think what finally relaxed her was my smile. She could tell I was OK with what was happening—that I wasn't grossed out or freaked out, that in fact I liked watching her pee her knickers. I was too shy to tell her she looked pretty pissing in her little undies, but maybe my face told her. She finally grinned back, and that's when I knew we had real possibilities.

SIXTEEN

She squats, savoring the knowledge that if she pisses on his hardwood floor, he will wipe her pussy with a silk handkerchief, and she will come against his hand.

He watches. Squatting there with her skirt at her waist and her panties at her knees, her smooth white bottom is an unbroken curve. Her piss comes down in a thick, broad torrent, and he licks his lips, imagining how gloriously wet with pee her unseen underside must be.

"You know, there's a word for that lovely position you're in: *retromingent*. Peeing 'backward,' etymologically speaking."

"Only you would know such a word."

"Thank you."

SEVENTEEN

He sits on the park bench with Julie on his lap, holding her snug. Soon she sighs, and he feels the first warm sprinkles—as arranged, his lover is peeing through her thong under her skirt, letting his trousers absorb her release.

She wiggles her ass on his thighs as she opens more fully, and now she is pissing freely. A passerby, if there were one, would never know. Only Mark's warm, wet trousers tell the tale of this delicious, planned panty wetting.

Julie pees and pees, wiggling her ass more and more erogenously, letting his hardening cock press at her sopping pussy through his soaked fly and her saturated panty gusset, even as she continues alternately to gush and trickle out, still emptying in spasms and spurts and lazy, extended showers.

Finally she has finished; and while Mark holds her tightly by the waist with his other hand under the front of her skirt, he rubs his wet-denimed erection along the tight, damp, thong-clinging hunger of her cunt lips, fast and intense, until they both come.

EIGHTEEN

The backyard pee-holding game that the two women had staged on this lazy afternoon was coming to its inevitable conclusion.

"Mmm ... come on in," said Alissa, as the wet warmth began to pool in the depths of her panties and leak out the leg holes of her shorts. "The water's fine."

Valerie, still doing frenetic jiggles and hip bumps, watched her friend melt into thick gyrations of pleasure. With her eyes on Alissa's crotch, Valerie held on just a delicious moment more before giving herself over to a fabulous release, laughing up at the summer sky while puddling the concrete.

NINETEEN

When Gene opened his apartment door, he was surprised to find it was Noreen who'd knocked. He hadn't expected to see her before their date the following weekend.

"Well, hello!" he said.

"I want to pee on you."

"What?"

"I want to pee on you, Gene. Can I come in?"

He stepped aside. Noreen entered, turned, and clutched her groin.

"God, I just had two pints in half an hour."

"I see."

"Can I? Can I do it? We could use the bathtub. Oh, man, I want to do it all over your hot body, all over your abs and your dick."

A minute later, Gene watched the freckles on Noreen's hips glisten in the bathroom light while she wet all over him, her head cocked in bliss.

"Oh, I love you, I love you," she moaned.

TWENTY

During their workdays on the ranch, she has observed him to be inordinately interested in knowing when she has to pee.

So one day, when the rain has kept them indoors, she rewards his curiosity.

Wearing only her Western hat and a white vinyl vest, she leads him into the bathroom, sits for him, and spreads her legs.

Ride that seat, cowgirl.

After pissing heartily she stands, so he can reach right under her smooth ass with a handful tissues.

Dab my wetness, cowboy.

Twenty-one

"Any ideas what to do tonight?" Penny asked.

"How does this sound?" he began. "First, you choose the outfit that you want to wet yourself in. Next, I pour you a twenty-ounce beer, which you drink as quickly or as slowly as you like, letting me keep you company as your bladder fills.

"Then, when you get to the point where you can't sit still from needing to pee, you take me upstairs and let me watch while you soak your pretty panties. I bet you'll be so aroused at that point, you'll come while you're doing it. Then I'll fuck your hot little pussy while you're still dripping wet.

"How does that sound, Penny?"

Twenty-two

Ian ran through the rain to his apartment at 4 a.m., deliriously incredulous at what he'd heard over the dance-club sound system. Could those lyrics really be what he'd thought? All the way home, he replayed them in his head as best as he could recall them, hearing the sex-saturated voice of the vocalist over her buzzing techno backing track.

He paused only long enough to take his coat off before switching on his computer and typing some of the words into a search engine.

There it was.

He rushed his cock out as he leaned forward to savor the text.

"Pee in Your Hand"

I had my panties down
'Cause I was ready to pee
When a fuckin' gorgeous dude walked in on me.
He stammered, 'Sorry, babe,'
But I said, 'Don't go away,
'I wanna pee in your hand, if you'll only stay.'
He grabbed my ass in his right

And cupped my puss in his left,
And then I sprinkled like a fountain till there was none left.
And while he squeezed my cheek
And I pissed in his hand,
It was almost more pleasure than this girl could stand.
He had the golden touch
To make my world complete,
And I was coming like a tiger on the toilet seat.
Pee in your hand,
I wanna pee in your hand.
Yeah, this woman's kind of kinky—
Do you understand?
I wanna show my stuff
By raining down from above.
I wanna hold it till I'm squirming,
Then I'll water you with love.
And when I need to go more,
Watch me pee on your floor.
I wanna wet my fuckin' panties for you
Till you roar.

Ian had come three times before even buying the download.

Never Like This

LINDA DANCED ON THE PORCH. "WHOO! I DIDN'T REALIZE HOW badly I had to pee. Do you have the key?"

Tynan put it in her outstretched hand. "Here you go." He grinned slyly. "Hey, why don't you take your other hand out of your crotch? I can do that for you—hold your pussy, I mean."

At this suggestion, she seemed to forget about unlocking the door. "Do it," she said quickly.

He replaced her hand with his own.

"Don't let go now, Tynan, because I might, you know … "

"Oh, yes. I know."

The hand cupping her pussy began to move solicitously.

"Turned on from holding your pee, angel?"

She bit her lip and nodded shyly.

As he stroked her through the trouser fabric, her thighs began to tremble, and the first dribbles seeped out.

"Careful, Ty! I'm—"

"But isn't that secretly what you want? To lose control, and wet your pants for me?"

"Ohhh," she said, in a way that validated his theory.

He continued to pet and rub her—her lips, her mound, even the part of the fabric that he knew corresponded to her huddled clit.

"Tynan, I'm really peeing! I'm peeing my pants, right here!" Her face was flushed; she was intensely aroused. He looked down to see the neat crotch of her herringbone pants beginning to darken.

She broke away from him and hopped to and fro before his eyes. "I'm pissing my pants!" she said, in a tone of gleeful amazement.

He caught her again by the pussy and resumed fondling her through her capris. Linda pissed away, squirming erotically until her flood was once again a seeping trickle—and she was coming like hell.

She recovered her breath. Piss dripped luxuriously from her herringbone crotch.

"Holy fuck, Tynan. I've peed—what?—a thousand times a year. But never like this. Never, ever like this."

The Most Fun You Can Have …

MAKING MOVIES CAN BE A DRAG, JUST LIKE ANY OTHER JOB. But I was having a good time with this one. Partly it was because my co-star was so easy to work with—and really hot, I might add. No, I had no complaints on this set. I don't think I'd made a single whiny phone call to my agent since production had begun.

For the kitschy '70s dance number in the film, they'd put Sherrie and me into goofy purple jumpsuits. The set had been dressed with enormous fabric plums, of all things, and I guess we were supposed to match the set in our slick, shiny purple costumes. Actually, they looked kind of cool—though it's not the sort of thing I'd wear to the supermarket, you understand.

These suits had been specially made from a strong but thin fabric, and Winnie the costume woman had said, with her usual frankness, that she didn't want to see any underwear lines. She showed us the lining that had been sewn into the crotch of each of our jumpsuits—ultra-thin but really soft, in a hi-tech way. "That should be comfortable enough even for *your* baby-faced asses," she said to me and Sherrie. "So no undies—got it?" Sherrie darted a flirty look my way as she replied, on behalf of both of us, "Got it, Winnie."

I had to admit, that lining felt *really* good against my bare cock. Soft. Smooth. In the privacy of my dressing room, I found myself gyrating my hips a little just to get a bit more of the sensation. And I couldn't help wondering if it felt equally nice against the crotch of my co-star. Her genitals, of course, were anything but similar to mine; but perhaps the sensations, at least, were similar. I tried not to think too much about this—if they didn't want to see underwear lines, I was pretty sure they didn't want to see erect-penis lines, either.

When I arrived on the soundstage, Sherrie was already there. Her costume had been tailored with exquisite accuracy to fit her delectable shape, and it molded her grapefruit breasts and suggestive hips to perfection. And though the jumpsuit wasn't quite tight enough to show the undercurve of each ass cheek or the raw charm of the crack between them, the overall roundness of her bottom was emphasized to inspiring effect.

I marveled at the way in which these ostensibly matching outfits made us look so very different. I appeared angular, while Sherrie was a symphony of curves. I wanted to fuck her even more than I had since the moment we'd begun working together.

As we showed off our well-rehearsed moves for the camera, I was almost distracted from my dancing job by Sherrie's fluid beauty. Every time her body glided close to mine, my head reeled with images of all the anatomical places where I wanted to run my hands over bare, smooth skin. It was powerfully erotic being so near her; and on the few occasions when our eyes met, I was afraid I'd ruin the shot by revealing an unsightly-to-the-camera erection bulging against my costume.

When we'd finished the scene, I didn't want to let her get away.

As was our habit, we chatted companionably on our way out of the shooting area. And, as usual, the small talk continued as we walked down the hall toward our dressing rooms. When we arrived at her door, I casually asked if she'd mind my coming in for a moment.

"Sure—come on in," she replied. She seemed a little surprised, but not displeased.

I stood just inside the door, while she sat down at her makeup table. "How does your costume feel?" I ventured. "Mine's *very* comfortable," I added meaningfully.

She blushed. "I know what you mean," she said with a giggle, and I thought I saw her ass squirming for an instant in her chair.

I closed the door and stepped forward. "It looks really nice on you," I said boldly. "I was having trouble keeping my mind on the dancing."

Her face suddenly turned serious—a sexy, happy kind of serious, like a new world had just opened up for her. She got out of her chair. "Yeah?" she asked quietly.

"Yeah," I echoed.

"Y'know ... me too," she said, coming closer.

As we kissed, it was hard to know where to put my hands first. I wanted them all over her. So I squeezed, stroked, and caressed hither and yon, making a tour of her marvelous landscape while our lips pulsated together more and more intensely.

When we finally stepped apart, it was clear that this was only so that we could move things forward. Her dressing room had a couch that would do nicely, and these sexy jumpsuits could now be dispensed with.

"Hey—the zipper on this thing is stuck," Sherrie complained.

"Oh!" I said. "Well, let me just get my suit off, and then I'll be more than delighted to help you with yours," I said with a horny grin.

But when I yanked at my own zipper, I found that I was in the same predicament. Sheepishly, I told this to Sherrie. "So much for hi-tech costumes, eh?" I said.

"What do we do?" she asked. She was unconsciously smoothing her hands along the flanks of her purple garment, looking sensual and very ready for me.

"One option is that we could call a tech, of course," I reasoned. "But somehow I think you and I and a tech with pliers would be a crowd, at the moment."

"What's the other option?" she prompted. She touched my chest as she asked the question.

"The other option is we get creative," I said hungrily. And I scooped up her jumpsuit-clad bottom and carried her to the couch. Here, we squeezed and cuddled and tickled and kissed playfully for a couple of minutes, before addressing the problem at hand.

Though I couldn't get out of the costume, I found that I had enough space around the waist that I could, from the outside, push and pull my cock into a standing position against my belly. Having done so—while Sherrie looked on with an alluring mixture of curiosity and lust—I lifted her onto my lap, so that her crotch wedged itself tightly against my stiff pole. I held her by the waist, so that as we embraced I could contrive to manipulate her body up and down, in such a manner that the friction between her pussy and my cock was direct and delicious, despite the encumbrance of clothing. It felt unbelievably good.

"Ohh … ahh … yummy!" said Sherrie, thus articulating my thoughts as well as her own. Her legs held my hips in a determined grip, which underscored her enthusiasm.

It was amazing how quickly we both came. And how reluctant we were to call it a day when we had. The jumpsuits had obviously been engineered to do a great job of absorbing moisture, and the sticky mess I'd made in mine soaked efficiently into the fabric. As a result, it was almost undetectable against my skin. I could assume that Sherrie's juices were being effectively wicked away, too; she certainly seemed in no hurry to shed the outfit now.

"Let's try something else," I suggested.

I had her lie on her side. As I lay down to face her, I lifted her upper leg to insinuate a leg of my own. Then I began to move my leg up and down while gyrating my pelvis against her, gently pumping her upper leg this way and that by means of the ankle I was still holding. This time, my erection must have been pressing directly on Sherrie's clit, and she was soon writhing in utter ecstasy.

As we frigged toward orgasm, our legs clamped open and shut against each other like two crazy pairs of shears. An observer, watching us hump each other at the juncture of our jumpsuits, might have had trouble telling where my body ended and Sherrie's began. To the external eye, we had simply become an erotic tangle of humping scissors.

But I knew who was who. And as my free hand snuck between us to touch her yielding pussy, albeit through the interface of a special Hollywood fabric, her feminine deliciousness was overwhelming to me. Before I knew it, I was making her come again, and I felt that my fingers could sense every spasm of her cunt, jumpsuit or no jumpsuit.

Now Sherrie took the initiative. She nudged me onto my back and climbed aboard. She wrapped her legs around me and somehow, miraculously, found a perfect point of contact yet again. As she began the slow friction of woman's jumpsuit crotch against man's jumpsuit front, the action of her mound against my erection was electrifying. Every stroke fed my engorged excitement as effectively as it nurtured the tinglings of her wide-awake love bud.

Stroke. Stroke. Stroke. She set the pace, and that pace quickened as the frenzy in her hot point caught up with, perhaps even overtook, my own level of arousal. Soon we were not so much fucking as vibrating together, a well-synchronized mechanical orgasm generator. She held my arms at the elbows as I came for her, and, just as I finished, she ground against me with intensified purpose and shrieked into her own paradise.

At last, we were ready to call for the tech and the pliers. While we waited for the knock on the door, we snuggled together on her couch.

"Most fun you can have with your clothes on," I commented. Sherrie laughed, and her hand petted my numb groin.

"You know, I really need to pee now," she said a minute later.

"Me too, actually," I reported. "Well, they said the tech would be down in just a couple of minutes, and then we'll be all set."

"No, I can't wait," Sherrie giggled. Abruptly, she stood up.

I looked over to see her wetting herself, without a shred of self-consciousness. It was a dazzling sight—her face radiant as the wetness spread down her body. And I realized, suddenly, that I couldn't wait, either—or maybe it was that I didn't want to. Without letting my eyes leave her, I stood up as well.

To piss in my jumpsuit would have felt embarrassing, had I been alone. But as I did it along with Sherrie, it felt exotically sexy. I was wetting with a beautiful woman, and that made all the difference. The thrill of knowing that we were jointly giving in to our private urgencies, with our bodies sealed all the while in these silly outfits, was remarkable. As my own wetness pooled and trickled around the juncture of my legs, I could see her pee caressing her in the same way, with what appeared to be an intensely pleasurable effect.

We just stood there and busily pissed ourselves empty, our eyes riveted on each other's bodies. Sherrie gave a sensuous little shudder when she finished. I reached my hand forward to pet her saturated crotch, and she purred.

Nothing surprises a seasoned Hollywood backstage crew member. When Jim the tech arrived with his tools, he gave no indication that it was peculiar to find a couple lounging cheerfully in pee-soaked jumpsuits. He greeted us with a casual camaraderie, efficiently broke our zippers open, wished us a good evening, and left.

As we ripped the useless zipper tracks apart on our respective costumes and slithered out of them, I thought about these state-of-the-art jumpsuits, now destined for the trash heap. *Technology*, I thought. *When it works, it's great. And when it doesn't work … it's sometimes even greater.*

"My shower's big enough for two," Sherrie informed me, squeezing me on the ass.

Pre/Post

"Mmm ... I have to pee."

He pressed his weight onto her. "What would you think about staying right here, right here with me on the bed ... being fondled and loved until you soaked those blue panties?

"I could squeeze your breasts. I could kiss your tummy. I could trace a finger down your gorgeous crack back there, and caress those cheeks till they were vibrating.

"I could tickle you a little under the arms, where you like it so much, and between the legs, where it always makes you shake with pleasure.

"What would you think of that?"

She wriggled under him as she considered it. "I think that would be very sexy."

"You're so wet," he said, stroking the warm dampness across her crotch and bum. "You did that beautifully."

She was clinging to his erection. "I love it that you have a cock to piss and fuck with." She laughed. "I don't have one, you know. All I have are these wet, wet panties."

"What would you think if I fucked you right now ... right now, while you were still freshly warm and damp for me?

"I could strip you and lick your thighs clean. I could get inside you, then slap the dewy curves of your bottom while you ground your sopping pussy against my balls.

"What would you think of that?"

She rubbed her soaked-blue-panty ass against his hand. "I think that would be very sexy."

Doing It for Olivia

"You want me to wet myself for you?"

"Yeah."

"Why?" Karen wanted to know.

Olivia shrugged. "Because I think it would be really, really pretty."

They were quiet for a minute.

"Does the fact that you had to ask 'Why?' mean you wouldn't want to do it?" Olivia ventured.

Karen had to think about this. "Not necessarily," she finally said.

The conversation resumed (as conversations do) later that evening.

"So, how does one usually do it?" Karen inquired.

"Do what?" asked Olivia.

"Wet oneself," Karen specified.

Olivia instantly warmed to the subject. "Well … first, I'd say it's a good idea to make sure you're wearing clothes that you feel sexy in. Ideally, clothes that are easy to wash, too," she added with a laugh. "Then you take your coffee, or tea, or wine, or beer … and you get yourself situated comfortably somewhere. You relax for a bit, until you start to think that you need to get up and go to the bathroom for a pee." Olivia said *pee* in a tone that suggested it was a magic word for her.

When she continued, the light in her eyes became more intense. "Only you don't get up. You stay put, relishing the way you tickle inside, without feeling inhibited about squirming around, clutching yourself, or touching yourself. You let your thighs, hands, and hips do whatever enables you to hold it for a while, in a delicious, ever-shifting equilibrium, to make the most of the sensations as they blossom. You just hang out and indulge those feelings."

Karen blushed, cast her eyes down shyly, and nodded her understanding. Olivia thought she saw a tiny smile on her lover's face. She took a breath and forged on. "Then, when you know that you really have to go—that you're about to lose control, or that it's simply time to give in ... you just do it, babe, right where you are, right in your lovely panties." Olivia was stroking herself as she experienced the raw thrill of describing this process in such meticulous detail—something she'd never been called upon to do before.

"It all sounds very sensible," Karen admitted.

That was all either of them said on the subject that night.

A few days later, the two of them were having a Saturday-night chill-out in the kitchen. As was typical on these occasions, Olivia was dressed simply in boy shorts and a form-fitting little T-shirt, which showed off her sassy tummy. Karen, on the other hand, was a bit more dressed up—she had put on her favorite miniskirt, and a cashmere mock turtleneck. As erotic music trickled softly in the background, Karen got up from her seat at the table and helped herself to a second beer.

"What's up, babe?" said Olivia. "You don't usually have more than one b—"

She stopped short. A hope had hit her like a ten-foot wave. "Don't tell me this means ... oh, Karen, are you ... ?"

Karen smiled enigmatically, slid back into her seat, and began to down the beer.

Two beers didn't take long to overtake a metabolism like Karen's. Around the time that her face began to glow with a tipsy magic, she started to jiggle from the hips down.

Olivia looked lovingly at her. "Do you have to pee, honey?" She spoke very quietly, but her voice was charged with incipient excitement.

Karen leaned in and answered in a sultry, conspiratorial

whisper. "Yeah, I have to pee. But I want to have to pee *more* before I do it. Until you painted that picture for me the other night, I never thought about how good it feels to just let it build for a while. Since then, I've been thinking about it a lot."

She was jiggling more sensuously now, with larger motions. And as she spoke, one of her hands disappeared under the table. Olivia reached her own hand forward to meet it, and together the two hands pressed against Karen's panties.

For several exquisite minutes, Karen enjoyed letting Olivia masturbate her through her knickers while her knees knocked together in a pulsating "hold it" routine. Her clit was tingling, and the tug of war between her persisting control and her impulse to let go created a precious tension that was absolutely ecstatic. She moaned in blissful ambivalence, unsure whether to wet now, or to come now, or …

Suddenly she realized how she wanted this to play out. "I'm going to put on a show for you," she whispered.

Olivia closed her eyes briefly in rapture. Though she was reluctant to remove her fingers from her darling's crotch, she knew it would be worth it.

Karen stood up and walked delicately to the center of the kitchen floor, holding herself with a lewd elegance. Soon she was rocking from side to side, with her skirt hiked up haphazardly and her hand wedged against her panties. "Mmm … I've gotta go," she crooned.

As she began to do a kinky dance across the kitchen tiles, Karen came alive with erotic energy, in a way that Olivia had never seen before. Her patter, stated softly as if to herself—though it was officially addressed to Olivia—was poetry to her lover's ears. "Oh, fuck yes, I'm going to wet for you. I'm going to wet. I'm going to pee my freakin' panties for you."

In one unforgettable moment, future tense turned to present. "Oh, glorious fuck, I'm pissing. Feels so good … so fuckin' good. Oh fuck, oh fuck, yes … "

Olivia, her hand in her boy shorts, was going wild with arousal and slamming her ass rhythmically against her seat. Karen was giving her a performance that was beyond her dreams.

"It's all for you, honey, it's coming down all for you," Karen was gasping, as robust rivers poured through her skimpy bikini panties. She realized with a thrill that she couldn't stop now, even if she wanted to. Her piss-soaked pussy was burning with libido, and her fingers sought her cunt as fast as they could.

When her orgasmic scream trumpeted forth from her trembling body, Karen noted with surprise that it was even louder than Olivia's.

Movie Night

THE MOMENT I WALKED INTO THE DEN AND SAW JOCELYN squatting on a plastic tarp in the middle of the room, pissing furiously through her lime panties—while she and the other women laughed uproariously and Steve Martin blithely continued his shtick on the twenty-seven-inch screen—I knew this was not your average party.

"What in the world is going on in here?" I blurted, my eyes riveted on Jocelyn's thick cascade.

"I *told* you this was 'Laugh Till You Pee Night,'" said my friend Tina. Tina was rocking in an armchair, and she was wearing only a T-shirt, underpants, and tiny crew socks—which rubbed together as she intertwined her ankles. "You said you weren't interested."

"I didn't know you meant it literally," I said.

"*Shh!*" said another voice, from the couch—Caroline's. I looked in that direction and, in the dim light afforded by the TV, saw a couple of pairs of bare legs crossing and uncrossing. On the coffee table in front of Caroline and Denise, a population of empty beer bottles flickered their part of the story.

"I just thought you were going to watch some comedies," I persisted.

Jocelyn had finally finished peeing. She stood up, smiling radiantly, and smoothed her hands over her soaked panties. "Hi, Ted," she said, acknowledging me nonchalantly before seating herself on a beach towel. She now turned her attention back to the movie, and I could see that she was beginning to gently stroke herself through the dampness.

I had thought myself lucky this May when I'd found out that the house Tina and I had arranged to rent for the summer was going to be populated with what I deemed to be four of the most gorgeous women on campus—Tina and her three best friends. The reality, though, was that none of them seemed particularly interested in interacting with me. So, aside from my casual friendship with Tina, I'd developed a habit of keeping to myself. This was why I'd turned down her invitation to join them for what I thought would be a run-of-the-mill movie night.

I swallowed. "Do you girls do this often?" I asked Tina.

"Quiet!" said Denise.

Suddenly, the TV went dead. No power failure, no unplugged cord … just an appliance deciding to conk out forever.

"It's not going to come back," Tina reported a minute later after fussing with the controls, her body dancing the whole time.

"*Now* what do we do?" asked Caroline from the couch, amidst a continuing flurry of crossing and re-crossing legs. "I've been looking forward to this all week!"

"I know. Same here," Tina replied. As she paced the room, I observed that her delicate minuet was approaching the scale of a tango. "I'm just about ready to do it, too."

"I'm not going to wet myself to a dead TV," said Denise. "I mean, what would be the point of *that?*" And with this remark she stood up from the couch, clutching herself, obviously ready to call it a night and head for a bathroom.

It took me only another instant to assess the situation and respond appropriately.

"I know some jokes," I said.

What Do You Want Tonight?

"*WHAT DO YOU WANT TONIGHT?*"

She loved it when he asked her that.

It was a little odd that he was doing it from around the corner this time, while he was out of sight in the kitchen … but this just made it all the more sexy. She closed her eyes, stuck her hands in her pants, and plunged in, enthusiastic as always.

"What do I want tonight? I want your cock teasing my ass crack. I want your tongue all over my nipples. I want your breath on my pussy." She paused, smiling at the images she had so easily conjured up.

"You know—"

"Tonight, Ben? I want to sit on your face and squirm till I scream. I want to kiss your butt cheeks and tickle your balls. I want to straddle your chest and piss my heart out while you finger my clit." Kate was enjoying the way her soprano raunch bounced brightly off the acoustic tiles and carried itself loudly and clearly to her husband in the other room.

"I think—"

"Then I might want to you to fuck me. Yes, I want you to grab my ankles and screw your fat cock in and out of my cunt, till I come five times. Oh, and I want—"

"Yes, Kate. Yes, of course. But what I really meant was, 'What do you want tonight *from the take-out place?*' I have them on speakerphone, and they're waiting for the rest of our order."

And/Or

In retrospect, it was funny that I spent an entire hour trying to decide which one of them I should focus on. In retrospect, I could have just relaxed, and given myself completely over to enjoying their combined company.

They'd seen me standing at the bar, singing along to Duran Duran while I sampled the foam on my ale—almost inaudibly, even to my own ears.

Jill had smiled at me, and Marissa had said something to her. Then Jill had beckoned me over.

"We can't hear your singing," she'd informed me. "And we think you probably have a nice voice."

The song was just ending, but nonetheless they'd encouraged me to take a seat.

"Now you'll never get to hear what my singing voice sounds like," I quipped. "That was the only song I know, and they'll never, ever play it again."

Marissa had vacated her side of the booth for me and was squeezing in next to Jill. As they settled in, they bumped together playfully, poking and elbowing each other's yummy torsos. I noticed that my bench was warm from Marissa's body.

Marissa had long red hair and scintillating green eyes. She was skinny yet strong looking, and her tight bicycle shorts emphasized her muscular but fleshy bottom. I was grateful I'd had a chance to observe this when she relocated.

Jill was softer—a little rounder in places. Her eyes were deep and dark, and she looked perpetually on the verge of laughter.

I could quite easily, and quite agreeably, imagine either of them wiggling wetly under me, or straddling my lap to take me in. Which one, which one?

A certain type of guy might have approached the situation from the calculating perspective of which woman he'd be more likely to "score" with. Hell, sure, I was hoping the night would involve some sex; but I was less concerned with "scoring," per se, than I was with figuring out which of the two I especially liked—and which one especially liked me. That, for me, was what made the sex worthwhile. It didn't have to be true love—it didn't have to be any variety of love—but I was turned on by *chemistry*.

After an hour of drinking, kidding, and comparing favorite songs (they even persuaded me to reprise "Rio," a cappella), it turned out that we *all* especially liked one another. This was underscored by what Marissa said during the third round of beers: "While you were getting our drinks, we decided we'd like to bring you back to our place." *We.* That simplified things. Or maybe, in the long run, it complicated them. Either way, I was in favor of it.

"Do you always work as a team?"

Jill giggled, and Marissa licked her lips. "Team, nothing," she said. "You're looking at a sophisticated, highly versatile, two-component stud-seducing *machine*."

"A well-oiled machine," Jill added. Both girls cracked up at that. I grinned, too, though half my brain was still reeling from hearing myself described as a "stud."

It dawned on me that they'd been working as a team all evening. Their conversation had included many compliments for each other ("Jill always burns the best party discs") and prompts to me—not that I required any—to notice details ("Alan, did you see what Marissa's T-shirt says?"). It made me like both of them that much better to recognize their cooperative spirit. Each was sincerely interested in seeing the other have a good time, in watching her friend charm my trousers off. I wasn't sure I merited this status as a shared objective, but it was certainly flattering.

"We work from the 'and/or' principle," Jill explained. "When we spot the right kind of guy, we invite him to play with Marissa and/or Jill. No hard feelings if it's an 'or.'"

"I think we can forget 'or,'" I said without hesitation.

"We were hoping you'd say that," piped in Marissa.

This wasn't my first threesome, but I hadn't ever cuddled so rambunctiously on a sofa with two women at once. They pulled me this way and that, rolled me around, clambered onto me. They hugged, kissed, humped, tickled, and groped their way all over my lanky topography, sharing me with mutual generosity. I touched them, too—a handful of ass here, a mouthful of neck there—but I was, to a large extent, the passive party … and I loved every minute of it. The scent of pussy—two pussies—was in the air, and the room rang with female giggles. When Marissa unzipped my jeans, the cock she discovered inside was a very stiff one.

We all moved to Jill's bedroom. I found it captivating the way each of them served as a spokesperson for the other's sexual desires. "Jill really digs getting her pussy licked," Marissa advised me, while managing to undress me and also undress herself. And, wouldn't you know it, Marissa was right.

Jill, who had wasted no time in shedding everything but a pair of red fishnets, reclined on the bed to allow me access. Her pussy was an adorable shade of pink, and it was set off deliciously by her dark bush.

Marissa sat beside her, cross-legged, wearing a white lace bra but no panties—a combination that I considered incredibly hot. Jill smelled wonderful, felt wonderful, and tasted wonderful as I visited every nook of her cranny with my tongue … but Marissa also held a place of honor, in my mind's eye, while I ate Jill out. And I assumed Jill wouldn't object to that. In fact, as she squirmed and trickled into my face, her shriek was "Marissa, he's making me come!" In this house, even one's orgasm was shared with one's best friend.

"Baby!" said Marissa, with comradely enthusiasm. It seemed

extra sexy to have licked Jill into mush with Marissa feeding off the vibe.

As soon as Jill's twitches subsided, I sat up and reached for her pal. I pulled her onto my lap, swooning at the tender beauty of her orange-furred mound, and I started bouncing her naked bottom. She kissed me hard. "Nice ... you taste like Jill," she cooed.

I tickled Marissa under her arms, then upended her so that her ass lay across my thighs.

"Mmm ... ass on my lap; lap full of ass," I said with relish, applying a soft pinch to an enticing cheek. No matter how I phrased it, it sounded good—and it looked even better.

I massaged her saucy derriere, rubbing and patting and squeezing till I could see her cunt dripping with need. While continuing to hold her on my lap, I moved a hand down to caress her slippery lips, then coax them apart. I inserted a finger, exploring her innermost skin, awakening every nerve. And as I finger-fucked Marissa, Jill breathed heavily in the background.

"More," Marissa gasped.

The tempo of my slick finger, then fingers, increased with her churning horniness, in a mutually ascending feedback loop. Finally, the scrumptious bottom bucked in my lap, the cunt clenched around my digits, and the redhead wailed euphorically.

Damn, I needed to fuck someone now. And I was fairly confident I'd have one or more takers, among present company.

Jill was physically behind me and strategically a step ahead of me. She pressed her breasts into my back and embraced me around the middle, taking my cock in hand. In a very graceful movement, she turned me so that we were face to face. In a second very graceful movement, she toppled onto the mattress, pulling me down with her.

Sliding into Jill was an indescribably juicy affair. She moaned as I slowly entered and we collaborated on generating, and ex-periencing, the crazy pleasure of hardness scraping past softness.

Her body, relaxed at its surface level yet seething with arousal, had the feel of a water bed beneath me. She responded to every element of my motion—not only the pulses inside where my cock filled her, but also the sensations coming her way from my squirming shoulders, my urgent thighs, and the friction of my belly muscles.

Marissa began participating by slapping me lightly on the butt. That made me even harder, and Jill "ooh'd" with appreciation for the additional expansion of my shaft within her. Then Marissa scooted around to tickle her friend's tummy while I pumped her pussy.

Jill was in heaven, writhing at the limit of tactile pleasure. I knew she was close—there was nowhere for her to go but into orgasm—and, sure enough, within another minute she was gushing and exploding in climax, with Marissa's fingers still between us. As for me, I couldn't keep control in the face of this tableau of feminine ecstasy, and soon I was giving Jill everything I had—and laughing into her chest in an eruption of good feelings.

What next? I wondered, when it was over.

"You know, Alan, Marissa likes to pee on our men," volunteered Jill, in answer to my unspoken question. "And I like watching."

"Please," said Marissa earnestly, not wanting to let the outcome of this proposition rest solely on Jill's advocacy. "Please, Alan, can I pee on you? God, I'm so ready to do it … " She clutched herself suggestively, rocking on her knees.

I accepted the thick bath towel that Jill had grabbed from a nearby dresser. I situated myself on top of it on the bed, face up. Bottomless Marissa shuffled into position, squatting above my crotch. She was holding herself with great erotic intensity now—there was no doubt that she had to pee, and that she was wildly turned on by the opportunity we'd arranged for her. Her face was pink with excitement.

Then the sky opened, and her sweet rain came rushing down.

She peed and peed, giving me a beautiful flood of womanly urgency. Never had I been blessed with such a perfect view of this awe-inspiring phenomenon.

"Oh wow, oh wow," she said blissfully, wiggling her hips so as to caress me with her water, and grinding her pelvis as if she were being fucked. She looked so joyous, and this made me very happy. Beneath her stream, my cock danced and straightened.

Out of the corner of my eye, I saw Jill masturbating at the edge of the bed. "Do it, girl," she said quietly to Marissa, while she furiously worked her own clit and slit.

Marissa was still pissing a little as she descended onto me. She hunkered down all the way, absorbing me in my entirety and letting me feel the raunchy intimacy of her ass cheeks, as they kissed me through the warm liquid that pooled on my lap.

In a moment, she dragged herself upward again, thereby establishing an exquisite fuck rhythm that caused me to wonder how long I'd last between her lovely, pee-sprinkled legs. I took hold of her ankles, and that appeared to crank her arousal a notch higher.

Jill, newly returned to earth from a solo orgasm, leaned forward and ran a hand along her roommate's inner thigh. She brought her fingertips to my mouth, then her own, and we each sampled a few delicate drops of Marissa's fresh piss.

"Oh, yeah," grunted Marissa. "Taste my water. Taste it. It's for you ... both." The last word was nearly swallowed by the beginning of a deep-throated scream. She was riding me full throttle at this point—it almost seemed as if she might fly off me and bounce onto the bed. But her pussy muscles were gripping me for keeps, and rather than careening away she twisted and pistoned herself into howling satisfaction. I spurted like a geyser.

Their shower had ample room for three: Jill and Marissa, comprising a paradise of buttocks, nipples, and smiles, framed me like breathtaking, glistening-wet bookends. None of us could keep our hands off each other, and soap suds flew everywhere as we scrubbed, teased, and fondled. I was stiff again by the time we'd rinsed.

Marissa joined me under the auspices of a giant fluffy towel, and we stood dripping together on the bath mat. Jill, wrapped in a towel of her own, crouched to pet my balls and lick the head of my cock. Claiming one knee of mine and one of Marissa's for stability, she began to suck me with extended, sensuous strokes. Her towel flared lewdly, and I admired the damp, sleek, squeaky-clean hair of her pussy.

She sucked me gently toward ecstasy—her hot, nurturing mouth coaxing my wildness forward—and Marissa had to hold me up when I came, lest my legs give out and I collapse on top of Jill in a friendly little heap. The two of them had worn me out, and I was the first to admit it.

I didn't want to presume that I could sleep over, but they virtually insisted. In the morning, I awoke with someone's slender fist grasping my hard-on. But instead of fucking just then, we all ended up snuggling in our underwear on the sofa, eating bowls of oatmeal, and this was glorious in a different way.

"We discussed it while you were asleep," said Jill, "and we'd love to entertain you here again tonight."

"And/or tomorrow night," giggled Marissa.

"From now on," I said, "you can assume the answer to every-thing is 'and.'"

"We were hoping you'd say that," said Jill. She reached into my boxers for that leftover morning hard-on, and I put down my oatmeal bowl.

Volume 4

Release

It's four o'clock in the afternoon, Lynne's pussy is on fire, and all she can think about is whether Julie is going to pee her shorts.

Her redheaded lover looks impossibly, irresistibly cute with that extra wiggle in her ass, serving the beers and mentioning to Lynne, in between customers, how emphatically she needs to pee. Mentioning it with a sexy smile, and not with any hint of discomfort. Mentioning it and mentioning it … but not doing anything about it. She undoubtedly knows Lynne could cover if she took a break; but clearly she's having fun making herself wait—and making sure Lynne knows about it.

She's done this to Lynne before. Julie absolutely loves to turn herself on by holding it until she's a pussy hair's breadth away from wetting herself, and it drives Lynne wild to watch her indulge in that kink—which, of course, turns Julie on even more. What makes it so perfect is that Julie knows her limits and is completely in control: if she ever *lost* control, like it seems she's on the verge of doing now, that outcome would be intentional as well. Intentional … and, in Lynne's opinion, fucking fabulous to watch.

Lynne is no stranger herself to autoerotic pee games. Like her girlfriend, she can hold it quite a long time without distress; and, in her last job, she discovered that a busy shift behind the bar could provide a good excuse to wait until one was practically dribbling in one's panties. She found it especially delicious when she went out to deliver drinks to the tables. When she arrived at the elbow of some cute customer, stepping gingerly with tray in hand, she would wonder whether it would excite the cutie to know that she seriously needed a piss: that standing inches away in her shorts and fishnets, Lynne was keeping it in—and loving it—while she dispensed the drinks and collected the cash, and getting more and more horny the longer she squeezed her thighs together.

They are a well-matched pair of girlfriends indeed, thinks Lynne, while she watches Julie's ass wiggle.

She recalls proudly that the two of them even met with their knickers down, peeing in side-by-side stalls in the employee restrooms. Lynne was lost in one of those moments where watering away into the toilet just felt so damn good, she couldn't help saying so. "Ooh, that's nice," were her exact words.

She knew someone had come into the stall next door right after she'd closed the door to her own—but she was so carried away by the sensuous bliss of her well-earned piddle, she didn't care. She'd already been aroused when she dashed in to hurry her panties down and lower herself to the seat, and the intensity of the experience had only grown from there.

The laughter-tinted voice that responded to her vocalization brought her back to reality. "Whoever you are, it sounds like you enjoy peeing almost as much as I do."

Lynne was about to reply, through her blushes and her surging libido ... but suddenly the woman next door was moaning—*moaning*—as she gave way to her own release.

This was clearly no hasty tinkle occurring next door, but a drawn-out pleasure pee. The woman seemed to piss forever; and as Lynne sat there dripping her last drops, she found herself hypnotized by the sound. She was almost afraid to break the spell by crinkling the toilet paper she required to wipe herself.

"I'm Julie," her neighbor finally said.

It thrilled Lynne that she'd introduced herself while they were still sitting there bare-assed. And it made her bare ass tingle to hear herself reciprocate. "I'm Lynne, the new bartender."

"It's a *pleasure*, Lynne," said Julie—and, on that evocative word *pleasure*, Lynne heard another gush of pee rush out next door. Her hand froze on the toilet-paper dispenser, while her other hand went to her wet pussy, where her clit was pounding frenetically.

Damn! exclaims Lynne to herself, after the lovely rerun in her head has faded out. *Now Julie's doing the dance.*

The customers will just think she's bustling around, being energetic and efficient … but Lynne knows Julie's pee dance when she sees it—that side to side, hip-shaking shuffle. It almost makes Lynne feel that she's going to wet *her*self, though she hit the bathroom just fifteen minutes ago. Flushed with arousal and buzzing with excitement, she can so vividly imagine feeling what Julie is feeling. If Julie doesn't head for the restroom soon, Lynne might just return there herself, to spread her hot, bloated lips and take care of things.

"I have to pee *so bad!*" Julie mouths to her, laughing silently even as she says it. She obviously doesn't mean anything bad by "bad."

The first night Lynne was scheduled to come home with Julie for a post-work party for two, Julie caught her heading for the pub's ladies' at closing time.

"I'm dying to go, too," Julie explained, "but I live incredibly close, and you're coming over anyway. Shall we just dash home?"

Her place *was* incredibly close. As they scrambled the few blocks, Julie clutched the front of her skirt and giggled.

She led Lynne into her kitchen and immediately sat on a bar stool, crossing her legs in such a way as to expose her flirty plaid panties.

"The bathroom is through there," she informed her guest,

gesturing. "Personally, I'm going to sit here and hold it a while longer. I'm enjoying it too much to give in just yet." She winked, then patted a second stool suggestively.

Nothing if not receptive to this overture, Lynne took a seat on the companion stool. She spent a moment letting her eyes run over Julie's compact, svelte form, contemplating how Julie was relishing the tickle between her legs, and meanwhile getting in the groove with her own full-bladder sensations. She caught herself toying absentmindedly with the strap of her bra—pulling it nearly off her shoulder as a teasy substitute for pulling her gusset aside, down below, to let loose.

Impulsively, she reached over and touched the front of Julie's knickers.

"Mmm … ," the other woman purred. "Careful, now—you know I have to pee." There was a playful lilt to her voice.

Lynne grinned naughtily and began softly stroking there. She kept stroking while she leaned in to kiss Julie.

"Oh, Lynne … oh yes … but I'm warning you, baby—I swear I'm going to—ohhh!"

The first spurt of heat and wetness kissed Lynne's fingers through the cotton. As the panties soaked it up, she caressed Julie's pussy with more vigor.

Another spurt.

A few more strokes and Julie's eyes widened, as her hips twitched in a complete loss of control. Then she shrieked a laugh and shuddered, gushing hotly and relentlessly into her knickers.

She danced in her seat as the pee squirted down her thighs. She kissed Lynne's face and neck feverishly as she peed all over the barstool.

"How did you know what I wanted?" she whispered in Lynne's ear, still pissing for all she was worth, bouncing up and down like a slow-motion horse rider.

Well, she *had* given some pretty clear hints, thought Lynne.

When Julie broke from the embrace to quiver through the final moments of her panty wetting, Lynne was torn by several conflicting impulses: Rip Julie's drenched plaid knickers off, and finger her the rest of the way to orgasm? Grab a towel, and start mopping up Julie's pretty puddle? Dash to the toilet, before she made a pretty puddle of her own? Or stay right there and make one?

She chose to go after her friend's drenched knickers.

But when she reached for Julie's crotch, Julie grabbed her wrist, winked at her again, and stood, pulling Lynne up with her.

Lynne ogled the inviting roundness of Julie's soggy ass cheeks, clinging like fruit to piss-stained panties within a now-transparent skirt. She had the urge to fondle them, or give them a few sweet slaps. But Julie was pulling her along too swiftly.

And now that her body was upright, Lynne was conscious of how long she'd been holding off herself. She felt an exquisite twinge between her legs, as if she might collapse any instant into a sensual squat and flood her valley.

Julie pressed her up against the kitchen wall and kissed her lusciously, squeezing her breasts and wedging a knee between her legs.

"Do you have to pee, baby?" Julie purred in her ear.

"Mm-hm," Lynne replied.

Neither of them moved. Julie continued to press her knee into Lynne's crotch, while teasing her fingers over Lynne's bottom.

"I bet no one's ever given you a bona fide panty-pissing orgasm," Julie speculated.

Lynne shivered as she felt the electrifying sizzle of her friend's words running through her body. Her nipples were aching, her clit was scraping the taut cotton of her panties … and, oh, did she have to pee.

Julie slowly undid her guest's skirt, then threw it aside. She toyed with the waistband of Lynne's knickers.

"Look at your tight little panties," she said approvingly, "stretched across your squirmy pussy while you hold your pee."

Lynne wriggled against Julie. She was frantic with anticipation.

"Oh, honey," Julie continued, "you're going to look so sexy when you do it. A pint and a half at the end of our shift, and you haven't tinkled a drop yet? You must be holding back a fountain."

Lynne moaned in the affirmative.

"Is this a nice place?" Julie's finger had crept just inside Lynne's gusset, where it was titillating the most sensitive part of her inner thigh, terrifically close to her pussy. "When I tickle you there, do you feel the water welling up? Pee for me, baby."

"Pee for me," she repeated, tickling. "Let it all out."

Suddenly her other hand was down Lynne's panties—fingers in her lubricated slit, thumb against her clitoris. Still tickling with her left hand, she masturbated Lynne with efficient precision with the right. Lynne knew she'd be having that "panty-pissing orgasm" within seconds.

"Make me pee!" Lynne requested—unnecessarily. She knew she couldn't stand all the tension and sensation one second longer, despite how good it all was. She had to let go.

She felt the pleasure of Julie's touch assailing her last shred of control from all directions, and she savored one last instant of squirmy anticipation before the climax rocked her core and a tidal wave of release surged through her.

Coming on Julie's hand and splashing over her tiles, Lynne was now experiencing perhaps the most intense jouissance she'd ever felt. She seemed to be wetting in slow motion, as the warm liquid collected in the snug panties and then poured out the leg holes, caressing her upper thighs. The bath of ecstasy her pussy was receiving felt unbelievably good in conjunction with the luxurious tingling that continued to sprawl through her pee muscles as they further relaxed.

She was going to come again—this time slowly, so slowly. She was practically crying from sensory delight as she orgasmed.

Afterward, Lynne relaxed into what she now recognized as the incomparable peace of a woman who has been pleasured until she wet her panties. Julie kissed her forehead.

Tommy is at Lynne's elbow, saying a cheery hello. The clock shows four thirty, and Lynne has forgotten that Julie's shift today ends right now, rather than at five. It'll be Lynne and Tommy from here on in. There's a lull in the customer traffic, so Tom gets busy beside her, drying glasses.

Julie will obviously be heading for the ladies' at this point, Lynne tells herself.

Won't she?

She sees that Julie's heading toward the back exit, not the restroom. And she's gesturing for her girlfriend to join her.

"Tom, I'm going to borrow Lynne for a minute, OK?" shouts Julie.

"Sure thing," says Tommy.

Lynne throws aside her dishtowel—then, thinking better of that, grabs it again—before following Julie toward the back door, which leads to a quiet alleyway.

The area immediately behind the pub is obscured from sight by a wall, and no one ever goes back there but the staff. With Tommy stuck behind the bar, Lynne knows they're as private as can be. Julie already has her shorts off by the time Lynne closes the door behind them.

She grabs hold of one of Julie's elbows and runs a forefinger along the elasticized hem of her panties, before pulling the fabric to one side and coaxing her pussy lips open. She kisses Julie quickly, then drops to her knees.

With the gusset just barely out of her way, she starts licking Julie's trembling pussy lips. Julie rocks for her, her knees slightly bent.

"Do it," says Lynne. "Pee right in my face."

Julie hangs on another minute while her girlfriend continues the verbal encouragement, in between licks. Varying direction, Lynne tongues up, down, and around her lover's fragrant pussy. On the brink, Julie moans.

At last it seems she can't hold on any longer, and her hardworking muscles give it up, letting the pee trickle out from her arousal-bloated nether landscape. Lynne looks up to see a priceless look of bliss on Julie's face, her mouth open in an especially low moan that can only mean the sweet rush of letting go.

In another instant, Julie's fountain is cascading wildly onto Lynne's face. Hot and urgent and voluminous, it floods over her chin. Julie grinds her hips while she does it, passionately chanting *oh fuck, oh fuck, oh fuck* as she pisses and pisses.

Never mind a faucet—Julie's gushing like a fire hydrant. It's so beautiful, thinks Lynne, as Julie gives out a roar of pleasure above her. The pee feels like champagne kissing her skin.

And she realizes that despite the momentous nature of what's transpiring, they've only been absent a minute or two—meaning Lynne will have plenty of time to eat Julie's pee-soaked cunt to climax before Tommy could begin to miss her.

So when Julie finishes, Lynne edges her girlfriend's knickers down to properly feast on her piss-warm, unwiped pussy. As she begins to mouth along those sensitive lips once again, Julie pees a little more, and Lynne catches it on her tongue.

Julie squirms and squirms again, then soon melts once more in release—this time orgasmic release. Lynne keeps licking as best she can while her lover climaxes on her tongue, making sure Julie gets every iota of ecstasy she can take. She pees yet again while she comes—until finally she can't pee or come anymore, and her tired little pussy just twitches against Lynne's lips.

Thank goodness for that dishtowel, thinks Lynne. She stands up, wipes her face, and prepares to finish her shift after a quick wash-up.

"See you at home," says Julie breathily, after she's restored her clothing.

She blows Lynne a kiss and walks away, leaving behind a magnificent puddle.

And a very adoring girlfriend.

Co-Education

The supplementary co-ed bathroom at the far end of Janice's dorm floor was the next best thing to a private hotel room. Phil loved slipping in there with Janice for late-night sex in the stall nearest the door—the stall that featured a bathtub instead of a toilet. They'd yet to be disturbed here.

"Mmm, your fingers feel so good," Janice said at 1 a.m. on a Thursday night, as Phil teased the slick lips of her pussy with his warm, soapy digits.

Suddenly, the bathroom door creaked open. And through the gap between the stall door's hinges, Phil and Janice were able to see who had entered, catching a fleeting glimpse of her as she walked by: chestnut hair, a yummy midriff, and tight, round jeans.

"Oh, wow," said Phil in his lover's ear. "It's that hot chick from our French lit class." He and Janice had talked about her before. Janice liked hearing Phil talk about the women he found attractive.

As he spoke, they heard a stall door slam. Feet appeared in the cubicle next to them.

"Whoa—her jeans are down," Phil whispered.

A moment later, as a pretty splashing noise reverberated off the tile walls, he continued: "Oh my god, she's peeing."

"Duh, Phil," hissed Janice, her voice evidently holding back laughter. "What did you *think* went on in here?"

"I know, I know … but, wow, without any pomp or circumstance …"

"What do you mean, pomp or circumstance? You thought girls made a speech first?"

The lovely tinkling sound continued.

"It just seems too good to be true. That women come in here, and they actually pull their pants down and piss, just like that. They really do it." Somehow a part of him had expected the world around him to fade to black rather than really showing him this.

"Phil, you goofball—it's what she came in here to do."

"Oh, fuck, yeah. I know, I know," he repeated blissfully.

The peeing music finally abated, and the girl in the next stall sighed sexily. Then she chuckled.

"I hear whispers!" she called out cheerfully. "Are there two of you in that tub?" she added, with the vocal equivalent of a wink in her tone. "I hope I didn't disturb you."

"Not at all," groaned Phil, as Janice pulled firmly on his hard, hard cock.

Night of Treats

SHE HAD NEGLECTED TO LOCK THE DOOR, THE HALLOWEEN party was noisy ... and I accidentally walked in on her.

She was at her most exposed. She'd finished peeing and was just standing up to yank her cherry-red panties back into place. Not only did I see the inside of her panties, I also saw her handsome auburn bush. I even thought I saw a wayward drop of pee trickle down.

And I saw her face. A face I'd never seen before. A face that looked startled but ... vaguely pleased. I saw all of this in the split second it took for her to say "Excuse me!" and me to say a simultaneous "Sorry!" We both sounded as apologetic as one can sound when surprised.

And then I was back in the hall, with the bathroom door closed discreetly behind me.

As I headed upstairs to the other bathroom, I noticed that the experience had left me more than a little aroused. Maybe this was because of the vibe I'd received—the sense that she didn't mind that it had happened. And if she didn't mind, I sure didn't. Maybe she, too, felt like she'd just stumbled onto a nice little treat on this Night of Treats.

She was sweetly beautiful. Her face was soft and dreamy, and her eyes were kind and bright. Believe me, I would have noticed her even if her pussy hadn't been exposed. But, having taken in such a preciously sexy sight, I was not just smitten—I was unable to think about anything else. She became an instant obsession to me, by virtue of having inadvertently flashed me ...

and having looked like she didn't regret it. What had begun as a typical Halloween party had become a quest to find the girl I'd met with her panties down.

More than an hour passed before I saw her again. She was by herself, ladling out a cup of hot cider, across the living room from the much more popular beer station.

It's a funny thing when the first part of a Halloween costume you notice is the inside of the panties. It makes the rest of it a little anticlimactic. Still, this costume was impressive even with the panties demurely out of sight. It consisted, essentially, of a silver-lamé minidress, with red go-go boots that matched what I now could not see. Her green eyes sizzled sympathetically with some glass jewels that dotted the outfit. Overall, the effect was that of a '60s pop star from outer space.

As I approached her, she looked at me like we were longtime pals. I was a little nervous, and so I was glad to know that I had an easy conversational opening.

"Hey, I'm really sorry about walking in on you before." Though I knew that I actually wasn't sorry—and I truly believed that she wasn't either—it seemed like the appropriate thing to say.

"Please don't be." Though others might have said this out of politeness, she said it as if she meant it.

Before we'd even introduced ourselves—Faye and Scott—it was evident that we had chemistry. The next hour seemed to pass in a few minutes while we sat comfortably on a corner sofa, making an effort to let our conversation catch up to our hormones.

After a while, I returned to the subject of our original encounter. "Just think," I said, "if I hadn't opened that bathroom door … "

Faye smiled enigmatically. "Speaking for myself, my only regret is that you didn't walk in on me sooner."

She was charming, and her electricity was giving me a huge hard-on. But I was puzzled. "What do you mean?" I asked.

"This may be an odd thing to say to someone I've just met … and you may find it hard to understand … but when I see a man

I'm attracted to, I get this kinky desire to pee for him."

Offhand, I could not remember a woman ever telling me anything like this before.

"I don't usually get the opportunity, of course," she continued with a laugh. "Tonight was the closest I've come recently. Anyway, I know it's weird. It's just some kind of fluky, animal expression of sexual desire, I guess." Faye looked into my eyes. "Do you think I'm bizarre?"

I clarified the situation for her. "I think you're the sexiest woman I've ever known." And I kissed her.

After we'd said our goodbyes to the host, we climbed into Faye's car to extend the evening on our own terms. It was peaceful in her parking space, around the corner from the house with the loud party. The night was unseasonably warm, and we had the block to ourselves. A full moon allowed us to see every expression on each other's faces.

"Mmm … wow, after that cider … " Faye crossed her legs significantly.

"No worries," I said. "Go ahead and start the car. I know which of the convenience stores in this neighborhood have public restrooms."

To my surprise, she shook her head, smirking mischievously, and got out of the car.

When I came around to join her, she was rummaging for something in the backseat. Her ass was jiggling—because she had to go, I reasoned.

"Aha!" she said, and she emerged with the thing she'd been looking for. It was an empty plastic jack-o'-lantern, like kids carry when they go trick-or-treating.

"I was going to bring this in to the party, just as a prop," she explained. "But I decided there was really no use for it, and that it would be a nuisance to carry it around all night." She held it up so that I could see it better. "I've had this since I was a kid."

"It's in great condition," I said. "Cool."

"Yeah," she agreed. "But what's even cooler is that I'm going to pee in it for you."

And without further ado, she set her prop down on the

deserted sidewalk. She hiked up her shimmery dress and hastily peeled her panties. This time, they came all the way off, and I had the privilege of clutching them to my chest.

She straddled the plastic pumpkin and let her water flow.

If she had looked like a pop star in her sexy costume before, she now looked like a goddess. Watching her shapely body pissing, I couldn't imagine a more beautiful thing for a body like hers to do. And the spectacle she had brilliantly engineered could not have been more dazzling. Her fountain, shimmering like her sparkling outfit, plummeted majestically from her tender, naked crotch into the bright orange receptacle, which grinned lasciviously at me as Faye rained down. I imagine I was grinning back, but with an expression of intense awe and reverence that no plastic candy pail could possibly share.

When the breathtaking display came to its inevitable end, I thought she would ask for her panties back. Instead, still holding her skirt high, she turned her bare ass toward me. "How about a little kiss before we get back in the car?"

So I dropped to my knees and kissed the perky, delicious cheeks in an assortment of places. And I reached in to feel the pussy she'd so recently sprinkled from, before wiping her dry with my handkerchief.

I couldn't wait to get back to her apartment and touch her some more.

When she fucked me on her bed an hour later, she still had the costume on, complete with the cute little boots. Only my old friends the cherry panties had been sacrificed, somewhere between the ass-fondling and pussy-licking phases of our evening.

After our flesh had cooked, climaxed, and lazily disengaged, Faye continued to straddle me. Now, as a final act of the night's lovemaking, she sensuously peed all over my lap, consecrating our bond.

It was a very fluky, very sexual, very animal ... very wonderful thing.

Beer or Wine?

WHEN HE'D ASKED WHICH SHE WANTED—BEER OR WINE—
he hadn't expected quite this sort of answer.

"What do I want?" said Marigold. "I want you to give me
beer and let me wet myself for you. Yes, Jim, give me beer and
make me pee."

He remembered the time he'd come home to find her
squatting over her fresh puddle in his dining room, fingers
furiously masturbating inside her drenched, clinging panties, her
other hand twisting at a nipple. He had pulled the panties off her
to fuck her then and there. Afterward, she had pissed heartily
again, now wearing only her unbuttoned white waitress blouse.
Her naked haunches had been mere inches from the floor, and
a thick, robust column of water had poured out of her as if she
were an inverted bottle. He had noticed how smooth her skin
was around her furry blonde mound.

Tonight she was wearing just panties and a blue oxford shirt.
As she finished her beer, she leaned forward to speak softly in
his ear, her hair fluffy on his neck, her breath hot and slightly
alcohol-tinged.

"Jim," she whispered, resuming her monologue, "I want to
wet my panties for you." She kissed a spot just below his earlobe.
"Would you like that, Jim?"

She kept talking as she took his hand and guided him up
from the couch with her.

"May I do that—wet myself in front of you? Right here? I
could do that, you know. You wouldn't have to do a thing. I'd just

stand here and piss my boy shorts … pee my panties … soak my knickers.

"Would you enjoy that? If I wet myself, and then you licked me dry—licked me till I came? I've held it almost as long as I can, Jim.

"Oh, Jim. I'm pissing myself, Jim. Oh, Jim … "

Quick Tinkles

One

Alicia greeted me with a grin and a handshake. "Make yourself at home," she said brightly as she stepped aside to let me in. "I'll be right back. I was just about to pee."

I had entered from the hallway directly into the kitchen, a space made pleasant by the low-volume cool of some modern-jazz disc. Alicia now disappeared through a door on the far side of this room. I crossed to the table and seated myself facing the windows, through which I hoped to catch a final glimpse of the sunset.

Sitting there, I became conscious of the titillating music of Alicia's fountain as it tinkled exuberantly into the bowl.

For a moment, I wondered if it would be courteous to avoid listening—I couldn't help hearing, but I could try not to listen—yet I had a feeling that she wouldn't mind. So I relaxed, and I noticed how the sound of her intimate cascade mingled with the round, cheerful vibraphone notes that bubbled softly out of the speakers.

Our eyes met when she emerged. It was obvious that I must have heard her music. She blushed a little and smiled, shyly but impishly. Then she broke the tension.

"You haven't lived till you've listened to me urinate," she laughed.

Two

With her thighs holding her own hands down in voluntary

suspension, Marilyn stays passive and lets the pressure in her crotch float to the surface.

She watches serenely for the appearance of a wet cling of release in her panties, as the tension of holding on breaks into the exquisite relaxation of peeing.

The cotton slowly darkens, in an intense, creeping oval; and as the warm wetness bathes her pussy lips and tickles her clit, Marilyn feels herself jerking forward, her crotch dancing with the sexual tingle of stimulation. With her thighs still flattening her palms, she slowly pisses herself into an orgasmic sizzle.

THREE

Just as he started to fidget in his desk chair, his phone lit up. Tracy.

"Hi, Donny." She giggled.

"Hi." His heart raced.

"Well, I don't know about you, but I'm ready to do it."

"Me too. Can you hold on for five minutes?"

"I think so."

"I'll be right over."

Tracy was a genius, thought Donny, as he walked quickly across an array of quadrangles toward her dorm. They'd both needed to get a little bit of work done, on their own computers. It was her suggestion that they apply themselves to their homework until one, or both, had to pee; this would signal them to reunite in Tracy's private bathroom, where their shared pee break would officially end the homework session in a ceremonious fashion, inaugurating the recreational part of the evening.

He was holding himself by the time they bustled past the sink—but he was looking forward to feeling his water continue to pulsate inside him while she took first turn at the toilet.

He gestured for her to go ahead, and Tracy grinned hungrily for him as she pulled her pants down.

FOUR

From across the restaurant table, Randall kidded his

colleague. "Coffee … beer … and now lemonade with dessert? I can't imagine taking all that in. Do you *want* to wet your pants on the walk back to the hotel, or something?"

Amy took another slurp through her straw. "I hadn't really thought about it, Randall. But thanks for the invitation."

Randall laughed. But she saw that his face was red. Evidently, he hadn't realized what he was getting into when he'd opened the door to this topic with an offhand joke.

"OK, admit it," she ventured. "You'd enjoy seeing me wet these shorts on the way home, wouldn't you?"

Randall's blush deepened. "Huh? Uh … well … I mean, *you'd* have to be enjoying it too … but, all right, under those circumstances, I guess I'd … "

"Mmm … well, yeah, I always do enjoy it."

"You mean you—"

Amy shifted in her seat. "It's a pretty sexy image, isn't it?"

"Oh, f-fuck yes."

She could tell. All Randall could think about now were the sensations in her crotch … the tickly alertness inside her shorts … the possibility that she might jiggle and wiggle as she held it.

Yes, she was now officially a Pretty Woman in Shorts Who Had to Pee. And though she couldn't entirely explain why, she was the first to admit that it *was* sexy—and, as usual, being the PWISWHTP was turning her on.

"Let's pay up and take a slow walk back," she suggested.

Five

By now, she was sure he recognized the evenings on which she was planning to wet herself for him, just from the way she comported herself—the way she smiled, the way she sat, the way she drank her second glass of white wine.

"I have to pee."

By telling him, she'd given the need an explicitly erotic quality. She'd put his consciousness under her skirt and between her thighs—at the nexus of her womanhood, the apex of her panties. Now it was an acknowledged, intimate secret, the pulse in her underwear a cherished bond of kinky love between them.

She put a delicate hand in her crotch and sipped her wine, relishing the anticipation.

When her urgency began to overtake her, she positioned herself, peach thong visible under her skirt. Squatting proudly, she continued to hold herself in check.

"Tickle me."

He crouched beside her and ran soft, roving fingers over her breasts and tummy, offering her the sensual gift of a loss of control. Soon she shuddered. She whimpered while she wet, afloat in a sea of heat and pleasure.

He ceased the now-superfluous titillation and watched reverently as her thong, overwhelmed, became the merest threshold for her rushing heaven of pee—a tiny speed bump, a thin lip of the cup that ranneth over.

Six

The hotel's elegant indoor pool area—deserted at this hour—was the perfect venue for the tryst we both craved. As we enjoyed the chill-out music that wafted in, we kissed, fondled, and undressed at leisure.

The last garment had hit the tiles. Gabrielle's nipples and my penis were at maximum tension, and her pussy kissed my fingers with sweet juice. I began to lead her to a lounge chair, so that we could properly mingle.

"I have to pee first," she said.

I prepared to bide my time, thinking she would throw something on, excuse herself, and find a restroom.

But Gabrielle had other ideas. She glanced quickly around the pool lounge and spotted a pile of fluffy towels. She grabbed a medium-size towel and, standing gloriously naked before me, she shoved it, still folded, into her crotch, where she held it tight with one hand and both thighs.

As I watched in amazement and delight, she kept her outer muscles taut and relaxed her inner ones. Within moments, she was pumping a powerful river of pee into the towel, humping it rhythmically all the while.

Though she pissed a long time—an expression of sexual bliss

creeping onto her face as she did so—the towel absorbed most of her flood. Only a few small, titillating trickles headed down her sturdy legs or dripped languidly to the floor.

Seven

Walking back to his car, Phil turned the corner into the restaurant parking lot and saw a peeing peach—a beautiful bare bottom that squatted in the delivery lane, its lovely owner releasing her copious torrent to the asphalt after the evening's worth of cocktails and lemon water he'd seen her consume inside.

He stopped in his tracks, fascinated. The phrase *peeing peach*, instantly coined in his head upon stumbling on this sight, continued to resonate in his mind.

When the woman noticed him she winked, wiggling her smooth behind.

"Haven't you ever seen a peeing peach before?"

Eight

She's wearing a body stocking with a hole cut out behind—an oval windowful of crack and cheeks.

She puts a feather in my hand. She mentions that the oval might lend itself to a little tickling.

She places my other hand on her crotch, where the mesh hugs her.

She confides that she's put off taking a leak while waiting for me, because it feels sexy.

She wonders if having her ass tickled a little bit will make her pee.

She says it like a question. But she's wiggling to show it's the feather she wants, not an answer.

Nine

He positioned himself below his woman's charming ass and pulled her gusset to the side.

He was surprised when, instead of a delicate trickle, a veritable faucet opened above his face.

"Wow!"

Elaine laughed. "What—you didn't believe me when I said I really had to pee?"

"I just had no idea you could do it like … I mean, I always imagined you girls gently tinkling." He was impressed, awed, and intensely aroused.

"Heeheehee! Not after two beers and a lengthy subway ride, we don't. *Ahhh*, fuck, that feels good," she added, as she pissed heartily all over him.

TEN

Helen was lying facedown on the bed in her tap pants, reading a book, when George came upstairs.

A moment later, he was lying on top of her, pressing his weight down on her cushion of an ass and kissing her neck.

"Welcome home, darling." She squirmed under him. "Hey, I have to pee, so hold your horses a second, 'k?"

George shifted his weight so she could get up, but Helen didn't move. Instead, she took hold of his index finger and placed it inside the leg of her panties.

"Seriously, George," she said breathlessly. "I'd really better dash to the bathroom."

Still she stayed put, using a hand on his wrist to guide his finger to her pussy lips.

"I'm warning you, baby: you keep touching me there and I'm gonna pee." She settled into the bed and urged his hand on, spreading to welcome him.

"Oh, god … "

She was doing it, grinding herself against the mattress while she wet into his hand.

ELEVEN

Pam and Katy had agreed they would go bottomless for today's pee-holding contest. With their pussies nude, the first driblet, trickle, or leak would be instantly obvious—no secret dribbles into panties this time. Pam loved this twist: it excited her so to imagine wetting her pants, only without any pants ... to be that exposed when she had to go.

The usual ground rules would apply, of course, such as the all-important "no pain" rule, which stipulated that either participant, if she found that her situation was beginning to turn to one of true discomfort, would let loose immediately. They'd also decided, on this occasion, that they'd both wear wedge heels, as a treat for their friends the judges. Pam and Katy both felt that their naked, wiggling arses would look particularly delicious when elevated and angled by the heels.

There was an extra treat in store for Katy and Pam, too: it had been decided that if they both lasted long enough, they'd get to lie across the judges' laps for a few sensuous ass slaps and feather tickles—a guaranteed way to bring the contest to a speedy conclusion. Undressing for the event, it made Pam tingle with arousal just to anticipate the feeling of having her pussy brushed with a feather, followed by that of peeing uncontrollably on a handsome man's trousers.

Really, thought Pam, there were no losers in a contest like this.

TWELVE

There was a bathroom in the back of the bus, and Hannah knew she could wake the sleeping prince who was seated between her and the aisle if she really had to.

But why bother him, she said to herself, when instead she could sit there clamping her muscles closed for a while, feeling herself getting turned on by it.

Even when he woke up, perhaps she'd still wait to pee. Maybe it would be more interesting to be squeezing her thighs together to hold it while she flirted with him, feeling the tight tickle under her skirt.

One of her fondest memories was silently wetting her pants one midnight in the backseat of a boyfriend's car—knowing he wouldn't mind, and knowing that although home was a little too far for her to hold it, it was close enough that the damp jeans would not become uncomfortable.

Now, looking at the slumbering hunk beside her, she wondered if it would turn him on to see a pretty girl wet her panties with a smile of pleasure on her face.

Her decision made, Hannah sat back and watched the scenery, looking forward to the moment when her neighbor would awake and she would quietly start to drip, drip, drip in her knickers, while he remained oblivious to the fact that she was discreetly wetting herself.

Oblivious, that is, until she locked her eyes on his face to tell him.

THIRTEEN

Using her fingers to control her stream, she makes it last—pissing slowly, thinly out the leg of her panties, softly undulating, relaxing even, while she pisses ... and pisses ... and pisses at leisure, letting substantial parcels of conversation occur between them while still she elegantly pees.

He's been watching her intently from the beginning, when she raised her skirt with her left hand, then abstracted her gusset and separated her outer lips with the right.

The way the pointed toes of her shoes turn inward while she pees is adorable. And the way she makes a subtle stamping motion with the right foot—as a way of encouraging her flow? as an involuntary expression of sensory pleasure?—goes straight to his cock.

FOURTEEN

"How was your evening with Clarissa?" I asked Jocelyn.

She filled me in. "Did you ever sit there in your slacks, trying to hold your pee in while a gorgeous woman straddled you in her underwear and rubbed herself against your mound?"

I smiled and shook my head *no* to her gender-specific rhetorical question. My dick was already hardening.

"Let me tell you, it was the best game I've ever played. Now, I knew from the start she was going to make me pee my pants, one way or another. I knew it from the moment I arrived, when

I saw the neatly piled stack of fresh clothing she'd laid out for me—knickers uppermost. But there she was right on top of me, Michael, and—oh, wow—then *she* started pissing, wetting my crotch right through her panties. I could feel her warm pee seeping onto my tensed-up pussy, while I watched the orgasmic expression on her face.

"Mmm," I said approvingly.

"Well, needless to say I lost it. I told her I was wetting myself, and she clamped my hips tight with her thighs. From then on, it was like we were pissing as one."

I swallowed appreciatively. "Clarissa is a true friend, isn't she?"

"The best."

FIFTEEN

She looked surprised. Not displeased; certainly not repulsed; just a little surprised.

"Did you just say you'd like me to piss on your face?"

Francis nodded. "Allow me to elaborate: We wait for a suitable opportunity—to wit, when you really need to go—and we adjourn to your bathtub. I lie back, and you, my dear, position your pretty ass right over my face so that your scrumptious cheeks are a feast for my eyes. Of course, I'll also be able to see your pussy—your darling pussy, hovering over my face, all ready to do it. And then your water, when it comes, will dazzle my chin."

She considered this a moment. "Yes, I see," she said agreeably.

Later that evening, a portrait of statuesque ass and full bladder, Muriel posed gracefully in the tub, bracing herself. Her own innovation was to invite Francis to hoist her right leg and cradle her thigh while she squatted above him.

She laughed, warmly and kindly and sensuously, as her downpour splashed onto his sealed lips, kissing and kissing him.

Detour

We'd just finished our second round at a favorite pub. And as we stood to leave, Mandy confided that she needed to pee. But the loo was occupied, and rather than wait she suggested we start walking homeward.

I think we'd covered about half the two-mile distance when she stopped us short in front of an alley, pressing the front of her miniskirt.

"Well, that was stupid of me," she confessed. "I should've waited my turn at the pub. Now I'm not going to make it home." She did a little gyration, emphasizing the problem.

It was a quiet summer evening, with little traffic in the streets and no other pedestrians in sight. Mandy's eyes roamed our surroundings. Then, with a cheeky shrug, she turned into the alley. "Come on," she said.

I was impressed with her instincts. The buildings that lined this alley were windowless, and we had about as much privacy as one could hope for in a public place.

But Mandy held off.

"What are you waiting for?" I asked.

Without answering, she lifted her skirt, revealing a pair of blue boy shorts. But still she hesitated, crossing her legs to hold it in rather than committing to what she'd come here to do.

Even as I puzzled over her behavior, I noticed the flush in her cheeks and recognized the hint of a quirky smile at the corner of her mouth. Mandy was enjoying this. She was turned on.

"Just take your knickers down and go," I said, still somewhat focused on the task at hand.

"But what if someone comes down the alley?" she asked, dancing in place with her underwear in view. "Anyone could turn in here and see my pussy." She was sporting a full-fledged smirk now.

I realized that Mandy was using her situation to tease me—and I loved it. My cock got harder as I wondered what would happen.

I decided that if she was making a game of this, I would gladly play along.

"Come on, Amanda," I coaxed. "Pull those panties down and pee. You know you want to."

"No." She stuck her tongue out. "No. I'll just do it like this."

And she did. Before my eyes, Mandy stood there, clutching the edge of her skirt, wetting her knickers.

It started slowly, but with a couple of pints in her she soon pissing buckets, drenching her boy shorts and pouring herself down onto the bricks like a waterfall.

Never had I been given such a good view of my beautiful girlfriend taking a leak, and it was incredibly arousing. The fact that she was doing it through her panties added a kinky touch that put it over the top.

But the best part of all was her face. She was evidently in ecstasy, savoring the release and luxuriating in the feel of the damp cotton against her pussy.

"Ooh, Dennis, it feels so yummy," she said, laughing her horniest laugh.

Though *I* didn't have to pee, I found myself nonetheless needing to take my cock out. I stroked it as I watched the show, raining knickers and pee-splashed bricks and sopping crotch and radiant face.

By the time she finally trickled to a halt, my dick was ready to explode. But the show wasn't over. Mandy did another little dance now, a sensuous one, pressing the dripping fabric against herself—rubbing down and in and over her pussy, then up across her mound.

Then she looked me in the eye. "Fuck me, Dennis."

And *now* she yanked her panties down, tossing them behind her.

I advanced toward her, eating up the sight of this raunchy, randy creature who'd gotten so aroused by pissing herself that she couldn't even wait till we got home to have my cock up her.

She looked wildly gorgeous waiting there for me, and as soon as I could get a condom on I was clasping her bottom and brushing the head of my dick against her warm, pee-slick pussy lips.

"Still worried about being seen?" I teased into her ear.

She slapped my ass as a reply.

Mandy was extremely wet inside her pussy, too—wet with excitement. She grooved around me while I slid slowly up and down within her, repeatedly filling her with my shaft, showing her just how hard she'd made me.

Not surprisingly, given how keyed up she'd been, she was soon close to coming; and she reached behind herself to pull one of my hands off her arse and move it to her clit.

I remember thinking it was a good thing those buildings didn't have windows, because her scream would have rattled every one of them.

As for me, I came for a long, long time …

It was as if Mandy's sexy marathon piss had inspired my spunk to clock a record performance of its own.

After Tennis

PLAYING TENNIS WITH CANDICE WAS ALWAYS HARD WORK—for both of us. We each hit the water bottle a lot during those generous summer Sundays on the court. And then sometimes, when the sun began its slow late-afternoon descent and we were ready to relax the pace a bit, we'd pull a couple of beers out of her cooler.

On one such occasion, it became clear at the end of yet another close match that Candice and I were both jiggling for a good piss, as the brews and H2O coursed through us.

"Do you have to pee as badly as I do?" she called to me from across the court. This end of the park was empty except for us, so she was able to shout this fairly personal question without any inhibitions. It sounded sexy, though, to hear my lover shouting to me in the open air about how she had to take a leak. I'd had the good fortune to observe that Candice embodied a particular kind of erotic beauty on the commode, her soft, intimate regions the source of a shimmering fountain. So for her to mention the need was always enough to turn me on.

"You know it!" I grinned, as we met at the net. I noticed her left hand darting momentarily to the front of her shorts. Her knees were pressed together. She smiled in a way that looked a little kinky.

"Wanna try something?" she asked.

"Sure," I said. I didn't know what she had in mind, but that question—and that smile—had always led to nice things.

We headed off the court in the direction of the changing

rooms, and Candice took my hand. "I thought it might be fun to do a double wetting," she said softly.

I didn't get her drift. It had sounded like she'd said "double wedding," and the two of us had barely discussed marriage. But I was too intrigued—and too eager to take my dick out of my shorts and let the beer flow—to hold things up with a lot of questions.

To my surprise, she led me right past the locker building, into a secluded bit of lawn beyond. A moment later, while we swayed and held ourselves, she surprised me further by sitting me down on the grass ... and then seating herself on my lap, with her back to me. Feeling her ass on my fly made me start to get hard, but I was still ready to spill over with pee any second.

Candice jiggled on top of me, and at last I realized what she had in mind. "OK," she announced, with a touch of breathless anticipation in her sexy voice. "When I count to 3 we both let go, all right?" She didn't wait for an answer, but began to count. "1 ... 2 ... 3!"

I heard a lewd hissing from under her, and I did my part by relaxing every tensed muscle in my lap. A warm, wet bliss rolled over me as my tennis shorts soaked up Candice's flood of womanly water and my own bladderful of fluid. Her saturated crotch generated a river that merged with my own spreading wetness, creating a confluence of mutual release that mingled intimately where her throbbing cunt pressed through our flimsy clothing, urgent against my pumping hose.

Even while we were still wetting, her moans indicated that her enjoyment had crossed way over the line from the basic physical pleasure of urinating into something powerfully sexual. And when we finally, finally finished, we could not peel our soaked shorts and underwear fast enough. I had quickly developed a huge erection, and her piss-glistening pussy was slick and hungry.

With our pants at our ankles, she wriggled her ass back down toward my lap until her wet lips kissed the tip of my member. After an instant of this titillating contact, we screwed our sexes further into place and began a juicy bounce. Her back, warm with perspiration, pressed tightly against my chest, and her ass squirmed against my abdomen.

I heard the sounds of pee-kissed flesh squishing to our rhythm. As I fucked her right there on my lap, I reached around to finger her nipples through her tennis shirt, taking care also to tickle her under her arms, which was guaranteed to send Candice into ecstasies. Her climax and mine came rushing through us mere instants later.

Scarcely had the orgasms receded when she hopped off me, squatted mere feet away, and let loose another torrent of pee, this time onto the dry grass. She giggled frivolously while I watched the luscious stream roar out of her; her bare ass pulsated as it watered the terrain below.

Microminiclimates

I KNEW IT WAS AN INDEFENSIBLE FANCY OF MINE THAT CLARA could only have existed in San Francisco. But it was a harmless one, and I clung to it like a teddy bear.

It was Clara who first explained to me about the microclimates—how, even within central SF, a damp, rainy day in one neighborhood could coexist with a warm, sunny day elsewhere, at the same moment … that, if she were to be believed, this sort of thing went on all the time. And venture farther afield around the bay, she maintained, and a veritable "meteorology's greatest hits" was on offer.

"You can't really understand San Francisco unless you understand the microclimates."

I didn't doubt it. But I'd never said I intended to "understand" San Francisco. It seemed that to aspire to this might smack of hubris. After all, I wasn't sure I would even claim to "understand" Erie, Pennsylvania, though I'd lived there my entire life.

My knee-jerk response, I'm sorry to report, was to dismiss the microclimate paradigm as "silly." That was my typical reaction, in those days, to anything I was reluctant to make room for in my world. It wasn't that I didn't credit what Clara was telling me; I just didn't feel any need to embrace the phenomenon. Clara was disappointed by this, and she vowed to seduce me with the charm of her beloved microclimates.

She began, early in my visit, by instructing me in area geography. This I was receptive to—especially the way she taught it, using her body. The left leg was Oakland; the right,

San Francisco. Spread on the toilet seat while she shaved her pussy, they left me a good view of the bay below.

"And what's this?" she quizzed, setting her razor down and poking a finger into her smooth, juicy hole.

"That's easy," I popped back. "Treasure Island."

"Correct—on both counts."

I kissed the nipples of San Rafael and San Pablo, and the map that was Clara enfolded me.

She was a woman for all seasons, at least the locally represented seasons—equally comfortable in chilly or scorching weather, rarely needing to dress for any particular meteorological eventuality. And where most of us are water-resistant—that is, we don't melt in the rain—Clara actually seemed 100 percent water*proof*.

So it didn't surprise me, that morning in May, to see that Clara had dressed for our outing in a berry-colored T-shirt and a denim microminiskirt, though I was in long pants and a windbreaker. She had adorable knees—among other things—and she looked positively delicious.

"I checked the forecasts," she said—*forecasts*, plural! I noted with East Coast disbelief—"and today should be perfect."

We ambled out of her apartment building. It was cool and foggy here in the Sunset District, and though we were within walking distance of the ocean, our sight line up the street provided no hint of the vast Pacific. But Clara led me in that direction just the same, taking the ocean on faith.

"Fog," she said, when we stood on the sand, viewing the water now through a cheesecloth of grayness.

"Yes, I *thought* I recognized it," I teased.

She poked me in the ribs, her way of applauding my wit. I noticed that the beach was devoid of people, as far as the eye could see—which, granted, was not very far.

"A blanket of fog, as they say." She gave particular weight to the word *blanket*. "So, Davin, do you want to crawl under the fog blanket with me?"

Without waiting for an answer, she spilled herself onto the sand. And, microminis being what they are, Clara was all panties:

a fresh crotch of smooth pink cotton, crisp but soft between randy thighs, ready to be devoured.

It was still relatively early by my standards, and, despite a cup of coffee consumed at the apartment, I didn't have a tight grip on my consciousness yet. And so I felt, indeed, that I was in a fog as I dropped to my knees to sample Clara's morning-fresh thighs. But the brisk, savory aroma filtering through the knickers as I kissed her legs accomplished what the coffee had not ... and soon my intellect was sharp, not to mention my cock. Her bubblegum-pink bikini briefs were a bright spot in the gray environment, and I homed in on them, eager to taste the color.

She wriggled playfully when I stretched her gusset aside and greeted her sensitive lips with my tongue. She tasted like dawn, sweet and private, a secret treat to be enjoyed beneath an umbrella of mist. I licked her with rigorous dedication, following the trail of her juice and the rhythm of her spasms, continuing the tongue bath until she locked my head in place and humped herself to climax against my mouth.

She was a yummy mess now. The rear of her skirt had scooped up fistfuls of sand, and her panties became instantly moist when she pulled them back into place. She sat up, clasping my crotch, where my hard-on was creating an interesting regional topography within my jeans.

"Where would you like to be fucked?" I asked suavely, cherishing the thought that these pink panties enclosed a couple of possibilities.

"In the Mission District," Clara answered. "Come on."

"Mission and 24th," she told the cab driver. Then, acknowledging my patience, she began to stroke me through my pants. "Soon," she mouthed.

We left the fog behind as we climbed eastward, and sunlight bled erratically through the dirty windows of the taxi, alighting on Clara's light brown hair from time to time, almost turning it blonde where it licked her. She twisted herself toward me, her body wrapped tight in the skirt, and whispered, "My panties are so wet I could come."

Beneath her tide-me-over touch, my cock ached with delight and anticipation.

We coasted downhill again and arrived at our destination. I stood by while Clara leaned in through the front passenger window to settle up. Her decision to pay from outside the taxi was, I knew, an intentional gift to me—a bending-forward, ass-in-panties, short-skirted act of premeditated seduction.

Even with the lion's share of my attention focused on Clara's pink-fabric hemispheres, I was struck by the fact that it had turned into a bright, warm morning. Or rather, as I had learned from Clara's micro-minilectures on the subject, we had gone across town to where a bright, warm morning was already in progress.

I nudged her rear with my jeans front just as she straightened up. She spun around, grinning. "This way."

We zigzagged through the district for about five minutes, until Clara found the block she was looking for. She halted in front of a nondescript bar, closed at this hour. "I'm friends with the owner," she explained.

A minute gap—barely an alley—separated this building from the next, and I followed Clara down the channel the way my shaft yearned to go up her slot.

Behind the building was a tiny patio, obscured from view by walls on every side. There was a café table with two chairs back here, where bar employees might take breaks.

"No one will bother us here," said Clara. And she promptly bent to grab the top of one of the metal chairs, enticing me with all the ass she had to offer.

The denim of her skirt was warm to the touch, thanks to the generosity of the Mission District sun. The cotton of her panties, I found, was warm as well—though at their center, the heat was clearly originating from within rather than without.

"It's incredible," I said. "It actually is hot and dry in this part of town." Not the best foreplay talk, perhaps, but I was truly impressed.

"Hot, yes," she said, wiggling her derriere at me. "But, speaking on behalf of the pussy and myself, I'm going to challenge that word 'dry.'"

I laughed. "You're such a smartass. Just look at you, you smartass, in your smartass panties."

She wiggled some more, making her roundness irresistible, and I gave her a lusty slap on the aforementioned unmentionables.

Then I yanked them down. Clara stepped out of their sphere of influence while I, at last, unzipped and emerged.

The bliss of having something close and giving around me was like a strawberry milkshake on a summer day. And, fucking Clara behind the bar building, I could have sworn it really was summer. I'd been in too much of a hurry to slip off my windbreaker, and my upper body was cooking pleasantly in the nylon; while, in the gap between my hair and the jacket, I could feel the sun's voyeuristic gaze on my neck.

I alternated between dragging myself slowly inward and outward—relishing the clenching textures of Clara's sensation-soaked cunt—and ramming her quickly, to let her groove on the incremental bursts of discharged energy that sparked off me as my lust uncoiled. She gurgled soft *ohyeahhhhh, fuckmefuckme*'s during the slow parts, and yelled clipped *oh-FUCK-oh-FUCK*s to the beat of the staccato thrusts.

When I was a hair's breadth from coming, I tightened my hold on Clara's waist—pulling her against me so her bottom compressed on my abdomen, and jockeying myself into her so that her cunt could taste each nuance of my frantic dance. I used my other hand to cup her mound, one finger on her clit, and her orgasm doubled my own.

In the aftermath of our exertions, the day seemed that much hotter. I shed my jacket while we strolled toward the BART station, enjoying the nurturing feeling of sunshine on my arms—and the inspiring sight of Clara's upper thighs, as she walked two steps ahead of me. Her stressed, stretched, and streaked knickers had been donated to the trash can behind her friend's bar, and I was getting hard again contemplating how little fabric stood between me and Clara's bare ass cheeks and vulva, right out here in public.

We had a subway car to ourselves. I chose to stand, while Clara, initially, sat, her legs pasted together.

"I have to pee," she confided with a giggle.

I swallowed, feeling a tickle in my gut. I knew it sometimes made Clara horny to hold it; and, from the privileged smirk on her face, I could tell this was one of those times. And of course it made *me* horny—hornier than I was already—to know that it was making *her* horny. As I watched her shift around a little in her seat, tapping her toe on the floor, I couldn't help squirming a bit myself.

We were still a stop and a half away from downtown Berkeley—our next venue—when she hopped up, allowing me an instantaneous glimpse of pussy in her haste—probably by design, I reflected cheerfully. She joined me at my pole and let me handle her tush greedily through her skirt, while she pressed her gotta-pee crotch against my leg to grant herself a combination of bracing, damming, and erotic stimulation. The sensations of jiggling and arousal that reverberated in tandem under her skirt were transmitted to me as if by telegraph pulses, and I felt included in every detail of her excitement.

When we darted out of the station, a surprise party of heavy rain awaited me. While I struggled back into my windbreaker and wrestled with its unruly hood, I observed that the precipitation, which Clara welcomed literally with open arms, had immediately made her nipples stand out against her top.

She pointed her jaunty nipples toward the university campus and marched forward.

Once inside the gate, she employed her keen instinct for privacy to guide us to an unused corner, where buildings shielded us from pedestrian traffic and trees filtered the deluge into a mere downpour.

There, beneath the largest tree, she turned to face me, spread her legs as far as her skirt would permit … and added her own rain to the surrounding performance. Hers was a thick, beautiful outpouring, a testament to the natural wonder of microclimates inside a micromini.

I stood frozen in libidinous awe, but Clara giggled again and beckoned me closer. She kissed me as she peed.

"It's not raining in the Mission, you know," she said didactically, to ensure that I comprehended the situation.

"I understand," I smiled. "It's only raining here. And"—I gestured between her legs—"down there."

I'd never fucked a woman against a tree in the rain before … but then I'd never practiced foggilingus before, or come within an inch of creaming my jeans in a 45-degrees-off-sea-level taxicab.

Yes, Clara was indeed giving me an insider's tour of greater San Francisco's outdoor environments. And as my cock was welcomed to the University of California at Berkeley by a wet snatch in a wet quadrangle, I noted that being an insider felt damn good.

"I Bet You Looked Hot"

GISELLE WALKED BRISKLY FROM HER SUBWAY STOP, EN ROUTE to the apartment she shared with Diana. Diana of the smiling green eyes and the floppy, straw-colored hair. Diana with the ripe-looking lips that Giselle longed to taste. Diana, whom she wanted desperately to corner with a certain question, "Do you, perhaps perhaps, like girls?"

Diana, for whom that question arose in Giselle's mind every morning … and lingered, unasked, every night.

Diana, who would be moving out at the end of the month, to begin graduate school in another city.

Giselle had been caught short, as they say, on her trip home this evening. But she prided herself on being a resourceful woman, and she was determined not to be daunted by her own bladder. So she suavely diverted herself into the recesses of a vacant, semi-overgrown lot.

There, she calmly spread her legs and, yes, she peed, standing quietly with an elegant feminine dignity, her posture mistakable at a distance for the businesslike stance of a prospective developer checking out the property. No big deal, thought Giselle. It had happened before, and it would happen again. Panties into the wash when she got home, and that would be that.

As she appeared back on the sidewalk, with her soaked crotch her own discreet, warm secret, she congratulated herself on this habit she had of wearing skirts.

During the walk home afterward, the wetness felt pleasant, almost arousing. She walked more slowly than usual.

Diana was in the kitchen, a room Giselle had to pass through on her way to the washing machine—or to any other room in the house, for that matter. Giselle said a quick hello, then tried to excuse herself, explaining candidly to her roommate that she had a pair of wet panties to contend with. "I had to pee myself on the way here," she said with a comfortable laugh.

Diana's eyes seemed to look at Giselle with increased intensity, and she laughed a different sort of laugh from her friend's casual chuckle.

Where Giselle's laughter had been low-key, her roommate's was imbued with some vital energy that Giselle struggled to identify.

"I wish I'd been there," Diana said liltingly. "I bet you looked hot."

And then Diana went to her room. Five minutes later, she left the apartment to work her evening shift at the restaurant. And three days after that, the end of the month arrived, and Diana moved away.

Giselle started a new job, one that gave her the means to keep the apartment for herself. And life went on. Diana's presence was now limited to a series of affectionate "Miss you!" messages in Giselle's inbox.

When the first e-mail arrived, Giselle deliberated over whether to send more than just a chirpy "Miss you, too!" in reply. But she decided that e-mail was not the best vehicle for asking your ex-roommate if she was a lesbian, and (P.S.) asking whether said ex-roommate in fact meant to imply that she'd be turned on by seeing you wet your panties. IM didn't strike her as the ideal way to approach these matters, either.

About a month later Giselle was walking home, as usual, and once again she needed to pee. This time, it was not so urgent that she ducked into the vacant lot; but she was very much looking forward to slipping her panties down upon arrival, and taking a womanly seat for thirty seconds.

In the bathroom, when she was impatiently peeling her silk and her ass was descending sweetly into place, the vision hit her. It was a vision of Diana, standing in the open doorway and watching, her eyes blazing and her luscious lips giving voice to that electric laughter.

A sizzle ran through Giselle's body, and she cried out in unscheduled ecstasy as piss flooded across her gates. She was as surprised as she was overcome upon realizing that she was going to have an orgasm. "I bet you looked hot!" her memory shouted passionately, in Diana's voice, just as she was about to peak. When she hit that threshold of tightly coiled, shimmering bliss that is so intense a girl almost can't stand it, Giselle's feet did a drum roll on the tiles, and her legs pulled wildly against the fabric of the half-dropped panties.

It was the type of giant soap bubble of erotic pleasure that could only sustain itself for a moment before exploding; and, in another instant, Giselle was a passenger on a massive, cunt-tickling wave of sensation that resonated with the water music of her urinary flow. Then she slouched into exhaustion, her ass cheeks resting wearily on the toilet seat as her puffy pussy dripped nonchalantly beneath her.

Several more weeks passed before it became an obsession. Certainly, seeing an e-mail from Diana, however brief, always made Giselle tingle a bit. And occasionally, when she felt that other kind of tingle directing her toward the toilet, a yearning would develop in her cunt, accompanied by thoughts of her ex-roommate.

Gradually, this sort of experience became less and less occasional.

Soon, Giselle could not remember the last time she had peed without imagining that Diana was watching. It happened at work, where she stole quick pisses with the hope that no important phone calls would be missed. It happened in public buildings, where she would sometimes wait a little longer than she had to, because it made her tingle more. It happened, of course, at home, where she was now in the habit of following almost every piss with an intensive self-fingering, even before she wiped. Wherever and whenever she tinkled, she felt on some level that she was doing it for Diana.

Often, she continued to imagine that Diana watched from a doorway. But sometimes Giselle pretended that Diana was crouching right at her feet while she occupied the commode, gazing between her delicately spread thighs and looking straight into her poised crotch. She liked to imagine Diana's smiling face less than a foot away, closely observing her most feminine flesh as it experienced the critical moment at which tension melted into release.

She began to say "Oh!" aloud, whenever she let go with a stream in the privacy of her own bathroom. And she knew that "Oh!" in her inner lexicon had come to mean "Oh, Diana!" Giselle recognized that she was obsessed, that she had allowed what might have been just an off-the-wall remark by a straight chick to turn her into a compulsive, autoerotic piss freak—with a fixation on a girl now a thousand miles away. It was ridiculous, she thought at times.

And yet, there had been that look in Diana's eyes, and that hauntingly exciting laughter.

In the shower each day, Giselle fantasized that Diana was tickling and slapping her sensitive bottom, and she pretended that this was what made her insistent morning piss emerge from its sleep. As it dribbled down the insides of her thighs, she indulged the fiction that Diana's caresses had turned on her intimate tap. Giselle's knees would buckle as she gave in to the cascade. She'd moan and tweak her clit as she felt herself nourishing the bathtub with her personal water. And, swaying in sensuous ecstasy, she wished that Diana could really be there, that she could kiss Diana's darling toes with her warm river.

And sometimes, very late at night, with a beer or two welling up in her tank, Giselle would stand in the tub again, this time decked out in a short dress and panties. Here she would pretend that she was back in the vacant lot, and that Diana was there with her. But where the original moment in the vacant lot had been characterized by poise and discretion, the fantasy-charged reenactments found Giselle quivering, shrieking, and pressing her dampening self into frenzied climaxes.

When Diana took advantage of a semester break to schedule a trip back to visit friends, Giselle did not even have to offer her old room: her former roommate invited herself. In an e-mail exchange the day before she was to travel, Diana politely expressed the hope that she would not be imposing. She naturally had no idea that Giselle was masturbating herself into jelly each night at the thought that Diana would soon be in her house again.

The plane was a late one, and the ex-roommates exchanged only the minimal greetings before Diana collapsed into her former bed. Breakfast the next morning was a blur of toast, orange juice, and a little bit of catching up. Just before Giselle left for work, Diana insisted that she would cook dinner for her that night.

During the afternoon, it took a bit of planning and pacing—not to mention a cup of tea and several trips to the office water cooler—for Giselle to ensure that a stop in the vacant lot on the way home would be almost, but not quite, necessary.

Outside her door that evening, she fumbled giddily with her keys. Her knees were trembling, her ass was jiggling, and her heart was pounding.

She could hear the sounds of Diana in the kitchen, immediately within.

As the key finally connected, Giselle's thighs throbbed purposefully against each other, and Giselle noted with satisfaction that she could just barely have made it to the bathroom in time—if that had been her destination. Turning the knob, she felt tears of joy in her eyes, complementing the precious droplets that were only now beginning to drip into her panties.

She hoped it would look hot.

One Afternoon
Near Sherwood Forest

"Ah, 'tis rapture thy face to gaze upon," said Robin when his beloved met him, as agreed, in a dilapidated castle.

Marian rolled her eyes. "Puh-leez, would you knock off the 'thee thy thine' crapola! You're not even doing it right. Besides, if you wanted to be authentic, you'd have to be speaking French."

"French?"

"Yes, *French*. During the reign of Richard I, the English aristocracy still spoke the language of William the Conqueror. What do they teach you in Merry Man school, anyway?"

"You're telling me the British nobility used to speak French?"

"Not British—*English*. In the twelfth century, there was no such thing as Great Britain."

"Oh. Nonetheless, I'm glad to see you." He embraced her, and they enjoyed a passionate kiss.

"Mmm," said Marian. "Your kissing is better than your knowledge of history."

Robin smiled. "It's a good thing we're here for a liaison, and not a lesson."

"Hey, not bad—*liaison*. Very posh."

With renewed confidence, the beneficent bandit once again clasped Marian to his chest, this time squeezing her round, folkloric arse.

"Wait," said Marian, wriggling in his arms. "Before we get too involved … did you bring your friend?"

"My friend? What friend?"

"You know." Marian blushed.

"Will Scarlet?"

"No."

"Alan-a-Dale?"

"No."

"Hmm … Friar Tuck?"

"Eww—*no*."

"Well, then I don't—oh!"

Having suddenly seen the light, Robin quickly delved into his tote bag,* removed something from it, and promptly handed it to his love.

"Perfect!" said Marian, as she took the porcelain bowl from his hands. "I knew I could count on you to bring 'Little John.'"

And without further ado, she set the bowl down beneath her, lifted her skirts, and tinkled merrily before her man.

*glaring anachronism

The Woman Who Loved to Pee

I SUPPOSE I'VE KNOWN OTHER WOMEN WHO WERE AS BEAUTIFUL. But what's special about my Lydia is the way her eyes lock with mine, so as to make me feel sexually linked to her merely by being in the same room. Her very presence makes me feel warm, intimate, and naked. She's a kind, lustful spirit bursting with wholesome erotic energy—a raw sexuality that I've never encountered elsewhere. A biologist would probably tell you that I can smell her sex, unconsciously, from thirty feet away.

In addition to her general qualities of highly charged magnetism, there is a specific thing about Lydia's sexuality that puts me over the top. You see, Lydia really likes to piss. If you'd seen her, just once, spraying the grass on a sunny day, her panties at her ankles, her head flung back to share her bliss with the sky, then you'd know what I mean.

For Lydia, the standard messages from her bladder several times each day do not represent a chore or an inconvenience. They represent opportunities for pleasure. As for our sex life—well, she certainly likes fucking. But what really lights her up is peeing in front of me. And being with me when I know that she's going to pee soon—or not so soon, if she's in a "holding it for fun" mood. After she's fully indulged her urinary eroticism and exhibitionism, the intercourse, we would both admit, is a joy that's terrific, but a touch anticlimactic.

Though I'd known Lydia for about a year before the night she peed beautifully into my lap at Sandra's party, our interactions had been minimal. Oh, I had been instantly infatuated with her, all right. But she was seeing someone else for most of that year; and so, on the all-too-rare occasions on which we happened to meet, I felt obliged to interpret her friendliness as mere friendliness.

The night of Sandra's party proved revealing almost from the start. Early in the evening, I happened to overhear Lydia talking with a friend. The conversation made it clear that Lydia and her boyfriend had broken up some months back, subsequent to when I'd last seen her. A few minutes later, while I remained within earshot, their conversation took another turn. As my jaw dropped and my erection rose, I heard Lydia mention to her friend that her idea of a nice way to indulge herself at home on a Friday night was to make herself a cup of coffee, throw a couple of towels on the floor, turn up the stereo … and then chill out drinking beer, slowly, until she wet her panties.

From across the room, her eyes met mine just as she was finishing this testimonial—to which her friend responded with a predictable shriek of "Too much information!" It must have been clear to Lydia, from my expression, that I had heard everything … and had relished it.

So, about an hour later, when Lydia sought me out and quietly invited me to accompany her to Sandra's out-of-the-way upstairs bathroom, I knew more or less where things were headed. Watching her miniskirted ass lead me up the stairs, I was already immensely aroused.

She closed the door behind us, then kissed me with an ease that belied the fact that it was our first. "Hey, come down here with me," she urged. She danced me down to the tile floor and unzipped my jeans. As she squatted into position, I could now see that she wasn't wearing any underwear beneath her enticing miniskirt. I reclined, and she deftly extricated my cock from my trousers. She scooted forward with surprising grace, looking lewd and elegant all at once, cunt exposed. She straddled my lap. She let go.

A paradise of warmth overcame me. I had never experienced anything quite like it, and it was wonderful. She peed for what seemed an eternity, and my cock quivered and twitched beneath her rain. I watched in fascination as the blond water gushed and dribbled out of her and her thighs trembled with the ecstasy of release.

Afterward, her crotch glistened with the last trickling drops, which clung magnetically to her intimate flesh as she shuddered in a quasi-orgasm of muscular relaxation.

"Don't wipe," I suggested huskily. She looked unbelievably sexy with the traces of pee still ornamenting her feminine landscape, and I lifted her forward and began to lick her pussy dry. Evidently this felt very good to her; and, though she had soon been neatly tidied of pee, her other private wetness soon took its place. She clutched at my dick.

"Lydia ... why didn't you look me up sooner?" I asked in a libidinous groan.

"I don't know. I guess I'm a little shy."

"You're not acting very shy now," I smiled.

"Hmm ... no, I guess I'm not." With her free hand, she delicately touched my jeans where she had soaked them. Her eyes held a dazzling sexual charge.

She mounted me. We fucked at full throttle to a shared explosion, my hands gripping her soft ass and the wet back edge of her skirt tickling the base of my shaft.

"You know, I was thinking of you when I was in bed this morning, with my fingers inside my pajama shorts," she confided afterward. "I was really hoping you'd be here tonight."

We went home together soon after—our clothes were not really what you could call "presentable," though we were careful to make sure that Sandra's bathroom was—and we stayed up all night talking in bed ... when we weren't otherwise occupied. Lydia told me a lot of things. In addition to the more conventional topics of personal experiences, interests, and ambitions, I learned all about how much she enjoyed "holding it," and how much she enjoyed releasing it. "I tingle when I tinkle," she explained.

Secure in her knowledge that I was deeply interested, she described for me, in delicious detail, what she did in her favorite sparkling, empty department-store restrooms. Here, after deliberately spending hours browsing in a short skirt without visiting the toilet, she would hover just above the seat with her panties still on, wiggling sensuously in a moment of glorious tension and anticipation, until she was almost wetting ... and then rip the panties down to her ankles and indulge in an orgasmic-quality release. And she painted a similarly detailed picture of how at home, in the privacy of her bathroom or her backyard, she would leave the panties on and sensually water them under her skirt. Or soak herself in a pair of capris, after enjoying an orgy of leg-crossing. "There's something so *cozy* about just giving in and tinkling warmly into my snug-fitting sexy clothes, without having to pull anything down," she told me. Sometimes she would challenge herself by holding her pee in every position she could think of, eagerly awaiting whatever posture would provoke the flood on a given occasion.

And so, in the months that followed, my Friday evenings with Lydia would typically begin in a predictable, but most welcome manner—a ritualized prelude to whatever sexual adventures the weekend would bring. Lydia would show up in one of her sexiest dresses, and drink a couple of beers while we talked, listened to music, and danced. Eventually, she'd deliberately piss her knickers, while I hungrily observed the ecstasies this took her through. Then, with her hot breath on my face and my hand caressing her damp panties, she would earnestly urge me to fuck her little ass off.

As if the thought hadn't already occurred to me.

As I spent more and more time with Lydia, I was treated to plenty of evidence of—and participation in—her special passion. Sometimes, when her bladder was full, I'd watch her slowly undress and then, gorgeously naked, indulge herself in little pirouettes in front of the toilet. It was exquisite watching her savor each moment she could hold it. Then, when she was about to lose it, she would hop nimbly onto the seat like it was someone's warm, waiting lap, and water the little pond beneath her. And, always considerate, she would gradually part her legs to improve the comprehensiveness of my view. With me present, she would engage in this intimate ballet as a performance; but it made it even sexier to know that she also did it when she was alone.

And I learned to expect the soft, erotic whimper that Lydia always made when she unclenched the muscles that held her bladder closed. And again when she had finished emptying it, after relishing the exit of every drop that flowed out of her.

Some days, I saw her do her first squirt of the morning right into a pair of shorty pajamas, as she stood proudly in the shower. And sometimes, if she was first to wake up, she would lie beside me in a short, sleeveless negligee, her thighs squeezed solidly together, cherishing her unreleased morning pee. When she was on the verge of leaking, she would wake me and lead me to the bathroom. She would then hand me her feather duster and accompany me into the shower, knowing that my gentle tickles would begin, at her request, under her arms ... whence they would progress to her crotch, her thighs spreading in welcome. Here, softly brushing her delicate feminine crack, my titillations would coax her waterworks open, having courted and won her ... having saturated her entire sensory system with pleasure, prompting her to dance gingerly from foot to foot and sway her hips with enchanting gyrations.

On other occasions, she would undress completely in our living room and spend some minutes clutching her crotch, before escorting me to the bathroom. I would lift her onto the seat, her ass wriggling lasciviously in my hands. Sometimes she would sit there and continue to hold her piss, still wriggling, until I tickled her toes and the backs of her knees, and she at last abandoned her muscular control.

And on summer Sunday evenings I'd watch her strip down to her T-shirt and panties, and step out into the secluded backyard with me. She would settle down on the grass with a beer and just wait, lying still and content, until she began to rock involuntarily with her inner waves. Meanwhile, she remained otherwise passive, even when her powerful stream finally bubbled out on both sides of the thin gusset that clung to her juncture. "It's the ultimate relaxation," she informed me after one such classic display on the lawn, as she gently pressed and stroked herself

220 | Jeremy Edwards

through a haze of bliss. I noted that she didn't stay very relaxed, though, as her increasingly intense strokes across the wet gusset quickly evolved into the hottest masturbation I'd ever seen from the sidelines.

When we'd been together for about six months, Lydia and I embarked on our first road trip together. On the first day of this adventure, we found ourselves zipping along the interstate in the arms of a sunny morning.

"I'm going to want to stop and pee in a while," Lydia said after a couple of hours. Instantly, I went a little bit hard.

Within just a few miles, a service area was announced. "Shall I stop here?" I asked.

Lydia said not to. "No, don't pull over yet. I want to enjoy it for a bit."

I was aroused, but not surprised. I checked with her again when a rest area appeared, fifteen minutes later. "Keep going," she smiled. She squished herself up against the car door and half knelt on the seat, her hand subtly pressing against herself and her toes bobbing over the edge. "I'll tell you when to stop,"

Lydia purred, rocking herself, her bare heels digging into the seat. She turned her head to look out at the landscape.

It must have been another twenty miles before she spoke on the subject again. "Pull off here," she requested abruptly. We were in the middle of nowhere, but an exit ramp was coming up. I took it.

"You can stop anywhere," Lydia said. I pulled off the road alongside a mown but deserted field. The sun kissed the asphalt, and a warm, gentle breeze greeted us as we scrambled out of the car.

Lydia ran about fifty feet into the field. It was all I could do to keep up with her. She peeled her shorts and tossed them to me, grinning. Then she stretched out her hands and pulled me toward her.

"Ever been kissed hard by a girl who's about to wet herself?" As she beamed at me, I noticed how her black hair was setting off her glinting green eyes especially well this sunny morning. And how her bright aqua panties fit her deliciously.

"Not yet today," I answered truthfully.

"You'll have to let me know how it feels." She promptly grabbed me and kissed me hard, as promised, her bare, throbbing leg vibrating against my jeans.

"Electric," I said.

Lydia giggled as she took a step backward. Her thighs were pressed together and her hips were swaying sensuously. She began hopping up and down, her hand now shoved deep between her legs.

"It's so ... beautiful ... here." Lydia's speech was coming in short bursts, as her dance became frenzied. Suddenly she planted her feet immovably in the meadow, with her legs far apart. She removed her hand from her crotch and rested both palms on her thighs. Then she stood there in her cranberry jersey and aqua panties and peed for all she was worth, laughing with abandon. She slowly bent her knees down, then up, in an erotic rhythm, as a Niagara rushed through her.

While I watched the rain come down for me, without a cloud in the sky, I unzipped my jeans and openly fondled myself.

Lydia had just enough breath to talk. "Have you ever had your dick pulled by a woman who's pissing her ass off?" This time she didn't wait for an answer. As I stepped forward she took hold of my cock, while still busily watering the field beneath her.

She was still pissing hard when I came in her hand.

When at last she was done, she smoothed the soaked panties into her crotch and rubbed herself till she screamed. We both stood there, shaking.

Lydia embraced me, her saturated panties pressing warmly against my cock. I knew I was in love with the woman who loved to pee—and that this was shaping up to be a very nice trip.

Volume 5

Jodi's Jeans

THE POP STAR HAD AGREED TO THIS SPECIAL INTERVIEW WITH the sexy magazine I wrote for, on one condition: that she get to tell our readers how much she loved peeing in her jeans. My editor had given me the assignment as a favor—though she confessed she would have liked to handle it personally, had she not been stuck in the office. "I sincerely hope you'll enjoy yourself, Ted."

"I go through a lot of water," the star explained as I sat alone with her in a backstage lounge. "Which means, naturally, that a lot of water goes through *me*," she laughed. I noticed that her legs, sheathed in tight indigo denims, moved restlessly as she spoke. "And there's nothing I like more than the feeling of needing to pee when I'm in a pair of my favorite jeans.

"Sometimes, when I wake up in the morning and I'm dying for a pee, the first thing I do is wiggle some jeans on and button them up tight. Ooh, yeah. Then I get the pleasure of *un*buttoning them when I hit the bathroom thirty seconds later. It feels so sweet to peel a pair of tight jeans off my hips so I can let the water flow."

"But we understand that sometimes you leave them on."

"*Yes.* That's a special treat, and I have to plan for it." She told me that she had an old pair of wine-stained jeans that she put on whenever she was going to piss herself. The massive discoloration from the night she'd spilled her Chardonnay made them suitable for little else; to wear them under normal circumstances would have been to invite the assumption that she'd ... well, that she'd done just what she now intended to do whenever she actually did wear them. "I love the way they fit me, too. They make me feel sexy right off the bat—and then I get to pee them!

"By the way, your readers might like to know that I always wear shoes when I'm going to play 'hold it' and wet myself. Just ordinary laced shoes, old ones. I love the way they clack on the bathroom floor when I'm shuffling in place and pissing my pants. Major turn-on." She was squirming now—squirming and smiling.

"Wow," I said.

Jodi then gave me some background. "In college, my house-mates and I would sometimes have what we called a 'pee-in.' We'd have a little cookout in our private backyard, wearing nothing but our undies and drinking our fill of beer ... and deliberately holding back from visiting the bathroom. We'd take turns making up sexy stories, getting each other worked up till we were wetting our panties right and left. *Good* times, my friend. Of course later on, by myself, I discovered the hidden potential of jeans. Oh. My. God."

"Hey," she said abruptly, before I could ask another question, "I seriously have to pee. You want to come with me? I waited, in case you might." I couldn't believe my good fortune.

Without waiting for a reply, she stood up; then, noticing that someone had dropped a pen on the floor, she squatted down, knees far apart, to retrieve it. I imagined her pussy warm and open against the inside of her jeans—I imagined Jodi wetting the denim in this position, pissing her jeans just because it felt so damn hot.

"Oh, yes, please," I answered without further hesitation, as she stood up again. Incredibly, she was actually dancing for me, pivoting her round little bottom with a hand at her crotch. "Ooh!" she said. "There's a little running down my leg. Man, that feels nice. But I don't want to really soak these pants, so let's go."

I trailed behind her as she scurried to the bathroom, already undoing the buttons of her jeans en route.

"Ahh, fuck yes, that feels good," she said, almost moaning as she faced me on her toilet seat, bare-assed, relieving herself noisily.

"You can tell your readers, Ted: Jodi thinks pissing feels reeeeeeally good."

Massaging Belle

CHARLENE WANTED TO PLEASURE BELLE TILL SHE WET her pants.

"Mind if I go first?" Belle had asked, when they'd headed for the restroom together in the bar. "I'm practically peeing myself."

Charlene was sure she could see a kinky sparkle in her friend-with-benefits' eyes as she made the admission. And as Belle entered the bathroom and glanced back to say "Thanks," it was with an expressive jiggle and a sultriness in her voice. "I'll be quick," she had added with a wink.

Take your time, Charlene thought to herself with a tremble as Belle closed the door behind her. *Enjoy it.*

From that moment, Charlene's dearest, horniest, *dampest* wish was to take her friend someplace private and, assuming of course Belle liked the idea—as Charlene was all but certain she would—tenderly and solicitously *make* Belle pee herself.

Yes, she wanted to take charge of Belle when the need was brimming between her legs, and love and fondle and encourage her till she was unabashedly pissing in her pants, right before her eyes ... flooding her folds, saturating her senses, and soaking her clothing.

Yes, she was quite sure it was an idea Belle would appreciate.

—❈—

"I know how tense things are for you at work right now," she told Belle midweek. Why don't you come over on Saturday? There's a special treatment I can give you."

"Ooh, that sounds nice," Belle chirped. "Some kind of massage?"

"Something like that. Oh, and wear that body stocking of yours." Charlene had chosen this attire for Belle after much tasty consideration of various options.

On Saturday, after they'd lingered in the kitchen over two pots of tea, Charlene led Belle to the den, where she'd prepared a special "massage" area with a gym mat and towels.

"Oh, maybe I should pee first," Belle said. Again Charlene noticed a glint in the other woman's eyes. "I don't know if I'll be able to lie still after all that tea," Belle added with a giggle.

"You're not supposed to lie still for this. Don't worry, you can get up at any time—if you want to."

She had Belle lie facedown on the mat, then lowered herself onto her friend's thighs. She began to lovingly massage her buttocks.

"Mmm," said Belle, "that feels good."

Charlene continued massaging the irresistible globes, adding the occasional gentle but lusty slap, which made Belle squeal and wiggle.

"Still need to pee?" Charlene asked after a few minutes. It thrilled her to hear her husky voice involving itself in Belle's private affairs.

"Yeah, actually, I really do have to go."

"Hmm." Charlene slipped a hand underneath Belle, right into her crotch. "Tell me," she said, her voice jumping half an octave with sexual tension: "does it feel nice when I touch you in here?"

"Oh, fuck yes. Only I—" Belle squirmed gorgeously.

"So do you want me to stop? So you can get up and use the bathroom?"

"No! Damn, no, I don't want you to stop. I'm just afraid it's going to make me—"

"And what if it did?" She gave Belle's midriff a quick tickle.

Belle giggle-shrieked, and then she lifted her head to look at Charlene, her eyes wide.

"Wouldn't you like to wet for me?" Charlene whispered.

Belle moaned in assent and let her head fall back onto the mat.

Without further ado, Charlene flipped Belle over and got her thighs open.

She kissed her friend's pussy through the body stocking. She tickled the space between her slit and her anus. She methodically stimulated all of Belle's most sensitive terrain, encouraging her entire nervous system to center in on the area between her legs, sensing that her attentions would give Belle's quickly burgeoning need to pee an exquisite edge of erotic urgency. Belle writhed and whimpered with excitement.

Then Charlene unfurled herself and lay nose to nose, toes to toes upon her friend, pressing down on Belle with all her weight and pawing the lucky woman's breasts. She saw Belle's eyes pop in incredulous delight as she began to relinquish control.

"Ahh-hahaha," Belle wailed, evidently riding that precious moment where she was beginning to blissfully leak but was still thrilling by holding on.

Charlene's nipples were sharp and her cheeks felt flushed. Her breath came in aroused hisses. As Belle wet herself, Charlene saw only her friend's face—her mouth open to an oval of pleasure; "*so good, so good*," it seemed to say. But though she couldn't see what was happening farther down, she knew that the body stocking was made of the perfect material for this— that it would be letting Belle's hot release linger against her skin for the perfect amount of time before carrying it slowly toward points south, north, east and west.

Belle shivered with joy as she leaked and squirted and pumped away all that tea, and Charlene knew her friend was feeling every gush of the pee tickling along her pussy and licking down her thighs. She knew the body stocking, like a magic carpet, was escorting the liquid to the backs of Belle's knees, to the crack and rounds of her ass, and all the way down to her ankles. How sexy it must feel to be so enclosed in warm wetness, Charlene thought. She felt her friend's legs pulsating underneath her.

"Thank you, thank you," Belle sobbed in Charlene's face as she peed herself silly.

Then Belle's hand moved hurriedly to where their pelvises met; and Charlene watched her friend's features shape themselves into a beautiful scream as she rubbed herself to climax.

Beer and Orgasms

Kenny showed up promptly at nine with the six-pack.

"OK," he said with a smile, after they'd kissed hello, "I brought what I was supposed to. Now I'm ready for you to deliver on *your* half." He gave her ass a promising squeeze. "When do we start?"

His playful but earnestly enthusiastic manner was just what Lauren needed—and the fact that he was so invested in things going right for her tonight made her more certain than ever that this relationship was a good one.

On their previous evenings together, Kenny had tried so hard to help her come that she'd had to insist they stop, when she was too exhausted to go on.

"Are you sure?" he'd said the last time. "I'd be happy to stay up all night, if it will get you off. Don't be afraid to ask. Don't be afraid to ask *anything*."

But she had a better solution than exhaustion, and she'd decided she knew him well enough now to be confident he'd go along with it. "Don't be afraid to ask *anything*," she'd quoted aloud to herself, as she got her nerve up for the phone call—the call inviting him here for "beer and orgasms."

"Works for me," he'd laughed. "But what's the connection?"

"I'll explain when you get here," she'd said softly.

The connection was that Lauren's one surefire way of getting off was to let her bladder fill to a point where, under normal circumstances, she'd be running, not walking, to the nearest bathroom. But when the circumstances were "Lauren needs an orgasm without further ado," the full bladder was where the fun began. She'd discovered years ago that escorting herself into a state where she could barely hold back the flood automatically brought her into a state where she could barely hold back her climax—which was quite a contrast with her usual recalcitrant mechanics. Her clit, normally temperamental, became a wild thing whenever Lauren was so primed she had to jiggle or dance or cross her legs, or squeeze her thighs around her hand to keep from leaking.

She would relish the tension and the tickle and the sexy pressure between her legs, getting more and more aroused by the sensations—and by the secret erotic flavor of what she was doing—until she had to give in. And when she gave in, a fingertip on her button as she soaked her panties over the bathroom tiles, the ineffable ecstasy of pissing charged through her like a sports car while the stratospheric *fuck-yeah* of coming screeched like twin jet planes in her ears.

And up until tonight, she'd always done it alone.

One beer, two, two and a half, all chased with gulps of water … it was a lovely private party with this man who kissed with passion, fondled with fire, and kept her grinning every minute. The series of drinks had reliably started her squirming here on the couch, and her cunt was slick with the anticipation of what was to come—and who would be participating. She was glad she'd covered the explanations during the first round of beers. Now she could enjoy unadulterated excitement, knowing that Kenny was on board with no misgivings.

Things were reaching a point where she could hardly sit still. Clamping her thighs together corralled the urgency but made it sizzle all the more sensually, and the indirect pressure on her clit made it buzz with alertness.

"Come with me," she said, when even dancing in place astride the couch arm was no longer adequate to the situation. With a wiggling ass she led him hurriedly to the bedroom, where she'd dressed the futon in special rain gear for the evening.

Lauren had also dressed herself with care: thin peach panties stretched tight across her flesh, under a clinging minidress that she wore without a bra. She was barefoot, and Kenny tickled her toes fleetingly when she lay down with her right hand wedged into her crotch.

"Ohhhh, I have to pee," she chuckled, rolling onto her side. She'd said this out loud, in exactly this sensuous fashion, many times in the past—but never for an audience.

Kenny's cheekbones seemed to glow with lust. She watched him shed his shirt while she rocked there for him, then squealed when he dived for the bed and positioned his face by her knees.

She felt his hand under her ass—right on the taut peach cotton that pulled across her tight-lipped, pee-holding pussy. She wriggled against his palm, so close to leaking, and so moist with the juice of her excitement. His fingers teased the panties subtly down the blushing smoothness of her bottom cheeks: just a few inches down ... then back up.

With his other hand, he gently pried her knees apart. She thought she might lose it here and now ... but suddenly the warm wetness of his tongue was on her gusset, bestowing a nurturing, rolling contact that made her cunt lips tingle while it coaxed her waters temporarily into submission. She moaned into her pillow.

The beauty of it was, she could let nature take its course. Kenny was licking her vulva through the fabric, and she was letting each velvety shiver of pleasure flicker through her, while hanging on for all she was worth. There was nothing to be anxious about: she *would*, when the moment was right, drench her panties, drench them right in Kenny's beautiful face, kissing him lavishly with her intimate stream. He'd sworn to her that he was looking forward to it, and the bulge in his jeans had backed him up.

It was the *inevitability* that made this work for her, she realized in her fever of anticipation. When you had to go, you had to go, and letting go was not merely the path of least resistance, it was the certain outcome. Not like the way it was with her "ordinary" orgasms, which demanded so much effort and then didn't even consistently reward it. With a tank full of beer like this, it took major effort *not* to just open wide and pee like a river. That was why holding it was such a scrumptious game; and by the time the inevitable, mind-blowing piss finally occurred, the mind-blowing orgasm would have earned its inevitability as well.

Kenny's crotch-pleasing tongue cruised over the elastic of her gusset to lap briefly at naked thigh, and Lauren shrieked with giggles. And then it was happening. She was convulsing with release, wetting and wetting as his mouth pressed itself even more firmly to her than before, his upper lip pulsing lovingly against the answering hyperbeat of her clit. It all felt so good, she almost couldn't stand it; she screamed and grabbed fistfuls of air, pumping her hips while the warm bath of her freedom mingled with the tremors of coming.

Kenny's hands found her breasts, and he pawed hot icing onto her orgasmic cake as she twitched into aftershock mode.

The song in Lauren's nipples echoed the last exquisite spurts into her underwear.

Secret Sexy-Underwear Smile

We were in the first week of rehearsals when I walked backstage and saw Evelyn stepping into the Belle Epoque skirt. A blouse hung on the wardrobe rack behind her; clearly she'd been asked to try on both garments, in case any alterations were needed. I'd had my turn earlier, when they'd put a couple of different dresses on me, along with a period hat.

Our eyes met just as my mouth formed an involuntary *O* at the sight of my fellow cast member in her luscious underwear: matching plum-hued bra and panties, lace tickling over mesh, cut to honor her breathtaking cleavage above and almost give it all away below. The smile she flashed seemed to say, *Oops, I guess now you've seen my sexy underwear, Lara.* We were theater peeps, of course, so in theory it was no big deal. For that matter, if we'd been roommates we'd probably have seen each other this way on a daily basis—and if we'd been jocks instead of drama geeks, we'd have seen even more.

But that smile of Evelyn's conveyed a certain meaning. It suggested she was acknowledging this moment as something more noteworthy than the typical undies-in-the-dressing-room, panties-in-the-dorm-room, or naked-in-the-locker-room situation.

As for me, there was no way I could even try to shrug it off. Damn, I'd been crushing on Evelyn since we were both cast in this period farce. Right away I'd noticed how her eyes sparkled like magic—how her whole face, framed by short dark hair complete with cute little faux sideburns, was pixielike, from the elfin nose to the impish mouth to the way the hair was cut over the ears to make them look adorably pointy. Though we were in few scenes together and had little overlap in these early rehearsals, catching the occasional glimpse of Evelyn's face—and, yes, her jeans-rocking ass—had been the highlight of my first month of college. And since we hadn't yet spoken, what I privately dubbed the "secret sexy-underwear smile" was in effect the first communication that passed between us.

And the next time I saw her, she did it again. She was fully clothed as our paths crossed fleetingly in a lecture-hall corridor, but still she smiled the way she had backstage. She did the same when I caught her gaze from across the dining hall at lunch the next day.

The hope of seeing that smile again, and again, became my primary motivation to get out of bed in the morning. I fantasized that every time she smiled at me that way, she was telling me that she was wearing another set of hot lingerie—that she wanted me to know, to imagine her undressed. Which I did, night after night.

I'd arrived on campus with a high libido. No sooner had I put on a pair of fresh, dry panties each day than things would start occurring to me that overruled their fresh, dry status—thoughts about what I longed to do to all the pretty girls I'd seen around since moving in. Luckily, I didn't mind spending half my time in damp panties—in fact, it made me feel sexy. But having anticipated this general state of affairs, I'd shrewdly requested a "single" in the dorm, so I wouldn't have to compromise my freedom to masturbate as uninhibitedly as I wanted, whenever I wanted.

And since seeing Ev in her lingerie, I was cashing in on that decision like nobody's business. In the fantasy version, Evelyn froze in place when I surprised her in mid–costume change. Our eyes locked rather than just briefly meeting … and soon I had my lips on that underwear smile and my hand down the back of those ass-cradling bikini panties. Evelyn danced with delight in my fantasies, one leg still plunged into the skirt, while I fingered the crack of her scrumptious bottom.

"Mind if I sit next to you?"

I looked up from my spiral. The psych lecture was due to begin in three minutes, and I'd been trying to make sense of the frantic scribblings that were intended to represent my takeaway from the previous session.

Evelyn was smiling at me—yep, *that* smile—and already snuggling her lovely booty into the seat next door. "I had to transfer into this class because of a scheduling conflict," she explained. "When I spotted you over here, I figured this was where the cool theater chicks were supposed to sit."

I laughed. But though her warm, witty manner put me at ease on one level, the fact of her proximity—and camaraderie—during this lecture, and the lectures to come, had me in a fever of blissful anxiety. It was as if I'd suddenly been served an unbelievably alluring dessert, but I wasn't sure where to dig in.

"Perfect," I ventured. "If the lecture gets dull, maybe we can run our lines for the show."

She greeted my facetious suggestion with a naughty chuckle of approval, and despite my cautious nature I felt all my hopes encouraged.

"Seriously, though, I'm a little stressed about adding this class so late. I'm going to be begging you to share your notes." Her eyes went to my face, then to the inky chaos of my notebook.

"Such as they are," I said sheepishly. "But no begging required. I'll be glad to share."

"Spoken like true show people," said Evelyn. She high-fived me, which made me giggle. "Meanwhile," she kidded, "I'll have to start thinking about what to ask you for next."

In the hour that followed, I struggled to keep my mind on the lecture. But, under the circumstances, I was aware that my notes would be even more incomprehensible than usual.

"I'm heading this way," I said to Evelyn when we exited the auditorium, inclining my head toward the side corridor.

"The bathroom? Ooh, me too," she said with relish. "I have to pee like a bastard."

The joint had two stalls, both currently vacant. As we approached our respective venues, Evelyn reprised her line from earlier on, with a wink: "Mind if I sit next to you?"

Through the partition, I heard her tight jeans *shhh* their way down to the tops of her boots. And though I was jiggling with urgency by this point, I waited a moment, ear cocked, while she situated herself on the toilet seat. I couldn't help visualizing her with her sweet pussy exposed, slowly relaxing into a delicious tinkle. The image made me horny as fuck.

Soon I heard an angelic moan, accompanied by the sound of sprinkling liquid. The idea that this beauty was hedonistically savoring her release made lightning strokes of lust shimmer from my clit to my nipples while I bared my own bottom to piss.

I tried to do my tinkling quietly, and my effort was rewarded when I heard Evelyn utter a sensuous *"Nnnn"* of satisfaction, after she'd eked every drop out.

I swallowed with the realization that this supercrush had made me so kinky I was getting off on listening to another girl pee. Nor did I regret it for an instant. On the contrary, I wondered greedily if we'd get to pee together after every lecture. My naked thighs quivered hotly at the prospect.

If Evelyn hadn't been waiting for me, I would have brought myself off then and there in my stall. As it was, I squirmed back into my undies and slacks and joined her, flustered and aroused, at the sinks. And there was that smile again—with, I thought, a new twist: *Now you've heard me pee, too.*

The following Monday, we began rehearsing the play with more continuity—an entire act start to finish in one session, rather than discontinuous groups of scenes that happened to share the same performers. This meant I got to watch Evelyn from the wings when she was onstage and I wasn't; and when the positions were reversed, it made me tingle to think *she* might be watching *me*.

Given the genre, the script was naturally chock-full of suggestive sexual situations, and both my character and Evelyn's had
titillating scenes with their respective male lovers. When the guy
Ev was paired with gave her a lusty slap on the rump at the
end of one scene (as directed by the script), I nearly juiced my
jeans. God, how I wanted my own hands on that melon-shaped
bottom of hers.

On Tuesday we did Act II, where there were several scenes
in a row in which neither of us appeared. Ev and I stood together
offstage, watching the action—which again featured plenty of
good old farcical sex business.

At one point the director halted the run-through to change
an actor's exit, and Evelyn giggled while we stood by.

"What?" I said, intrigued.

"I was just thinking ... since my character in the play is the
lover of your character's husband ... and your character is the
lover of my character's husband ... it's almost like my character
and yours are sexually connected."

I adored the way this woman's mind worked, and yet I wasn't
quite sure I followed her logic. "You mean like through the transitive principle or something?"

Ev's eyes danced with appreciation. "Yes! Exactly. We're
sexually connected through the transitive principle."

The way she'd simply said *we* were connected—no longer
our characters—sent an erogenous tickle through me as the
rehearsal resumed.

It was one of the racier scenes, wherein yet another elegant
Parisienne was straddling the lap of her husband's best friend
while he, the husband, spoke to her nonchalantly from outside
her boudoir door. Suddenly, while I watched the lovers with
interest, I felt a warm hand on the small of my back—right
above the waistband of my pants, where my untucked jersey left
me open to the cool air. I turned my head to face Evelyn, who
was gazing at me with a gentle, confident smirk.

I was so thankful she'd taken this initiative, my eyes were
tearing up. But tears or no tears, my "this is too good to be
true" grin was interpreted, correctly, as encouragement ... and a

moment later I felt a delicate finger teasing inside my waistband.

My skin sizzled under her touch. If I could have seen my butt cheeks, they would probably have been pink with excitation, blushing sweetly on either side of my thong strap. It was funny that she was touching me precisely where I especially longed to touch her—not that I was complaining about the way things had arranged themselves. Oh, no. I was in heaven.

While I rode the thrill of letting Evelyn's fingers pinch my flesh and dip under the ribbon of fabric to trace the path of my ass crack, I thought about how she must be aroused, too. I licked my lips thinking of her nipples hardening in her fancy bra, and her pussy anointing the gusset of her yummy panties with warm, sticky driblets of nectar.

Her hand had just made its way down and under, brushing my desire-puffed pussy lips inside my own rapidly dampening gusset, when something about the dialogue onstage commandeered my attention.

"Ev!" I whispered urgently.

"Mmmm?" she answered, practically licking the response into my ear.

"Aren't you on right after this bit?"

With the adrenaline-propelled efficiency displayed by any performer about to miss her cue, Evelyn yanked her hand out of my pants, assumed a Belle Epoque posture, and transferred one hundred percent of her focus to the play. And not a moment too soon: after the very next line, she was making her entrance.

Standing there flushed and dripping with arousal—once again—I remembered that this scene was immediately followed by another one involving Evelyn. This, in turn, was followed by one of my own scenes—at the end of which the act would conclude. We had at least twenty minutes to go, not counting director's comments. But I was determined, not disappointed. I just had to make it through the rest of this rehearsal, with my pulsing clit and my gaping pussy lips, and then get Evelyn back to the privacy of my room.

And now that I was certain she wanted what I wanted, I shed my inhibitions. As soon as the director released us, I grabbed Ev by the hand, making it clear I was on a mission. Her face glowed with excitement as she hastily scooped up her books and allowed me to lead her out into the hall—and then into the night.

She giggled again as we skittered across the quad to my dorm. "What's gotten into you, Lara?"

"The intention of getting into *you*, that's what."

"Oh, my!" she laughed. She broke free and dashed ahead of me—straight toward my building—as if even my hurried pace wasn't fast enough for her now.

We were both out of breath when we got up to my room, but neither of us seemed to want a break in the action.

"I think this scene calls for a costume change," said Evelyn.

And while I stood there, still clutching my keys, she began to walk back and forth in front of my bed—unbuttoning her blouse, then unsnapping her jeans, so that soon she was striding to and fro with open shirt and open pants, her lingerie shown off in seductive slivers.

Then, with a dramatic flair, she stopped her pacing, looked right at me, and swiftly shed the top and jeans altogether.

It was a different set of undies that now showcased Evelyn's intimate treats, but they were designed in the same boudoir spirit as the other ensemble, with the same revealing cut and lacy trim. This set was sea green rather than plum—and boy was I eager to dive into the surf.

"Do you always put on such sexy underwear?" I managed through my ogling.

Evelyn gave me the smile. "Not always. But I own a lot of it, and I've been wearing the good stuff every day lately."

"Oh. Any special reason?"

She burst out laughing. "What do you *think*, Lara?"

"Okay, I'll tell you what I think: I think I'm going to die if I don't get to touch your cute ass soon."

She turned three-quarters to wiggle it at me, and I let my keys drop to the floor. "Well then *what*, my dear, are you waiting for?" she asked. It was a line from the play—and never better delivered than at this moment.

I think *tackle* is the only word for what I did to Evelyn at that point. We landed together on the bed, yours truly sprawling on top, one hand already on her dreamy behind. I became a wild thing, pawing her juicy round cheeks and then also nibbling them—both above the low-cut waistband and below the elastic from which the delectable globes protruded. I was straddling her left leg, rubbing my aching pussy against her thigh through my thin cotton slacks. Fuck, she was delicious.

"Wow, you're a tiger," Ev shouted between giddy erotic shrieks as I tickled and slapped her buttocks.

I answered her with a finger in her flirty gusset, a finger that went straight for her honeypot. I humped her thigh harder as the digit worked its way into her, giving my clit some nice friction—and this made me even crazier with lust.

With my right hand busy as ever on her ass, Ev was sensibly taking care of her own nipples, which she'd popped out of the bra. "Yeah, fuck me, Lara, fuck me," she sang rhythmically, while she tweaked herself exquisitely left and right.

I made her writhe in ecstasy for a while on our little plateau. Then, sensing it was time to take things to the next level, I added a second finger to Evelyn's cunt, and I abandoned her ass so I could put my other hand to work on her diamond-hard clit. Judging from the way she moaned when I touched it, the tiny jewel was about as ready to trip the monster-orgasm switch as my own clitty was.

Things were happening fast, and I literally growled—yeah, like a tiger—a few seconds later, when Evelyn clenched her cunt around my hand, pressed my other one as tightly as possible to her button, and screamed a musical "Oh!" that was as round and beautiful as her derriere. I came like hell as she convulsed beneath me, wetting the back of her thigh with the pussy-soaked crotch of my pants.

I collapsed with Ev still under me, all the sexual tension of the past couple of weeks finally broken—at least for the moment. She wriggled sinuously, and looked up at me with her pixie eyes.

"Well," she said, "I knew I was going to major in theater, but now I know what my minor is."

"Really?" I said. It seemed an odd choice of conversation topic for this particular time. "What?"

"Math," said Evelyn. "Now that I fully appreciate the importance of the transitive principle."

I tickled her bottom again and she rolled both of us over, so that she was flattening me against the bed. I closed my eyes in anticipation as Evelyn eased my slacks and panties down, wondering what form of pleasure was in store for me.

The awareness of an elfin tongue between my legs gave me my answer.

Brief Sprinkles

ONE

My friend the erotic ballet dancer (tutu yes, leotard no) bursts through the dressing-room door in the brief interval she's offstage.

Her eyes meet mine only briefly before she has one foot expertly poised on the rim of the naughtily rococo chamber pot we keep handy, her tutu lifted with one hand, and her naked pussy lips spread by the fingers of the other.

Her bare breasts bob as she pisses powerfully, straight down. She "*Oh!*'s" several times with sensuous relief.

How I wish I could have the thick rope of Katia's pee rushing down onto *me*.

Looking again my way upon finishing, she winks but does not wipe. The door clatters shut behind the ass-flare of the tutu as she exits toward the stage.

Two

They both knew she intended to wet herself, to drench the pretty panties under her mid-length skirt. "I haven't had a good pants-wetting in ages," she'd said to him over their beers.

Yes, it had been so long since she'd treated herself to a panty-wetting, even alone … gulping the iced tea and the beer … jiggling around the house, crossing and uncrossing her legs, clasping her cunt and jutting her ass out … disco-dancing across the room while downing those final gulps … then finally shimmying in place with her knees bent until she dissolved into a paradise of hot, wet release, pissing uncontrollably on the kitchen floor.

Ah, a panty-wetting: there was nothing like a bath of hot pee from her pussy to turn ordinary panties into super-sensual pleasure panties, she'd learned.

Moving restlessly around the living room now, rearranging books and LPs, she let her ass bounce and a free hand visit her crotch. Her lover watched her crouch to look at something on the lowest bookshelf; she purred suggestively, as if toying with the idea of peeing then and there. But he knew she'd wait, wait until she lost control.

The insistent tickle between her legs was the most delectable of distractions. It was a sexy counterpoint to every thought and action: *I should turn the air-conditioning on. I have to pee. There, I think all the windows are closed now. Ooh, I have to pee …* And, physically, her constant motion was a dance whose every step was choreographed by the tide she was keeping back.

Eventually, they both knew, she'd begin to pee with her thighs still tightly crossed, leaving mere cracks for the warm liquid to trickle down. But shortly after that—they both knew—she'd be squatting spread-legged on the floor, her pee shower cascading fiercely through the underwear.

And he would have his head under her mid-length skirt, so that he'd be able to see her, really see her, wet her panties.

Three

"Hello? Oh, hi, babe. I'm just walking in the door."

I can hear the taut, efficient edge in my fiancée's voice, and I'm pretty sure I know which room she'll make a beeline for. Cynthia likes to make good time on the highway, and I bet she's been holding it all the way since New York.

"So, yeah, I looked over those notes about the property," she tells me. "I want to look at them more carefully once I get settled, but I think I agree with pretty much everything you said."

I hear the squeak of a door—our bathroom door, I presume. Her voice, when it continues, retains the clipped tightness in its timbre but comes to me now with the different dynamics of a small, windowless room. I close my eyes and try to visualize the exact moment when her bared ass connects with the toilet seat.

"Can we talk more about this when you get back on Thursday?" she asks.

"Sounds good." I deliberately keep my responses brief, not only because I don't want to miss what's coming, but also because I'm getting too aroused to speak well.

Having had the privilege of watching on occasion, I can see all in my mind's eye: My long-legged beauty—I picture her tonight in tall boots, bare legs, short skirt, white underpants— nearly ready to coax herself open, after clamping herself shut all the way home. Her furry pussy tensed while she squirms on the seat with her panties at her knees, readying herself, until the seal is broken. Her little pee hole then cracking open, to relieve itself in a trickle, a sprinkle, and then a forceful river.

How better to see the woman one loves let her hair down?

"Awesome," Cynthia is saying.

And there it is: the relaxed purr in her voice, telling me that my darling is peeing.

FOUR

"Let's do something different," Eleanor says. "You sit first."

She situates me on our big vinyl armchair, then unzips my fly to expose a good section of my briefs.

She reaches under her skirt and strips off her panties. Gyrating with her urgency, she goes to the kitchen, and returns with a tall glass of water. "This is sure to put me over the edge," she says.

Usually she has me sit on top: she waits until she really has to pee, and then she pulls me onto her lap. In that version of the game, Eleanor craves the weight of my body bearing down on her, pushing her hot bottom into the vinyl cushion and smother-ing her pussy into an airtight world of warm, wet, seeping release between her clenched thighs … of panty-soaking rapture aching its way through her crotch.

But this time she straddles my lap, letting her naked, tingling pussy press itself against the soft cotton of my underwear, squeezing her own softness against my increasing hardness.

Then she lifts the glass to her lips, and drinks deeply.

Five

Something in Lucille's sexual makeup made her yearn to tickle the bare asses of other women— elegant yuppie women whose scrumptious bottoms longed to be exposed and titillated … women who would make dates to come to Lucille's apartment on the promise of being pleasured specifically in this fashion. She loved the ways they'd dress for it—sometimes knickerless under their skirts, or with low-cut panties that revealed much of the upper portion of their cheeks, and plenty of the crack. One beauty had worn special mesh panties with a generous moon of flesh exposed; it made Lucille wet just to remember.

Sometimes they'd ask whether she minded if they peed a little, into their panties or down their creamy thighs, if they couldn't help themselves in the wriggling abandon of arousal and giggles. Of course Lucille didn't mind these dainty squirts. She would, literally, lap it up.

At the party this evening, she was looking around at all the women, wondering how many of them, in theory, might like to have their Friday night improved by getting their asses tickled. Oh, how she'd love to have every one of those eager women bottomless, if only she had enough hands.

And how wonderful, she thought, that all these women needed to pee sometimes. Tickling and peeing went so well together, in Lucille's opinion, and she fantasized that all these beautiful women here felt the same way. Though camping was not Lucille's thing, she visualized the whole group of them crouching outdoors to display their gorgeous feminine behinds, all in a circle, their faces stretched gloriously in ecstasy as their tight, naked slits opened to gush fresh piss in high-pressure fountains. She imagined fondling a bottom while this lady here, or that lady there, squatted and peed on the ground, with shorts and panties at her ankles—supporting the lady's silk-smooth derriere cheeks with her palms as her thumbs tickled the crack, her ears savored the giggles, and her eyes watched the stream splash crazily down.

Lucille would make sure she took somebody home tonight.

Six

In her short skirt, she seats herself on the metalwork bench in her hallway, where she holds on, cross-legged, until she starts slowly dripping through her panties.

It collects on the floor beneath her in what remains a rather small puddle. Yes, she's slowly, slowly leaking for me.

When she gives the signal, I embrace her, my right hand firm against her damp underwear, and carry her to the shower. Here I pull aside the panties to reveal the wet hairs and the patient, fiercely aroused vulva. Here I finger her lips and coax her to let go; and she pisses heartily like a fountain until, finished at last, her pussy celebrates its relaxation in sensuous aftertwitches.

Seven

He'd moved a stack of folders to see if his colleague had the report he needed on her desk—and, before he could avert his eyes, they'd involuntarily absorbed the contents of the personal-ad printout that the files had hidden:

> *Woman seeks encounter(s) with man, woman, or couple who, with her advance input and most enthusiastic consent, will engineer a safe, private situation that will culminate with her wetting her pants in front of them. She can promise she'll give a great display, and enjoy every minute of it—no tears or whimpers from this gal, just lots of super-hot leg-crossing, thigh-squeezing, groin-clamping, booty-squirming fun, and the sexiest jeans-soaking you've ever seen.*

He limped back to his own office, red in the face and rigid in the groin, knowing he'd spend the rest of the day wondering whether his friend was the author of the ad, or a respondent.

EIGHT

She waits until she's jonesing for a pee, then she changes into her favorite shift, sandals, and nothing else, save the remote vibrator. She gives Gerald the controls.

She sets herself the task of emptying the dishwasher while being teased by the twin tickles of the piss knocking at her between-the-legs door and the short, unpredictable sizzles of face-flushing euphoria whenever Gerald flicks the switch.

She's confident that long before the dishwasher has been cleared, she'll be orgasming over the floor with her legs apart and her sandals planted squarely on the tiles, wetting herself ferociously—her naked self, no panties—and howling with the interwoven ecstasies that have overtaken her.

NINE

With her nipples exposed to the cool air, and the warm jets of the hot tub pulsing through her skin-tight panties onto her vulva and the cleft of her ass, Dina is in heaven.

She repositions herself a hair, and now the jet servicing her pussy catches her clit at the geyser's fringes. As she wiggles with pleasure, Dina realizes that she needs to pee—and, alone in her private hot tub, that there's nothing to stop her from doing so.

The massage provided by the high-pressure water, in front and behind, continues to push her toward orgasm. And the saturated cling of her panties feels increasingly sensuous in its own right.

And, oh yes, she has to pee. She can't help it now, she's going to piss ... piss right into the water, right through her clinging panties, piss deliciously even as the jet nudges her clit over the edge and she screams in climax, bobbing her hips and coming and letting go and wetting the water, wetting everything, and coming and coming and dancing her ass crack up and down the rear jet.

TEN

Diane sits on Dave's lap in her kimono, the pout of her

underwear warm against his trousers.

She wiggles intimately against him as they watch the erotic film, with its scenes of lovely women frolicking and kissing and tickling and sometimes even wetting for each other. She's getting turned on—and she's holding her pee.

Eventually Dave feels the first hot dribbles as Diane starts to leak slyly onto his erection. For quite some time she slowly drizzles pee into her undies.

Then he rolls the wetted knickers down her thighs, and she begins to bounce with arousal—still spending her tension by increments, in squirts of piss that splash onto his crotch each time she lifts her bared bottom. It makes him wild to know how wet and aroused her pussy is.

And then she is glued to his lap again, absolutely flooding him, her eyes still locked on the screen, her ass so snug against his thighs.

ELEVEN

Meg peed as quickly as she could, she was that excited to get back to her date. And with her vulva tingling with the sensitivity of the early stages of arousal, the experience of pissing turned her on even more.

She was tempted to finger her lips as she finished—but in fact she hastened so to return to the party, she forgot even to wipe. She realized it as soon as she stood up, feeling tickles of warm pee striping her gusset; and though she thought of making a belated effort to clean up, she liked the idea of presenting herself this way—lightly marked for Alan with dabs of her own aroused urine, the intimate aroma of fresh pee perhaps faintly detectable by the nostrils of her new lover.

As they cuddled with their drinks and Meg enjoyed the raunchy, secret wet places on her most private flesh, she imagined peeing again later, in her apartment—and then hurrying back to bed to offer her unwiped pussy to Alan's face. Would he relish the tangy taste of the woman who has peed but not wiped?

She couldn't wait to find out.

TWELVE

From the exquisite sensation of dribbling a few spurts of relief down her panty hose while still in the car, to the ecstasy of parting her legs in her driveway and flooding the clinging nylon with hot piss, Marilyn knows what she likes.

This evening, after work, her bladder has filled while she's been speaking to her lover on her kitchen phone. So Marilyn lets the piss start to drip sensually into her knickers—precious little squirts from between clenched thighs—letting it well up in her panties and stimulate her clit.

She ekes out the release from inside the clutch of her business skirt. While she wets, her rocking ass is wedded to the vinyl of the desk chair at her phone table.

Now she's leaking rivulets along her thighs. By the time they get to their goodnights, the pee will be coursing briskly into her panty hose and she'll be coming in her panties, peeing and coming to the sound of her lover's voice.

It's when she first hears the sound of her splashing that she knows there's no turning back. She is not merely wetting her panties, not merely drenching her tights ... Marilyn is puddling the very floor beneath her.

Mentioned in Pissing

WE'D BEEN DATING ABOUT FIVE MONTHS WHEN ESTELLE mentioned in passing that she wanted to pee on me.

"OK," I shrugged. The idea didn't give me a hard-on, but it didn't repulse me. It sounded interesting, in a way.

"We could do it tonight, if you're up for it," she said.

I nodded, and she ordered herself another beer.

As she began to fidget in her chair, I asked if she'd ever peed on a guy before. A couple of times, she said. She smiled, and flicked her long hair out of her face, and said I couldn't possibly imagine how much she was looking forward to doing it to me.

She wanted me to understand that it wasn't a dominance thing, or extremes for the sake of extremes, and I said I figured, I could tell that. She simply found it ultra-sexy, in a way I personally didn't but could still comprehend.

After a while, though, as Estelle wiggled her way through that beer, I started to visualize her nude from the waist down with lots of pale pee gushing out of her—and damned if it didn't get me a little hard, especially imagining her face contorted in crazy pleasure while she did it. And I started to think about what the warmth of it would feel like on my body, as it splashed down from her sexy pussy.

Back at her place half an hour later, we stripped naked and she stood over me. She sweetly asked if it was OK if she peed all the way up to my chest. I said that sounded nice, and by this point it all really *did* sound nice. The prospect of her torrents pouring uncontrollably onto my cock and balls, in particular, was getting me going. By now I'd have been seriously disappointed if Estelle had suddenly called the whole thing off. It was turning out I was into this, and I wouldn't want to be stood up for some porcelain bastard of a toilet.

I flattened my bony self into the towels she'd laid out. Estelle chortled as she struggled to hold on a few seconds longer, clutching herself between the legs, asking me if I was ready. She was totally in position, and her eyes were huge with excitement.

She stretched herself open, and my heart thumped.

Waiting

Glenda is waiting patiently for the café's restroom.

No, *patiently* isn't the word. Glenda waits more than patiently. Glenda, in fact, is relishing the wait, savoring the intimate pressure that tingles in the gusset of her panties.

She makes eye contact with the skinny, shaggy guy who is the only person ahead of her. He's standing to the side where she can see his face, and she smiles at him. He grins affably, and she winks.

Yes, my tea went right through me, and now I really have to pee—and I'm rather enjoying it. Does that turn you on, cute shaggy stranger?

She hopes by this time he's visualized her with her pussy bared, emptying furiously, her whole body reverberating with shocks of pleasure.

Or maybe he'll guess that since no one else is in line, she'll let it out slowly, wallowing sensuously in the gradual release, before wildly finishing herself off, fingering her unwiped pussy to a luscious post-piss orgasm.

He's quite a cutie, Glenda notes. And now she imagines that instead of standing in this corridor, she's standing outside his door, dressed to impress in a miniskirt and a thong that she's about to soak. *Hot guy opens door to knicker-wetting vixen.* The scenario almost makes her pee herself then and there; yet still she's delighting in the urgency, the squirmy horny tension, the tickle.

The word *tickle* resonates in her mind. She wonders if this guy likes to tickle girls. Her bottom cheeks prickle with arousal as she contemplates having her tits pleasured with a feather while she wriggles on a toilet, or her ass crack gently titillated till she pees all over this cutie's lap.

The fantasies make her shiver, and a dribble of pee leaks out. She pretends the stranger's face is between her thighs, his nose pressed tightly to her panties, sniffing the aroma.

The restroom is free. "Would you like to go ahead?" he asks.

"Thanks, that's OK. I'll wait."

Now that she's alone, Glenda indulges her exhibitionistic expressiveness. She swivels her hips, bends her knees, even forces a hand between her legs. It feels so sexy to sizzle right on the verge of losing it, a breath away from giving in and letting the insistence of the liquid overtake her . . .

Very soon he emerges.

Though Glenda regrets the mopping up that will be necessary, she does not regret what she's about to do. She's sure that if the baristas could envision the intensity of her ecstasy, they would not begrudge her the cleanup. Their tip jar, she has noticed, currently has a lone dollar in it. Before she leaves, it will be augmented by a twenty.

"See?" she says with a grin. "I waited."

He smiles back, holding the door open. But Glenda stays put and lifts her skirt—making sure the stranger's eyes have traveled to her lavender panties before she proceeds.

"I waited ... for *you*."

She trembles with excitement as the flood comes.

Holding Forth

Though I hadn't exactly planned things this way, talking to Melanie about Alice that night in Toronto proved to be a door-opener—an opportunity to reveal my growing fascination with a little kink that, for whatever reason, I hadn't yet mentioned to my wife.

We'd both arranged to get out of work at noon so we could profit from an early start on our eighth-anniversary getaway. Now, after relishing the inaugural vacation-flavored drinks and dinner, we were back in our hotel room, naked in bed. It was foreplay time, and I'd volunteered to share a fresh fantasy.

"I saw Alice again today," I explained. "But let me start by asking you something about her…"

"Hey, I didn't know there was going to be a quiz!"

I managed to catch the pillow Mel had thrown at me. "It's only one question, and it's not even a trick one. Have you ever noticed how Alice always announces when she needs to pee—in so many words?"

"I don't think so."

"I mean, when we're all out having dinner and she gets up to go to the restroom, she doesn't say 'Excuse me,' or 'I'll be right back,' but always 'I need to pee.'"

"No, I guess I haven't ever noticed."

"Well, I have. And … I think it's sort of sexy."

Melanie appeared mildly intrigued. I continued.

"So the other night, after we'd been out with her, I found myself visualizing her when she has to pee … like, actually pulling down her pants in the bathroom." Just saying it made my heart speed up.

"OK." Mel was waiting to hear what came next.

"And then this morning, she came into the museum to show me some proofs. I was on the phone, and while she waited she was checking out one of the new exhibits near my desk.

"Uh-huh…?"

"She was wearing boots with her jeans, which made those elegant legs of hers look that much longer … and when she stood there with her back to me for a minute, lingering over one of the photos, she was kind of bending one leg up behind her."

"I can see Alice in that pose."

"It was pretty hot. Likely she was doing it just to stretch or something … but I automatically imagined that she had to—um—"

"Pee?" said Melanie helpfully. The word, in her feminine voice, sent my arousal up another notch.

"Yeah, maybe she had to … pee, I was thinking, and this gymnastic act was her way of masturbating off of that—you know, her personal flavor of the 'I'll hold it a little longer' fidget."

I swallowed, very conscious of my aching hard-on, which now bobbed up from my lap. "Is that at all sexy to *you*, Mel?" I asked, feeling exposed.

She pursed her lips thoughtfully and shrugged. "Maybe a little."

I could tell this was fact, not understatement. Melanie wasn't going to get seriously turned on by contemplating a woman holding her pee; but at the right moment she might feel a slight buzz. *I'll take it*, I said to myself.

"So anyway … during the drive up here this afternoon, while you were napping, I started to spin this fantasy where Alice and I both have to pee, and—well—for some reason we have to share the restroom."

"Ooh."

Now she was definitely becoming more interested. She spooned herself more tightly to my flank, so that I could feel the loving pressure of her mound against my hip.

I clasped her left bottom cheek. As the fantasy gripped me anew, the tale came with less hesitation.

"I stand aside for Alice, but she insists that I go first. She's clutching herself—she really has to go—but she says that she gets off on holding it. And she further confesses that she gets off on watching a guy piss *while* she's holding it.

Melanie began stroking my cock.

"So I go first. And as I piss into the toilet, I turn my head to look at Alice. She's jiggling and dancing, and intently watching my stream. I finish up quickly and gesture that it's her turn—but she makes a detour to the sink. Clearly, it's an excuse to hold it even longer."

"Why that kinky vixen," said Mel with a throaty chuckle. I felt an extra quiver of excitement in my gut at this sign that she was joining more actively in the fantasy.

"She smiles at me in the mirror; and meanwhile her ass, which juts out toward me now, gyrates while she takes her time checking her makeup—she can't stand still. Her bottom looks unbelievable wriggling around in those jeans."

"Wow, sweetheart, you're so aroused."

I grunted in agreement. "Finally Alice takes her turn at the toilet. Her jeans and panties are rolled down to her boot tops. She's very graceful about it all. Her thighs are squeezed shut—but I can hear her tinkling, loud and clear. Fuck, Mel, she's pissing right in front of me, looking straight at me and sighing with pleasure."

"It must feel soooo good for her to let it flow," Melanie observed sensuously, fondling my shaft with increasing vigor.

"Ohhh, yes. But even though I know that, I *ask* Alice if it feels good. I guess it's a way to … participate."

"Why not? It's your fantasy." She rubbed herself against me.

"Yeah," I said huskily. "And Alice replies, 'Ooooh, baby,' with a wink and a wiggle. She keeps peeing for a long time, and I—"

My wife sat up abruptly. "Time out! Damn, Lawrence," she laughed, "you know what they say about the power of suggestion."

She hopped out of bed and tiptoed toward the spacious en suite bathroom.

And then, with my cock pointing after the round of Mel's derriere, I heard myself speak a question I'd wanted to ask for so long.

"Can I watch?"

The Gilded Fountain

A FEW DAYS AFTER STEPHEN AND JOCELYN OFFICIALLY BECAME engaged, Jocelyn revealed that she had a weekend treat in mind.

"I belong to a private club," she said casually, "and I'd love to bring you as my guest on Saturday."

"That sounds delightful," said Stephen.

"I think you'll like it there. I hope so, anyway."

Jocelyn's club was housed in an impressive eighteenth-century building in a quiet street. The moon came out from behind clouds just as the couple arrived, and its glow gave the staid facade an exciting aura of promise.

They were elegantly attired. "There's no specific dress code," Jocelyn had explained. "Most people just find something dramatic or glamorous to wear—you'll see why. Everyone looks so interesting."

This was one of several hints Stephen had been given that there was more to this evening out at the club than met the eye. He was intrigued: what exotic world would his ever-fascinating Jocelyn be showing him here? She was hip to so many marvelous and unusual things. He'd resisted the impulse to ask a lot of questions, as he sensed that surprise was part of what Jocelyn intended him to experience. And he wanted to experience everything she had in store for him.

She was wearing a glittery, copper-colored blouse that brought out the humor in her eyes and interacted felicitously with her tiny gold earrings. A short but classy black skirt, stockings, and basic black heels completed her ensemble.

Stephen was wearing his tux, at his fiancée's request. "You're so delicious in it," she'd opined. "It makes me want to do special things to you." After that provocative comment, he had required no further persuasion.

The building's interior had obviously been redone in the twentieth century. The foyer blended elements of Art Deco, postwar Italian design, Renaissance sculpture, and contemporary-nightclub neon in a way that defied overall categorization but nevertheless worked. The effect was that of highly aesthetic, cultured decadence.

"Very nice," said Stephen sincerely. Jocelyn beamed and took his hand.

The first thing Stephen saw, as they exited the foyer through an archway, was a strikingly attractive woman in a sleeveless silk top and a jeweled necklace. Stephen was surprised to note that she was naked from the waist down—and even further surprised to note that she was engaged in pissing voluminously, from a standing position, into an ornate marble basin. Woman and basin were both situated atop a pedestal.

"Oh! We seem to have wandered into the ladies' room," he sputtered to Jocelyn, groping for the best explanation he could find.

"Welcome, darling," Jocelyn responded with a smile. "This place is *all* ladies' room."

"What?" As perplexed as he was, he didn't take his eyes off the unanticipated spectacle before him. The woman and her stream were captivating, together comprising a dazzling, kinetic display of feminine beauty.

"This is my club's raison d'être, Stephen." Jocelyn was whispering now, as if to avoid intruding on the public privacy of the woman—though she, too, was staring at the performance. "It's a place for women like me to indulge a taste for erotic, exhibition-istic peeing." She took a deep breath. "Are you shocked?"

Frozen in place, Stephen had to think about this. "Not in a bad way," he replied at last. The phrase "women like me" was reverberating in his mind.

He noticed that the pissing beauty's fingers were very active:

she was not only manipulating her lips so as to guide and shape her stream; she was also masturbating. Just as Stephen made this observation, the woman shrieked. She threw her head back, eyes closed and pussy still flowing. She was having an orgasm.

"What did you say the club was called?"

"The Gilded Fountain."

Stephen finally tore his gaze from the orgasmic pisser so he could proceed further into the club with Jocelyn.

In a corner up ahead to their right, where two complementary floral wall hangings met, a pair of nude, curvaceous women with Botticellian blonde hair were titillating each other everywhere with peacock feathers—and peeing heartily. And to the left stood a glamorous, rock-and-roll-style woman in a red vinyl miniskirt, who was surrounded by a group of male and female admirers and who clearly needed to spring a leak soon. She was rocking in place with her legs crossed, and pressing herself through the front of her skirt in a completely uninhibited manner. Far from looking unhappy while she held back her water, her lipstick-vivid face instead showed intense enjoyment, and her dark eyes sparkled lewdly at her fans. Stephen could see her erect nipples straining the thin cotton of her black T-shirt.

Focusing on this woman's face, Stephen remembered seeing a similar expression on Jocelyn's on one occasion, when the two of them were walking briskly home from the park because she needed the loo. Jocelyn had been on the brink of wetting her knickers, but she'd seemed to relish every minute of it—as if the cajoling tickle of holding it were foreplay for the orgasm of release.

Recalling that incident, he better understood why they were here. This organization was a magnet for erotically sophisticated women who found refined sexual delight in the rarefied sensations of holding, then dramatically releasing, their pee, in a variety of imaginative and visually astounding scenarios. Within these walls, their fetish could flower into a wonderfully bizarre genre of decadent performance art.

Nor, in this context, was piss-holding a source of distress, or public peeing a misadventure. No, these women were totally, cheerfully in control of their own kinky indulgences, expressing their femininity through their pee games … engineering themselves into squirming excitement and free-flowing ecstasies.

And Jocelyn was one of them.

The appearance of a team of three efficient employees—dressed as Victorian chimney sweeps, but with mops, buckets, towels, hoses, and spray bottles instead of brooms—answered Stephen's next question before he had a chance to voice it. Where the peacock-feather ladies had just finished frolicking, the crew got to work, and soon the entire area was pristine and florally fragrant.

"They have everything arranged here to a T," commented Jocelyn. "That's why the cover charge is so high."

Stephen continued to take it all in.

"Ooh, look," said Jocelyn, pointing at a man whose lingerie-clad girlfriend had backed him against the wall, where she passionately embraced him, grinding her pelvis into him while peeing her panties. "Nice kiss-and-piss there."

There was evidently some lingo to be learned, Stephen reflected, as he studied the woman's pleasure-enlivened ass.

"Let's have a drink, shall we?" Jocelyn suggested.

As they moved toward the bar, Stephen caught the rock-and-roll girl in his peripheral vision, wetting the floor with her knees bent as her laughter echoed off the ceiling. Right before he and Jocelyn rounded a corner, the rockin' wetter turned her face his way and winked.

It was difficult for him to concentrate on the drinks menu, for several reasons. First, behind the bar flowed a large artificial brook, the centerpiece of an expansive "outdoors"-themed adult playground. Various women, in various postures, were positioned along its banks, astride boulders projecting from the water, and even on a bridge. Some lifted their fashionable skirts to empty themselves; some had tailored slacks and silk panties halfway down their legs, and derriere cheeks proudly exposed, so they could piss ambitious, male-style arcs into the water; and some simply dampened their designer bathing suits as they danced in ecstasy on the shore. Nearby, women in crisp linen shorts played table tennis and croquet, all challenging themselves to make shot after shot while nursing their full bladders, each jiggling evocatively in place during her idle moments.

Nor did the bar's seating area represent a break in the entertainment. Almost every stool was occupied by a leg-crossing, crotch-clutching woman with a drink—all of them glowing with mischief as their bottoms wiggled and their feet twitched.

Immediately to Jocelyn's right, a redhead with a lager in hand was busily puddling her bar stool, her hips pumping in a high-quality business skirt, her panty hose glistening where trickles ran down them. She looked Jocelyn's way and grinned at her.

Stephen had never been so aroused in his life—and it was a revelation to him. If someone had asked him, the day before, if he appreciated the sight of a woman pissing, his response would have been a low-key assent like "Sure, I guess." And if he'd been asked whether it was titillating to him to contemplate a woman feeling the need to pee, he would have said something along the lines of "Yes, I suppose, as long as she's not uncomfortable." But no one had ever asked him these questions, and he'd never given these matters much thought: never given much thought to sensuous women who had to pee and deliberately hovered on the edge awhile … or horny women who intentionally wet their knickers … or remarkable women who had powerful climaxes from pissing in front of others. And now he'd been given all of this on a silver—no, a *golden*—platter, and he was incredibly turned on.

Jocelyn was glancing at his lap and smirking. "Sexy, isn't it?" she asked.

"Oh, god." He swallowed, and it took him a moment to say more. "You know, I couldn't have imagined London held so many women with these particular appetites."

"A few of them come in from the suburbs," Jocelyn allowed.

While Stephen had been absorbing the scene around him, she had ordered for them—scotch for him, and a pint for her.

"Cheers," she said.

"Yes, cheers!" said Stephen, thinking of the effect an evening of beer drinking always had on her metabolism.

"Would you like to see more of the club?"

He indicated that he would indeed, and so they grabbed their drinks and left the bar.

The next room used a shifting landscape of fluorescent lighting and a soundtrack of chill-out music to create an otherworldly mood. And here the carnival of erogenous pissing continued, now familiar in its theme but ever stimulating in its variations. A kneeling man in 1960s paisley and beads held his lover's vintage minidress up at the rear, kissing her all over her bare bottom while she peed straight into the panties at her knees. Not far from them, a muscular woman squatted over mirrored floor tiles, gyrating her hips and fondling her own breasts through her lace teddy. As Stephen and Jocelyn walked by her, she reached between her legs, cleaving the split crotch of her matching panties, then cleaving her own fleshy lips. She poured like a spigot, managing all the while to churn her pelvis athletically in time to the music.

Jocelyn spoke wetly into Stephen's ear. "I have to go, too," she said. Her pint glass was nearly empty.

Stephen smiled. "I believe you've come to the right place."

She squeezed his hand. "I'm not going to do it yet. I'm going to wait, until the release will blow my mind. But I wanted you to know. I want you to be thinking about it. I want you to be watching me as the need becomes more pressing, waiting for me to do something about it—and wondering, with a club full of opportunities, how exactly I'll choose to do it when the time comes."

As she finished her monologue, they arrived outside a majestic set of inner doors.

"Let's go into the theater," said Jocelyn. "It's almost time for the show." She gestured toward a poster.

"'Tonight at 9:00, Maggie performs her trademark piss-tease act,'" read Stephen aloud. "What in the world is a 'piss-tease' act?"

"You'll see."

The cabaret within the club was, like everything else, lavishly and artistically decorated. Red velvet hung everywhere, and the tables and chairs evoked fin de siècle Paris or Vienna. Here and there sat and wriggled other patrons.

The lights dimmed, and for the next ten minutes they watched an act like no other. Maggie, a stunning, somewhat androgynous woman with short black hair, long legs, and small round breasts, strutted out wearing only a pair of frilly, bikini-cut black panties and plenty of eye makeup. She stopped center stage, acknowledged the applause, and then addressed the audience.

"Ladies and gentlemen, I have to pee," she announced importantly. She clutched her crotch suggestively and let an erotic shiver run through her.

A murmur of sex-charged approval greeted this proclamation. Then a curtain behind Maggie opened to reveal a sparkling, silver-plated commode, its seat ready to receive the quivering arse of a piss-rich woman.

"And perhaps," Maggie said softly, "some of you have to pee, as well." The audience tittered knowingly.

Maggie sat down on the toilet seat—still in her knickers—then instantly got back up. She laughed, and again squeezed herself.

Over the next few minutes, Maggie walked laps around the stage, parading her condition, stopping now and again to cross her legs or squat teasingly, often smiling or winking at the audience, and generally playing the situation like an acrobat on a tightrope. With knees rhythmically knocking together, she slapped her own buttocks and tweaked her own nipples. She took delicate, gingerly steps and great, bold strides. She pulled her knickers down, then up, then down—flirting now with pissing on the stage, now with doing it in the commode, and making a show of pretending she couldn't decide where, when, and how to let go.

"You never know if she's going to do it on the floor, in the loo, or in her knickers," Jocelyn told Stephen. "Sometimes she even lets the audience choose."

Tonight, after suitable deliberation and debate, it was the floor. And as Maggie's ostentatious waterfall shimmered in the spotlight and the cabaret star roared with the divine pleasure of giving in, Stephen heard the liquid hisses and heartfelt sighs of the several women pissing in tandem with Maggie.

He saw that Jocelyn was fidgeting next to him. "Are you going to do it?" he asked eagerly.

"Not here," she said. "Come on." She stood hurriedly, dancing in place and giggling while she waited for him to scramble up.

He followed her out of the theater and along a space-age corridor, in a direction they hadn't explored yet. Just beyond a bench occupied by a platinum-haired leg-crossing enthusiast in a fine black raincoat and tense white panties, they stopped at a service window. Here Jocelyn addressed a club official, a handsome woman with penetrating eyes.

"I have a room reserved for an engagement ceremony," Jocelyn informed her.

Stephen felt a stirring in his heart—and, because of the possibilities promised by their location, another in his groin.

The official consulted her computer. "Ah, yes. Jocelyn. So you'll need four volunteers?"

"That's right." Jocelyn smiled, blushing slightly.

"You two can go on in," said the official. "I'm sure it will only take a minute to round up some friends. Everyone loves these ceremonies," she added to Stephen.

Jocelyn opened a door across the corridor, and escorted him inside. She closed the door behind them.

The room looked like a cross between a traditional private library and a postmodern sanctuary. There were oak bookcases along two walls, and heavy-framed paintings and mirrors on the others. There were deep couches and chairs around the perimeter; but the middle of the room was dominated by a sort of asymmetrical gazebo, lit theatrically by floodlights. Lounge music, incongruous yet appealing, was piped in through speakers.

Stephen sat on a couch, but Jocelyn did not join him. "I'd better not sit," she acknowledged. "At this point, if I don't keep moving I'll probably soak myself ... and that would spoil what I've planned for you." She chuckled seductively, pacing back and forth, petting herself through her clinging skirt as she savored her delicious restlessness. "Oh, fuck, I'm turned on, Stephen," she whispered.

Stephen had the insight, at that moment, that Jocelyn was not wearing any underwear, and his cock tingled as he imagined the sexy sensations his fiancée was experiencing as she touched her pussy through the thin skirt while enjoying the urgent thrill of teetering on the verge.

The door opened, and a procession of four women snaked in. One wore an iridescent evening gown, two were in bright little cocktail dresses, and the fourth was sleek as a cat in a turtleneck and slacks. Jocelyn, playing hostess, greeted them, introducing herself and Stephen. Then, without even waiting for them to give their names in return, she clapped her hands with enthusiasm: "Let's do it."

And they all knew what to do. The four smiling women converged on Stephen's couch. He relaxed, mesmerized, as each of them took one of his extremities in hand. Jocelyn, now digging her fingers deep into her crotch, waddled forward and leaned in to kiss him. "I love you," she said.

Then she scurried out of the way, allowing her four attendants to carry Stephen, face up, to the gazebo, each of them using both hands to support his weight.

"He's gorgeous," volunteered one woman.

"Mmm, yeah," agreed another.

"Wow, I really have to wee," giggled a third.

"Me, too."

"Me, too."

"Me, too."

Jocelyn moved into Stephen's field of vision, and the four women lowered him just enough so that she could step over him with one luscious, stocking-clad leg and then remain there, straddling him. And just as he focused his gaze on the magnificent image of his woman standing open-legged and knicker-free over his waist, he saw her face relax; and a dribble, then a cascade, of woman-warmed piss descended onto him.

"Baby," she cooed, looking into his eyes with a blissed-out expression of release and adoration.

And, like a string quartet playing the first measure of a piece with synchronized precision, Jocelyn's volunteers all suddenly switched on their sprinklers.

Stephen found himself at the center of an extraordinarily lewd tableau. The cocktail-dress woman holding his right foot was shuffling gracefully in place and wantonly splashing the floor, and the bearer of his left foot was pulsing around a darkening, slowly leaking trouser seam. Both women moaned—in harmony with Jocelyn, who appeared to be melting with pleasure. Behind him, he heard the burbling downpours of the other two goddesses, who were releasing their personal floods while still holding his arms.

"Ooh!" a pretty voice squealed at his shoulder—involuntarily, it seemed.

"This feels sooo fucking good," crooned the woman in slacks.

The whole room seemed to vibrate in a cosmic ecstasy built of abandon, sensuousness, and between-the-thighs female luxuries that were too recherché for a man to fully understand.

In counterpoint to this grand effect, the immediate caress of Jocelyn's water on Stephen's tuxedo trousers was the most intimately sensual thing he had ever known. Inside his clothes, his erection throbbed gratefully while his lover rained on him.

As Jocelyn and her lovely attendants, full of beer, pissed on and on, Stephen felt he was in paradise.

"Look at the lucky man," said the woman in slacks, breathlessly.

"We'd better finish soon, or he's going to come before she's ready for him," chirped the sweet-voiced woman holding Stephen's right arm.

Finally they all trickled to a halt, ending almost as precisely as they'd begun—like a string quartet gone slightly sloppy from imbibing.

"Let this outpouring be a symbol of my endlessly flowing love," chanted Jocelyn, her eyes tearing up.

Before Stephen could respond, she was unzipping his trousers and springing his cock free. Now it was his turn to moan.

Jocelyn dipped her fingers into her sopping crotch, then

grabbed his prick again. Then she steadied herself, standing solidly above Stephen, and nodded to the women behind him.

They took the cue, as did the women at his feet, and the four piss goddesses began to elevate him. Jocelyn guided his cock between her lips as it came up like an obelisk on a mechanic's lift, and Stephen trembled with the velvety satisfaction of being claimed by her.

When she'd taken him about halfway in, she nodded once more, and the attendants held him steady.

Then Jocelyn began to bend her knees.

He'd never been fucked like this, so exotically and from such a physically passive attitude. Jocelyn brought herself up and down, milking his shaft with expert sensitivity. Stephen's gaze moved from her piss-streaked stockings to her bliss-streaked face ... then to the sympathetic figures holding his ankles, whose countenances were radiant with the damp raunchiness of what they'd done for him. He thought of their hard little clits in their warm, dripping-wet underwear, envisioning the orgasms that would crackle through them as soon as their hands were free.

Jocelyn had her pee-dabbed fingers on her own clit now; and though Stephen was close to exploding, she beat him to it. A bonus gift of piss poured out of her as she came, sobbing with joy, and Stephen howled as he shot into her, completely wallowing in the extravagant eroticism of it all.

The attendants put him down gently and left the two of them alone, exiting the room with pussy-gratifying hands already active in their wet junctures. With his trousers a pond of sacred water and his groin beginning to pulse with a pleasant, watery ache of its own, Stephen licked Jocelyn's pussy—tasting everything, and feeling so very, very engaged.

Mariel's "Fountain"
Scene from *The Pleasure Dial*

"OH, THIS IS GOING TO BE SENSATIONAL, ARTIE! ELYSE WILL be the hottest thing on the pleasure dial. I'm so excited, I could pee."

"I mark that's the third time in our young friendship you've made an out-of-context allusion to peeing. This is not a complaint, mind you—merely an observation."

"See, that's another advantage I have over Trixie—mannequins don't pee."

"But getting back to *The Elyse Heffernan Show*: I have to hand it to you. I was considered a pretty sharp idea guy in New York. But you don't just think in ideas, you think in Concepts with a capital C. My hat goes off to you."

"And your pants, too, I've been pleased to note. But Thank You, Artie—with a capital T. And you know what? I think I really *do* have to pee. *In* context."

He thought she would reverse direction so they could stroll back toward the public conveniences. Instead, she stepped onto the grass, retrieving a cream-colored handkerchief from her skirt pocket. As she lowered herself into a squat, she sent a hankie flourish his way, as though she were waving *bonjour* (and definitely not *au revoir*) from the deck of an ocean liner.

"Right here? But someone will see you."

"I sure hope so," said Mariel.

He instinctively averted his eyes.

"You're kidding, Artie," she said with disappointment, as faint sounds documented the displacement of skirt and lingerie. "Oh, well, lead a horse to water…"

As she enunciated the last word, he heard the beginnings of her stream trickling down to the ground. And having absorbed the indisputable evidence that she *wanted* him to look on while she watered the grass, he decided to unavert his eyes.

"Oh," chirped Mariel, "are you back? The show's just started, good seats down front." She broke into laughter as a shudder of pleasure cut into her narrative. "Ahahahaha. Oh, bliss! Honestly, sometimes I think sprinkling is better than sex."

"Sprinkling," nothing, thought Artie—Mariel was now pouring like a spout. No one had ever shown him before how thickly, how forcefully a woman could pee. The torrent of release was a revelation overwhelming in its majestic—and, he found, intensely erotic—beauty. The acute, intimate ecstasy she was evidently taking from the process brought him a shudder of his own, a tickle of arousal that seemed to travel from his balls up the spine to his shoulder blades. His eyes were now locked on her river, his mind contemplating the pleasure Mariel was feeling between her legs.

When she sighed and reached up and inward to wipe herself with the handkerchief, he felt as if she were pulling her fist up the length of his dick.

There was nobody else in sight. "Give me that," he requested quickly, before he'd even thought about what he was saying.

Mariel stood, grinning with enthusiasm, and handed him the streaked hankie.

"Oh, god," he said appreciatively, bringing it to his face to savor the rich aromas of cunt and fresh, feminine pee.

In another instant his cock was out of his pants, wrapped in the woman-wetted cloth. He jerked himself off in a half-dozen strokes while she watched him, answering his frenzied grunts with delighted "oohs."

"We liked that, didn't we?" she said when he'd finished.

The Pleasure Dial is a full-length erotocomedic novel in Jeremy Edwards' inimitable style. You have just enjoyed (we hope!) the only watersports scene from *The Pleasure Dial*, but if you are interested in humorous, sexy erotica set in 1930s Hollywood, you may enjoy the entire novel.

Bronze Medalist,
2014 Independent Publisher Book Awards

The year is 1934, and amiable New York gag writer Artie Plask has taken the West Coast plunge. His first day on staff with a top radio show introduces him to the irresistible Mariel Fenton, a wit among wits who immediately takes an interest in all aspects of Artie's life—especially his private life.

As Artie finds his feet in a world of blustering comedians, pansexual sex goddesses, timid screen legends, exhibitionistic scriptwriters, and self-infatuated geniuses, Mariel leads him on a zany journey up and down the pleasure dial—a giddy romp through Hollywood that's chock-full of airwaves showdowns, writing-room counterplots, devious impersonations, naked meetings, and a sensuality-drenched assortment of erotic escapades.

For more erotica by Jeremy Edwards, both novels and short stories, visit his website at http://jeremyedwardserotica.com.

For other fine stories of quality erotica, visit the website at http://1001nightspress.com.